WYTCH BORN

CWC Collaborative Fiction Novel
Written by 22 International Authors

ISBN: 0-9863159-7-4
ISBN 13: 978-0-9863159-7-8

ABOUT CWC

Collaborative Writing Challenge is aptly named to describe what we do. We bring aspiring writers together from all over the world to collaborate on a full-length fiction novel. We accept writers of all ages with varying degrees of experience, as we believe everyone has something to offer.

Each chapter is written by three or four different writers, and each week, one chapter is selected to form part of the ongoing novel. The experience is challenging and unique, as the writers never meet or discuss their visions for the story.

The book is guided by a story coordinator, who checks names, facts, and integrity, and who works with each chapter writer to get the best results. This story has been kissed by many hands who have yet to read the completed novel.

We also introduced a new element to CWC, a short story competition, to give our writers a chance to submit a stand-alone story to be published in the novel of the same genre. At the end of this book, you will find 'The Choosing' by **James Dinsdale**. His story was selected as the winner. Our close runner-up was collaboratively written by **Jean Grabow & Evelyn Pentikis**, titled 'Retribution'. You can read 'Retribution' on the CWC website. Congratulations to all of you.

For more information, please visit:
www.collaborativewritingchallenge.com

IBBY

This is CWC's fourth project. 10% of profits from the sales of this book will be donated to the charity IBBY. This is a wonderful organization, dedicated to providing children from all over the world access to books.

We will be donating to the specific project called the **IBBY Fund for Children in Crisis,** which provides support for children whose lives have been disrupted through war, civil disorder, or natural disaster. The two main activities that will be supported by the Fund are the therapeutic use of books and storytelling in the form of Bibliotherapy, and the creation or replacement of selected book collections appropriate to each situation.

Please see further details about this charity by accessing their website: **www.ibby.org**

DEDICATION

This book is dedicated to all the writers who dared to get involved in a CWC collaboration. The interest in each new project is phenomenal, allowing us to start multiple projects of varying genres. This has resulted in better-quality submissions, giving the collaborations the best chance possible at being successful.

I would also like to mention my online writing friends who have brought so much fun and inspiration into my life. This encourages me to continue growing CWC and bringing people from all walks of life together!

And, of course, our CWC Story Coordinators, who work tirelessly to make each project successful. You are all a pleasure and an inspiration.

Laura Callender - CWC Founder

THE WRITERS

We had over 65 writers sign up for Wytch Born, and had 53 chapters submitted in total, 32 of which were selected for the story. The authors came from 5 different countries: America, Canada, UK, Greece, and Australia.

Rather than fill these pages with details about all 22 authors, all their pictures and bios can be found on the CWC Website. Please do stop by and learn more about our talented contributing writers. Some have very little writing experience, and some have reels of accomplishments under their belts. I think you would be hard-pressed to identify their individual chapters, and it's just possible that your favorite chapter could have been written by a fresh-faced, up-and-coming writer. There are certainly a few names that we will be looking out for in the future.

With CWC projects, it is inevitable that some writers will have their chapters rejected. We had some incredible submissions that we just couldn't use. These chapters are always integral to shaping the story, as the variety in chapters gave us the chance to find the best fit. These writers are as much a part of the teamwork that brought this project to completion, so to those who go unnamed: Thank you for your wonderful contributions and effort!

ACKNOWLEDGMENTS

This project has brought together so many talented people. I would like to thank **Jason Pere**, who had his starter chapter Wytch Born selected by his fellow writers from over 10 submissions. His work inspired so many great submissions, resulting in a fresh new take on Wytches and Magic.

As always, our chief editor **Kathrin Hutson** has done an outstanding job getting Wytch Born ready for publication. It is a pleasure working with you.

My biggest thanks must go to **all of our writers** who agreed to participate in this project. With each new project, demand increases, but so far, we manage to find a place for everyone. Some writers are not always proficient in the genre we are writing, but often their creative minds produce work so wonderful, they surprise themselves. We are very proud of all your work.

This novel contains a drawing titled 'Griffin' by LaguzLake. You can find more work by this artist and a link the the CC license here: http://laguzlake.deviantart.com/art/Griffin-72526552

A NOTE FROM THE STORY COORDINATOR

Wytch Born is CWC's fourth project, which was eight months of magic and emotions and amazing characters. It was our first fantasy collaboration. The starter chapters lit up many creative minds and the possible plots were endless, but when Wytch Born was chosen, I have to say I never expected it to go in the direction it did. The first week was one of the most difficult because the beginning of a story is the most important.

Writers definitely stood up to the task, though, creating new characters and continuing the story as if they had been writing it themselves since the first chapter. This collaborative novel started with a Paladin and a Wytch, but as the story continued, more Wytches came with secrets, and the Paladin's background grew with it all. Naturally, some chapters were more surprising than others because so much was revealed, and so many questions were answered that not only shocked other writers, but shocked me! When a Wytch's worst enemy discovers they share the same blood, and then that information is backed up with a history and a devastating past, I'd have to say everyone shared the intrigue and excitement. Drama came with fantasy, and energy with action. Week two and three and four and five flew by, and the more questions there were, the more challenging it became to choose the best chapters, especially since I had mixed emotions sometimes.

I couldn't tell if I was excited or nervous when two chapters couldn't be narrowed to one. The two-chapter winner weeks were hard but definitely worth it. Every week, writers continued to impress and expand a story that began in a saloon with a drunk and a deck of cards. Numerous plot twists allowed an odd pair to fight a larger force together despite differences.

There were a few weeks where writers didn't send notification that they couldn't submit a chapter, and I have to say those weeks were the most difficult. Thankfully, a few extraordinary writers waited for a call and a plea, and they somehow managed to dish out a chapter that not only followed the storyline but added something else to the already incredible piece. Oh, and they did this within twelve to twenty-four hours. Two thousand words.

The similar chapter submissions made some weeks hard because the submissions started mixing together and I couldn't remember what had and hadn't happened. It was always a relief when a chapter dove right into the story as if the author had just written the previous chapter. I didn't have to wonder because my mind picked up right where it had left off!

Weeks turned into months, and our characters went from enemies to unlikely allies. What's more, their emotions toward each other had an explanation, one that came from the incredible writers who put so much thought into their chapters.

As the story came closer to ending, writers had more challenges—they still had questions to ask while also having the task of "predicting" what would happen next because they only had a week to come up with their chapter when their turn came around. Needless to say, they did more than succeed, and even the final chapter had options for me, which were narrowed down by necessity in the end because some of the chapters were incredibly well done.

CWC isn't just a project where writers can write something and have their name on it. It's a heck of a workout and it takes determination and loyalty. It's a community where people have a chance to challenge themselves and grow by developing their creative minds through a story they can be a part of at every turn and every stage. All writers should have a voice no matter their background in writing or their credentials as an artist. And that's what CWC allows. Not just that, but it's where opinions matter because everything is voted on and everything is chosen.

It's not hard to say there's talent in the CWC community, and this was only Project 4. We're more than halfway through The Map, which is Project 5 right now, and Project 6 is sneaking up on us. It's been a crazy, amazing journey so far, and I can't wait to see how much it grows, because it's definitely growing.

Cayce R Berryman
CWC Story Coordinator of Wytch Born

CONTENTS

Short Story Winner:

CWC's Fifth Collaboration:

CHAPTER 1

T he saloon was filled with its usual nightly ruckus—the laughter of men plied by drink, a slightly out-of-tune piano keeping a lively melody, sultry murmurs of the prostitutes looking to lure a patron upstairs, and the occasional outbursts of men in dispute. Once again, above all the other commotion in the Frontier House of Vice, Sal heard the same voices.

"Hit me again, Charlie," called the disheveled coal miner at the bar. The man had been making a spectacle of himself since Sal had dealt the first hand of the evening. No less than six times this night had he caused a deafening scene of drunken buffoonery. The coal miner was a local by the name of Dan Pearly, and this was a usual occurrence. The reason Charlie, the barkeep, put up with Dan's inhuman volume was due to the fact that every bit of coin Dan earned at the coal mine went right into Charlie's pocket.

"That man clearly doesn't mind making a scene in public," Sal muttered.

"Dan don't mean nothing by it. Now, deal them cards and let me win a hand," said the railway worker beside Sal.

"Now there's the spirit. That is the kind of poker player I like to see at my table." Sal bared his perfect, white teeth in a joyous grin. He shuffled and cut the deck, but before he could deal the next hand, an enchanting voice took him aback.

"Gentlemen, is this seat taken?"

Sal turned to address the owner of such an alluring voice. He stood as he laid his eyes on her, her elegance and beauty more overcoming than any he'd ever seen. Her bright, orange petticoat matched those of the saloon's prostitutes, but Sal had to believe this woman was more than a simple lust-trader. Her thick, raven hair flowed softly around bright green eyes and fell against her skin, its soft tan like a perfect clay in the dim saloon. Apart from faint lining around her lips and eyes, she wore no makeup; she did not require any. Sal squinted at the ink of tattoos partially obscured by her mesh sleeves, but he could not tell if the tattoos were tribal or oriental in origin. He would have sworn that this woman carried Gypsy blood.

"Ma'am, a creature as lovely as yourself is free to sit where she pleases. It would be our privilege if you would join our table," Sal said as he stood and placed his gray hat over his heart.

"Oh, sir, you are too kind, indeed," the woman said with a practiced bat of her long-lashed eyes.

She raised her right hand, and Sal immediately picked up on the signal, taking her hand in his. "I wouldn't be so quick with that compliment. You don't know me yet." Sal gave her his best smile. "Please allow me to see you supplied with whatever drink you might fancy to keep those exquisite lips of yours from getting too parched by all this desert heat."

"If I said you were too kind, would you be agreeable this

time?"

"Ma'am, if you keep on batting those eyes at me, you will find I am agreeable to all kinds of things."

"My, I have to say it is a pleasure to make your acquaintance, mister…"

"Folks around here call me Sal."

She threw him a breathtaking smile. "Interesting name. Is Sal short for something?"

"Why yes it is, but only my best friends call me by my full name," Sal said, returning a playful smirk.

He wanted to maintain a bit of mystery about himself, though he could tell she was the sort who was used to having men answer her every whim without challenge.

"Oh, can't I be your friend?" The woman mocked distress, and he considered continuing their game, but the curious eyes at the table caught his attention, and he acknowledged them with a nod.

"Ma'am, just sit and play a hand, and I'll show you how friendly I can be." Sal cleared his throat. "I will confess you do have me at a disadvantage. You are stunningly beautiful and have the voice of a lark, but I have not the pleasure of your name."

She retreated into herself for a moment, glancing hesitantly at her lap. "A lark, you call me. A lark is a beautiful bird with a beautiful song. Sir, you may continue to call me a lark."

"As you wish, Miss Lark." Sal pulled the empty chair out for her to sit. "The game is Brag, ma'am. Are you familiar?"

"Why yes, Mr. Sal, I am acquainted with Brag. I confess that game has never held my fancy. It's too…gentle for my tastes. I prefer Pochen."

Sal raised an eyebrow. "I appreciate a woman who knows

her way around a deck of cards. Pochen it is, providing you gentlemen are agreeable to the Lady's Choice." Sal glanced at the surrounding men, and all the other card players nodded their heads vigorously in agreement.

They played for hours. Sal and Lark continued their shameless flirtation. To their credit, neither Sal nor Lark managed to relinquish the slightest shred of personal information. Even the every increasingly boisterous outbursts of the inebriated Dan Pearly were a muted hum and blur of faded colors next to Lark's divine voice and radiant beauty.

"That's the snake who cheated me!" came a shout above the roar of the saloon.

Things immediately quieted. The town sheriff, two of his deputies, and a man who Sal had relieved of his money much earlier made their way through the saloon's swinging doors and headed for Sal.

"I don't reckon I know you, stranger," said the sheriff.

"My good Sheriff, folks call me Sal. I assure you, there must a misunderstanding."

"For yer sake, I hope so." The sheriff held back a snarl as if he were ready to spit. "We don't take to card cheats, do we, Ross?"

"No we don't," one of the deputies said. "Cheats get their hands brought down to the blacksmith's. Big John likes that."

Sal took a moment and pulled at his shirt collar, which had grown tight around his neck. "That sounds unpleasant. It is a good thing I'm not a card cheat. We all have a run of poor luck from time to time. When you have been drinking hard, the head becomes cloudy." Sal grinned lightly at the man who scowled at him. "My good man, why don't you have a good night's sleep, let your luck replenish itself, then tomorrow you can find me here and win some of your money back. If it will ease your mind, I'm sure my good friend Miss Lark here would be agreeable to shuffle, cut, and deal for us." Sal turned his smile to the stunning woman. She returned the gesture with a smile of her own before casting a seductive look in the posse's direction. "For now, why don't you let me buy you another drink?"

It took a moment for Sal's fast-talk to set in, but his accuser hinted at growing favor to the proposal. Sal fought another grin as the man glanced at the radiant woman beside him. The glance from Lark had sealed the deal.

"Why not? Never pass up a drink," he said.

"Please, a bottle of whatever my friend here cares for," Sal called to Charlie at the bar.

As the saloon returned to its usual hum, the sound of Dan Pearly pierced above all once again. "Charlie, more rye!" It looked like this time Dan had overdone it. Without warning, he clutched his belly and doubled over, retching and howling toward the floor. The onlookers waited for the standard spew of bile, but a long trail of flames shot from the coal miner's gullet and put the room in a fearful silence. It burned hot and long for several moments, roaring with life like a dragon's breath, then faded.

No! You have just killed us both, you damned fool! Sal thought, frozen in his chair.

"Wytch!" The sheriff pulled his pistol and fired a shot into Dan's belly. The coal miner fell while blood soaked his coal-dust-stained shirt. "String this monster up and burn him!"

The posse pulled the bleeding Wytch into the street amid terrified screams of onlookers. Sal's mind raced. He could already feel powerful hands tighten around his heart and the blare of the Wytch's First Tenet echo in his mind.

My name is Magic. I am your mother. You are my children,

my blood, a Wytch. Should any Wytch spill the blood of our kind or stand idle while our blood is spilled, their life is forfeit. This I command above all else.

Sal pleaded, hoping he could manage to aid his fellow Wytch without calling attention. He closed his eyes and called upon her.

Mother, as your child, I ask of you, let the winds of your brilliant blue sky and the breeze across your vast meadows confuse the minds of all here with false whispers of forgetting, so it may serve your blood and your children.

She did not answer this. Sal called upon her again.

Mother, as your child, I ask of you, let my brethren's skin be as your enduring mountain's stone and his constitution be that of your great valley's Redwoods, that he may withstand the flame of those who would harm him, so it may serve your blood and your children.

She did not answer this. Sal grew desperate. He pressed his eyes tighter and called upon her again.

Mother, as your child, I ask of you, tear your clouds in the starlit heavens asunder and bring forth a deluge to hinder those who threaten your children, and let the your purest of waters that course beneath the flesh of my brethren heal his wounds, so it may serve your blood and your children.

She did not answer this. Sal could see them fix the noose around Dan Pearly's neck and light torches. He gritted his teeth, clenched his fists, and called upon her one final time.

Magic, I call upon you by my true name. I, Salem Taker, last of the Taker Bloodline, ask of you, as the sun's morning rays warm the endless face of your prairie, let that kiss of fire fill my hands and boil in my veins, so it may destroy your enemies.

This, she answered.

The doors of the saloon exploded from their frame amid a shower of splinters as a cannonball-sized orb of fire launched from inside, striking the sheriff in his chest. The man's body immediately set ablaze, and he fell to the ground screaming. Another ball of fire came through the saloon doorway, engulfing Deputy Ross.

Salem exited the saloon, holding a fireball in each hand. Flames burned in his eyes, and thick black smoke trailed from his mouth and nostrils. The last remaining Deputy went for his gun, but Salem threw a fireball and let the man burn before he could draw.

Salem sent a grand burst of sparks and fire into the sky. The supernatural display gave any lingering spectators cause to run for shelter, so Salem went to the fallen Wytch.

"You didn't let them burn me," Dan said with a sad smile etched on his face. His eyes glazed, but a burning pain remained in him, and Salem tightened, recognizing the effects of a silver bullet. Salem went to call on Magic again, but it was too late. Only a silver bullet could take a Wytch's life so quickly, and nothing could save Dan from it.

The gun beside Sal's head brought him slowly to his feet. He turned to see Lark holding an ornate pistol carved out of dragon's bone, the trademark weapon of a Paladin—a Wytch hunter.

"I'm guessing Sal is short for Salem Taker," Lark said triumphantly.

"And I reckon I should call you Dame Lark," Salem replied. The Wytch and the Paladin smiled at each other.

CHAPTER 2

Salem shot the Paladin a challenging glare, but on the inside, he desperately sought a way out of the situation. The fire still raged within him, but he could not move with the dragon bone pistol six inches from his head, loaded with a pure silver bullet. No alloy in this one; Salem could smell it, the rancor of pure silver emanating from the weapon. This Paladin was deadly, with a reputation that preceded her. If legend proved true, she would have forged the bullet that was meant to take his life with her own hands. He sensed it was true. She was Komodromoi of the ancient Romni gold and silver artificers. He had been right. The tattoos he had glimpsed before were Romni; the Paladin carried Gypsy blood and as such was kin to the Wytch Born.

Salem warily leaned back on the hitching post frame in a relaxed pose, crossing his strong arms and hoping to catch her unaware. Neither of them looked down at Dan Pearly lying at their feet, where he had bled out his life's blood around her silver bullet. Salem smiled at her suggestively. "Before you kill me, Dame Lark, enlighten me as to why you hunt your own people?"

The barb struck home, and the pain of his words flashed across her face, but she recovered quickly and said in her most charming voice, "You know nothing of me, Salem Taker, or you would never have asked that question."

He slowly stood up straight, dropping his arms. He had seen that momentary crack in her composure, the way she had let the gun barrel drift... He had no opportunity for action, however, for the smile never left her face and the dark expression in her emerald eyes was unchanged. Lark's gaze never left his, and he could not look away from her. They were drawn to each other, and he recognized that beneath that hardened and polished exterior was a woman as overpoweringly attracted to him as he was to her. Their common bond was the blood of the ancients. Salem smiled ruefully at the knowledge.

The Paladin raised the pistol. "It's a shame we didn't meet under other circumstances, Sal, but I fear it's time." She smiled with regret as she tightened her finger on the trigger.

Salem had no choice; he pulled from the inferno inside him and raised his hands. The fireballs spiraled within his palms—he had to end her as well.

Magic felt the plight of Salem Taker as keenly as she felt the death of Dan Pearly.

"Stop!" From the recesses of his mind, Salem heard the Mother, Magic, and felt her harsh command. "You cannot have him, Simza Adenah. Salem Taker is a Favored Son. The Taker bloodline does not end with him!"

In that moment, the Paladin hesitated; she felt her true name spoken. Salem recognized this in her pale face, knowing that

22

Magic had spoken to them both. A song of the ancients beset the woman, and her countenance changed. The smile became a determined glare. She was methodical and heartless, honed from eons of training and war with the Wytch. Simza Adenah did not need permission…but the dragon blood of the ancients held her fast and would not let her take this Wytch's life. Putting both hands on the weapon, she struggled to pull the trigger that would end this wretched day, but could not.

Magic wended her way unhurriedly toward them, flitting down the cobblestones of the murky street and whisking between the buildings. Salem knew he was the only one who could see her now. Magic had felt the presence of the ancients alongside the Paladin, and she acknowledged them. The Time of Healing and Restoration was at hand.

Magic materialized in her ghostly form before him and smiled. He was taken aback; he had not seen the Mother in centuries. Then his own smile widened as he glanced at the attractive Paladin.

"You're fixin' to be sorry you ever met me at all," he drawled.

The beautiful woman, so seemingly sure of herself, pointed the pistol that had been her father's between his eyes. "Either way, you…" Her sentence hung in the air unfinished as the Wytch's physical form shimmered into translucence. "No!" she screamed.

***

The gun went sailing from her hand, almost as if she had flung it herself, far out into the muddy street where a few brave people had gathered to watch the spectacle. With the breath knocked out of her, the Paladin was propelled backward off her feet as the weapon flew away from her, and the Wytch disappeared. She landed helplessly in the squishy mess of the street, her bright orange petticoat and the expensive indigo silk dress ruined. She heard the echo of the Wytch's laughter, mocking her.

"Damnation!" she shouted as she nimbly stood from the muck, shaking off the clinging mess.

She strode purposefully through the crowd, swearing under her breath, her eyes seeking her weapon. The crowd parted, un-speaking, as she trudged on until a child offered the weapon from under the yoke of a wagon. She bent and grasped it gently.

"Thank you, Mistress," she told the child in a sweetly con-trolled voice.

The Paladin then turned abruptly and, with a most unlady-like scowl, tramped back through the street, dripping muddy water and leaving a trail of dirt clods falling from the backside of her dress. No one dared say a word, but everyone stared.

She checked the cylinder of her weapon halfway across the street, threw her hands up, and swore again. "Hellfire!"

The Wytches always emptied the silver bullet if they could get their hands on a Paladin weapon. Apparently, Salem Taker had found a way to do the same. She blustered back through the ruined doors of the Frontier House of Vice, fighting her clinging petti-coats. She stomped directly to the bar, her weapon already dis-creetly out of sight.

"Whiskey, please, Charlie," she said quietly through tight, thin lips. "What a waste," she said to no one, shaking her head as with one quick shot she swallowed the whiskey the barkeep had placed before her. Then she motioned for another, laying a coin on the bar. "Damned arrogant Wytch, Salem Taker," she muttered and slammed down the second glass.

With that, she walked out of the saloon and toward the

boarding house on the far end of town. She was a sight, mud-splotched face and flailing hair, kicking the muddy mass of dress and petticoats away from her legs so she could walk.

She made it to the back door of Mathilda's board home and knocked loudly.

"I already got yer bath drawn, Missy. Just strip down out there," came a rough female voice from the back hallows of the house.

Simza was impatient with herself, stripping her ruined clothes to her bare skin, and left them in a bedraggled heap on the ground. She pulled at the combs in her raven hair, and it fell in waves to the middle of her back. When she shook her head vigorously, fragments of mud and debris dislodged, and the thick locks fell like silk against her dampened skin.

She lightly stepped up to the porch, where the round-faced Irishwoman met her with a large basin of warm water.

"Rinse yerself, darlin'. You'll be traipsing mud all about if'n you don't."

Simza only shook her head again fiercely, sending a few more twigs clattering onto the porch.

"What a mess!" the woman added.

Simza sat back in the warm, scented water with a sigh. This was one of the scant luxuries she allowed herself, and she reveled in the heated water while she soaked her sore limbs. Her body was hard, taut, and disciplined for warfare. Her blood was old and self-controlled, and she did nothing to excess.

This had been a strange time, and it both confused and frustrated her. Why would the ancients stay her hand? She knew the Wytch, Taker, had been correct; their families converged somewhere, possibly along the Caldarari lines. That would explain why the draw between them had been so strong. The Caldarari family was old, with an obscure and secretive history, and her roots ran much deeper and further back in time than even that family. As did the Wytch's, most likely. Those roots were the source of Simza's power.

"How did Taker know?" she whispered to her muddy reflection.

He had known before she did, and that troubled her greatly. Had she been so blind? She saw again the perfect smile and the allure in his eyes, cool at the point of death. He had courage, she had to admit.

"There will be another day, Salem Taker." Even as she spoke, she saw him in her mind's eye, leaning against the hitching rail, his strong arms folded across the wide breadth of his chest. The Paladin shook herself from the reverie and scolded herself. He was a Wytch.

Her water had cooled and she welcomed the scalding pitcher Mathilda brought for her. It pulled her further from her reverie. Simza paid the woman well, and Mathilda showed her gratitude with gruff but never-straying attentiveness. The Paladin stayed here often in her travels, and over the years, the two had forged the closest thing to friendship two fiercely-guarded women could manage.

Simza sighed again and relaxed against the warmed tub. A sort of malaise suddenly enveloped her and, bewildered, she heard the ancients sing for the second time that day.

"As it was of old so it is today—Ki shan I Romni—Adoi san' I chov'hani. Wherever the gypsies go, there the Wytches are, we know."

Portents came disguised as far more than one Romni folktale, repeated to wide-eyed children by firelight, and the rhyme formed a hard knot in her stomach. She had always dreaded those words, which flitted about the edges of her memory, unremembered just the same. Somehow, she knew in her spirit, it was truth. Simza could remember no more of the tale or why it was important to her, but she shivered even in the hot water.

"It is a strange time," she whispered.

She had not been allowed to embrace her Romni power, being of mixed heritage. She had little memory of her mother, but she did feel in her memory the happiness she knew as a young child among the Gypsy wagons and around the dancing firelight. Her father had raised her—a Paladin who despised Wytches and told tales of horror to his young daughter. Simza was never allowed to visit or even go near her Romni relations after her mother's death. It angered her father greatly if she even spoke of them, but he could not deny the formidable power that welled within his daughter. Eventually, instead of demanding separation, he had taken to demanding her discipline and control.

A Wytch had taken his life when Simza was yet a very young woman, long ago. Devastated, she had held his hand as the life departed his eyes. That day, the woman-child had become a hunter. She had stepped into her father's shoes against the wishes of every man in the trade, and today she was better than most.

***

Magic took Daniel Pearly's body to the place of resting, and Salem followed quietly behind her.

"He was tired, Salem. So very tired. He did not truly live after the death of his Sari. It is unwise for a Wytch to fall in love with a mortal. A strong love will always condemn a Wytch to walk alone."

"I never knew he had been married," Salem said solemnly.

As Magic let Daniel go, she smiled. "Perhaps he will find her in the beyond." They began the long walk back, and Magic gifted him with a story. "Sari gave him twin sons, and the power was strong in them. Their aura drew the Paladin who murdered both mother and sons and burned their bodies. That moment was branded on Daniel's soul. His madness consumed centuries of his life, hunting Paladins, until even the shedding of their blood brought him no relief from the memory. And only a child ended his wrath—the child of the last Paladin he shredded upon his blade, forced to watch her father die. Daniel never killed again nor knew another sober thought. His weariness was his last possession."

Salem had always thought Dan a buffoon and jokester without much substance, but Magic knew all, and she'd given him the gift of knowledge—and of empathy.

"There is nothing like understanding, is there, Salem?" Magic whispered in his mind. "This is why I have brought you home. First, go eat. The table has been set with all your favorites." She smiled down at him, her form wavering even in this place on the astral plane. "It is not often I get to break bread with one of my Favored Sons," she said aloud, then disappeared from his view.

Salem was a little nervous; it had been centuries since he'd come to the astral plane. He had never known another Wytch to visit the Mother once their powers had been honed, after they were ready to go out into the worlds. He didn't think too much on what she called him. Favored Son. She had never said such a thing before, and he hadn't done anything to earn such a title.

It is a strange time, he thought.

The image of the Paladin Lark came unbidden to his mind. He knew it was the drawing of the blood, but he had never experienced anything like the need he felt for her now. He scratched his head in wonder and laughed aloud as he dug into the meal.

"Just hours ago, she held a pistol to my head." He chuckled around a mouthful of honey-dipped bread. "And here I am, day-dreaming of her beautiful eyes. A strange time, indeed."

Magic felt his laughter in the courtyard, and she smiled. When the meal was finished, Salem met her there. She sat in her favorite chair, staring out over the expanse of the mountains and valleys which belonged to this in-between place.

"Thank you for the meal, Mother," he said aloud.

"I sense you know this is not a visit truly without purpose, Salem, though I have always been glad of your company. You have done well in your time, harming none if you could help it and saving all if it was in your power to do so. I am proud of that strength and courage, which is why you are here."

He sat on the lounge beside her, and she whispered into his mind. The revelation appeared more in pictures than in words. The Mother showed him the early time of man, the ancient bloods, and how the tribes began. The Father of the Romni, the Duke exiled and doomed to wander with all his people. The enmity that developed between the Duke's two wives, and between their children, until the two tribes had nearly destroyed the Romni as they were in those days. Centuries passed, and the tribes remained at odds. The day came when the enmity evolved to murder. The ancients punished the tribe that stole the lives of their brethren by taking away their Wytch Born powers. Thus, in time, the first tribe became known as the Wytch Born, and the second as the Paladins. In that time, the ancients decreed a day of rebirth in a future time—a reunification of the Romni.

"It is nearing that time, Salem. It will be a war like no other in all worlds, in all dimensions. There will be many lives lost before there is understanding."

There was such a long pause that he thought she had finished, and he cleared his throat.

Then she spoke aloud. "Once, I walked as you do upon the Earth, Salem, and I loved a man. We had a child, a girl. My power was noble, the greatest of all the Romni, and when the ancients punished the Paladins, I became Mother of the Wytch Born, blood of my blood. I was to guard and guide until the Day of Resolution. The man I loved lost part of his soul when they took me. He cut our daughter off from all contact with our people."

She stopped speaking, and Salem could feel her pain as she looked at him.

"The child who watched Daniel Pearly slaughter her father was Simza Adenah. That child, that woman, is my daughter."

"She is a Paladin!" Salem averted his gaze from the Mother as he realized his mistaken outburst.

"She is both, Salem. Wytch and Paladin," Magic answered softly.

Salem saw the tear course down her cheek and thought it wavered in and out of this plane. He could not touch her or embrace her in her pain, though his heart went out to her, so he hung his head and waited.

CHAPTER 3

Time did not flow the same in the Mother's realm. While Salem's visit with her felt like it had lasted hours, only seconds had passed on the physical plane. Fortunately, although Salem could not control the time of his return, he had slightly more leeway with the exact place he chose to re-enter, or else he might still have been looking down the barrel of the Paladin's dragon bone pistol.

He emerged inside his own still-locked room above the saloon of the Frontier House of Vice, which he rented by the month. He had few possessions. His most precious were carried on his body—the Hex tattoos inscribed in his flesh, similar to the Romni's, and a testament to their common ancestry though enchanted and invisible unless conjured.

As Salem threw his spare clothing into a worn leather bag, he kept thinking of the secrets the Mother had shared with him. A reunification of their people was coming, she'd said—a rebirth. But with it, a war like no other in all worlds. Was he meant to warn the other Wytch Born and rally them to prepare? Or was it a secret meant for his ears alone, to give him an advantage of prior warning not afforded others? Salem wasn't sure what purpose that would serve, but Magic always had her reasons. Why hadn't she told him what to do with this information? Why hadn't he asked? Because, he chided himself, he'd been thinking too much about her. His "Dame Lark". Simza Adenah. He rolled the sounds around inside his mind, as if caressing them. Now that he knew her true name, he would be able to track her. The trouble was, if she had any Wytch Born powers, and even a child's knowledge of how to use them, the same was true for her.

And for the same reason, Salem thought, Brothers would soon be coming. He dismantled the non-physical traces of his presence; the wards and charms he'd put on the room for safety would continue to drain his power unnecessarily if he did not remove them.

Brothers would come through the astral plane, and perhaps some even in person, to ask him why Dan was dead. All Wytch Born knew in their hearts the moment a Brother died, but those who actually knew Dan personally and knew he and Salem had both been living in Reunion Pass for some time would want an explanation. How much should he tell them?

His own mind was empty of the answer, and Magic volunteered nothing to fill the space. He could not call on her and demand one so soon. Audiences as long as his had lasted were a rare privilege, even for a "Favored Son". Salem snorted. He sometimes wondered what, if anything, he'd done to earn that title beyond being the last of his line. It was at times both a blessing and a curse, and this time the curse was knowledge. Knowledge he was ill-prepared to use, which didn't sit well with him. Salem was a man who liked to convert knowledge into action as quickly as possible.

He moved toward the window, keeping out of sight behind the dark, velvet curtain and listening to hear if the commotion in the street had died yet, reminding himself that in the time of this plane, only a few moments more had passed since he'd faced the Paladin over the corpse of Dan Pearly. The only remaining question was how soon before it would be safe to leave the room and slip out of town without causing another scene.

As soon as the streets appeared empty, Salem unlocked the door but left the key on the table and exited by the window instead. The Frontier House of Vice was one of the few two-story buildings in Reunion Pass, but even so, it wasn't so high that a drop from the second-floor window would injure a man like him. Salem had the added advantage of Wytchcraft to break his fall and landed softly as a cat in a crouch, looking in all directions before rising and starting at a swift pace for the edge of town. They had played cards deep into the night, and if not for the small crowd that had gathered to see the confrontation between Wytch and Paladin, the streets would have been deserted. They were empty now—the onlookers had retreated after the spectacle ended in an anti-climax—and black in the moonless night.

Before Salem had gone even five yards, however, he heard a set of hurried footsteps behind him. He whipped around to see a thin figure stop abruptly behind him, a lantern still swinging in its left hand. A boy of about sixteen stood there, almost as tall as Salem but only half as broad across the chest. He looked like an under-stuffed scarecrow with long, twig-like limbs, his unkempt mop of coppery hair colored a shocking orange by the lantern light. His narrow jaw hung slack, revealing too little room for all his teeth, which were packed together and pushed forward as if trying to flee his mouth.

"Excuse me, sir," the boy said in a tone that struck him as oddly un-frightened, given what had recently happened on just the other side of the Frontier House of Vice. "You wouldn't happen to be the one they call Sal, would ya?" And before he could answer, the boy added, "It's about Mr. Pearly."

"Dan Pearly's dead," he said, "and if you're wise, you'll ask no more about it." He turned to continue walking, but the boy followed him, the pool of light cast by his lantern swinging around him.

"Yes, sir, I heard. It's just...I came from O'Malley's Boarding House, y'see. Mr. Pearly had some debts with us..."

"His debts died with him," Sal said, picking up his pace and glancing around, hoping the boy and his bobbing lantern didn't call any undue attention to them. "I don't see what concern it is of mine."

"Well y'see, sir," said the boy, who spoke in the same slow, flat drawl even as he increased his pace to match Salem's with no apparent effort, "Mr. Pearly led us to believe you'd go security for him..."

Salem cursed the memory of Dan Pearly under his breath, then offered a silent apology to Magic for speaking ill of a fellow Wytch, even in death. "He said nothing of the sort to me, so go tell your father—"

"I ain't got a father, sir," the boy said matter-of-factly.

"That'll come as a shock to your mother," Salem said.

"She ain't alive neither," the boy said, giving no indication he'd heard or understood the sarcasm or lack of patience in Salem's voice. "I just work for the House, sir."

"Then why don't you go back to work and stop trying to collect O'Malley's money from me?" Salem snapped, breaking into a fast jog. Ahead of him, where the last few buildings of Reunion Pass tapered into the wilderness beyond, he planned his escape from the boy. He was so close.

The boy followed him with the slightest hint of bitterness in his tone as he tried to get Sal's attention, which stood out in stark relief from his otherwise unfeeling tone.

"I'm sorry about your family," Salem said, stopping to face the boy again. "But I can't do nothin' for you." He turned and started walking again.

"Mr. Pearly's debts, sir…"

Salem stopped and turned around. The boy stopped directly behind him, as if commanded, and returned the look blankly. His mouth still hung open slightly, even when he was silent, but not because he was surprised or confused about why Salem had tried to evade him or why he now had stopped. He appeared incapable of confusion or surprise about anything, no sense of the bizarreness of the situation, nor any thoughts or feelings save for the task he'd come to accomplish. Salem had to conclude that he was either dim-witted or extraordinarily single-minded—or both.

"Now listen here," Salem said. "Did you hear nothing about how Dan Pearly died? How fire shot from his mouth? How a ball of fire burst through the saloon doors and three more men perished in the flames before it was over?" He was careful not to mention exactly who was responsible for what, only saying enough to scare off the boy.

"Yes, sir, I heard folks saying it was Wytchcraft, plain and simple. But Mrs. O'Malley said she didn't care if I had to go down to the very bottom of Hell and collect from the Devil himself," the boy said, as though this was something which happened daily at the O'Malley Boarding House, "except that I get due payment."

Salem was so taken aback by the boy's complete lack of fear that his own mouth fell open. Before he could reply, a shout rang out from the street behind them, and the sound of running footsteps followed.

"That's him!" a man's voice yelled through the darkness. "I thought he was just a cheat, but he's a Wytch besides, and now he's killed an officer of the law. Get him!"

Salem recognized it as his former card partner, the man who had brought the sheriff into the Frontier House of Vice in the first place. He ran toward them with two other men, all of whom appeared to have guns drawn. A bullet from the barrel of the least patient or most careless man's gun exited with a crack and bounced off a nearby wall.

"You didn't know what in hell you were walking into," he muttered to the boy, stepping around him to one side, extending his arms, flames already sparking in his palms. So, he would have to double his body count tonight. Three more men and a clean get-away was better than a whole mob after him.

Before he could release the fireball, however, three more shots rang out in the dark street, one shortly after the other. Two grunts and a cry followed, and the men who had moments before been hot in pursuit all fell to the ground and were still. Salem looked at the boy, who still held the lantern, hardly swaying in his left hand, but in his right was a freshly-smoking pistol.

"Well, y'see," he said, "I ain't too bad a shot myself, sir."

***

Simza Adenah heard three shots from her room at the back of Mathilda's boarding house. They would have woken her, had she been asleep, but she wasn't. Despite lying in the simple, narrow bed with covers drawn up, Simza could not sleep. The memory of the near miss, of her prey slipping right through her fingers, was still fresh, and she found it difficult to let go of things. Things which took a form like that of Salem Taker were especially difficult.

Gunshots weren't an uncommon sound in these parts, but tonight she was apt to give any sound special consideration. She pulled on an overcoat, both as protection from the cool, arid air and to hide the stark white glow of her nightdress, and slid her pistol into its pocket. She slipped out the back door of the kitchen on the pretext of not passing Mathilda's door, though she knew the woman would not try to stop her. Mathilda knew better than that. For some reason, though, Simza did not want to face her even so. Perhaps it was because she feared seeing in the other woman's eyes a reflection of the thing she now felt. Over the long years of chasing and hunting, it had become so foreign to her that now its presence seemed almost an otherworldly spirit possessing her mind. The feeling of her own doubt.

CHAPTER 4

The clanging of metal announced the arrival of a wagon. Normally, this would raise the curiosity of the town populace, but after the Wytch's fire attack on the Sheriff and his Deputies, the arrival of a single wagon was of little consequence in the gossip circles. This was not the ordinary farm or pioneer cart. It was a stockpile of metal implements; frying pans and branding irons hung from a wooden frame, buckets of nails sat next to a potbelly stove, and a stack of mining tools buried themselves in an unstable pile.

The draft animal pulling this mobile store was a beautiful horse unlike any other seen in these parts. Black and white piebald coloring with a silky mane of pure white, which matched the feathering hair covering each hoof, this beauty cut a swath down the street, stopping in front of the Frontier House of Vice.

The driver hopped down to stand in the street. He was tall

and thickly built, broad-shouldered and narrow-hipped. Dust stirred on the ground, a constant nuisance in the valley, but it failed to touch the black pants and scaled boots of the stranger.

He surveyed the front of the Frontier House. The remains of the door lay scattered into the middle of the street, the burnt edges of the doorframes and boardwalk all bearing witness to the power and temper of a Wytch. The charred bodies of the three poor lawmen had been removed, but the smell of roasted meat hung in the air.

A few of the menfolk in town were busy with cleanup after the events of the day, scurrying in a frenzied dance. However, the dancing workers carefully avoided one area of the street, averting their eyes and hurrying past to the next task of restoration.

Viktor Chavdar calmly walked over to the shunned patch of darkened dirt. Kneeling down, he stretched his right hand above the spot and closed his eyes. A crimson dust devil formed, spiraling upward and connecting to the palm of Viktor's extended hand.

Images flashed in his mind's eye—the final moments of a Wytch after being shot. The form of another Wytch throwing fire-balls explained the exploded entrance and the odor lingering in the street. The final impressions of the dying man played forward, the fire Wytch kneeling over the body with a look of concern and fierce concentration on his face. As the light began to fade, a gun pointed at the Wytch's head—a Paladin weapon. But far more interesting were the tattoos on the inner arm of the Paladin herself. He concentrated on the image, his left hand absently stroking his short, pointed beard.

Viktor released the connection, and the dust devil dissipated. He stood and turned toward the Frontier House but stopped. Something in the air tickled his senses. He felt the fire magic in the air, an excitable, consuming energy. It clung to the wooden splinters and twisted metal piled in the street, waiting for permission to reignite. Understandable—the use of magic always left a residue, but there was something else there. A calming energy flirted around the edge of his senses. He recognized this energy. How could he not? All those initiated into the realms of magic and alchemy would recognize the presence of the Mother.

***

Business resumed as usual at the Frontier House of Vice following the fiery events of the day. Two girls circled the room, eyeing the fresh crop of miners drinking and playing cards. Lou played a lively piece on the piano and sang about a girl in St. Louis. Drunken laughter added to the sense of normalcy everyone sought after the Wytch attack. Charlie wiped off a glass and set it down on the bar as the tall stranger strolled through the blasted door.

"Evening, stranger. What can I get for ya?"

"Brandy, please, if you have it."

The stranger smiled at the bartender, but Charlie noticed the warmth did not extend to the cool, gray eyes. "I have some in the back, sir. Just a moment." Charlie exited through a door behind the bar, returning a few seconds later with a dusty bottle.

"I just arrived in town," said the stranger. "I am looking for a place to stay for a few nights. Is there a boarding house?"

Charlie poured the brandy and set the bottle on the bar. "Mathilda O'Malley rents a room to travelers, but she has a guest right now. Probably try the livery stable down the street and behind the mining office," Charlie said, pointing with his dishrag to the right. "Old Zedekiah has a room in back he sometimes lets out."

"Much obliged," came the reply with a smile. The man

slowly pivoted to face the room. "Say, what happened in here earlier? Drunken brawl?" he asked as if only half-interested.

"We had a Wytch attack. Damn Wytches killed the Sheriff and nearly burnt down my place."

"Word on the street said the fight was over a woman."

"Nah, that ain't it. Saw it myself. One Wytch tried to conjure and set the floor on fire. See?" Charlie pointed at a scorch mark in the wooden floor, two feet in front of the stranger. "Sheriff James shot the Wytch before he could do more damage, but another Wytch appeared from nowhere and started throwing fire at everyone. He chased the Sheriff out to the street and killed him and his two Deputies before disappearing into thin air."

"Then why are people saying a woman was involved? Was one of the Wytches a woman?"

"There was a woman in here enjoying a game of cards. Pretty little thing. She tried to help after the fight spilled into the street."

"You must have incredibly brave women in this town," the man remarked, tossing back the remainder of his brandy and setting the glass on the bar top-side down.

"Oh, she's not from here. She's a traveler. Just stays at O'Malley's when she's passing through."

"Thank you for the information," the stranger said, placing two gold coins on the bar. "I shall call at the livery stable as you suggested." He tipped his hat and exited the building to the sound of a slightly out-of-tune piano.

***

Darkness descended on the town, but instead of settling

down for the night, the lights burned brighter. The sound of laughter and the occasional gunshot punctuated the stillness.

Viktor emerged from the livery stable, purposefully striding away from town. He held no lantern and, with the new moon rising, was virtually invisible to anyone sober enough to notice. If Charlie were to cross Viktor's path tonight, he would have noted a change in eye color. The pale, gray eyes now burned a deep violet.

Clearing a rise, Viktor descended into a dried creek bed, the sounds of the town fading in the distance. He walked until the town was but a distant memory, emerging from the creek bed onto the desert proper. A coyote yipped in the distance, but otherwise the desert was still.

Viktor stopped walking upon reaching a level area free of the many cactus plants dotting the landscape. He lifted his hands to shoulder-height, palms facing the desert floor. Slowly rotating to the left, he closed his eyes and swiveled his hands until his palms faced skyward, then pushed his palms out. The ground shook with his movements; all the plants and rocks within a twenty-foot radius uprooted and threw themselves outside of the newly cleared ceremonial circle.

Finishing the rotation, he sat down in a lotus position. Closing his eyes, he chanted, hands circling in the air before him. "I call upon the power of the Blacksmith. Use your earthen forge to change and shape the desert sand into creatures at thy servant's command. Putere Fierari este Eternă. Putere Fierari este Tot."

The ground shook, and two whirlpools of sand formed on either side of Viktor, ten feet in diameter an d rotating at an ever-increasing pace.

"Putere Fierari este Eternă. Putere Fierari este Tot."

A great clay hand reached from the depths of the first whirlpool, extending from the maelstrom and resting on the desert.

A second extremity, hammer-shaped, emerged just before the head and shoulders of a sand golem appeared.

"Putere Fierari este Eternă. Putere Fierari este Tot."

An arrow-like appendage shot up from the vortex of the second whirlpool, followed by clawed pincers seeking purchase on the sandy ground.

"Putere Fierari este Eternă. Putere Fierari este Tot. Dușmani Ai Grijă."

Sand exploded upward, the swirling whirlpools replaced by the conjured creatures. A giant sand scorpion stood to Viktor's right, pincers clenching and unclenching, its stinger poised and ready to strike. Opposite the scorpion, a fifteen-foot-tall golem waited. Hunched forward, it pounded the ground with fist and hammer.

Viktor marveled at the servants brought forth at his command. The sand skin of the golem was cool to the touch but rock-solid. Closing his eyes once again, he brought forth a memory of the Paladin standing in front of the boarding house. Laying his palm on the scorpion's forehead, he inserted the image into the creature's consciousness with the command to retrieve the girl at all costs and bring her back to the place of its creation. Moving to the golem, he implanted the same information.

Removing two ruby crystals from his pocket, he set them in the faces of the golem and scorpion, covering each with his hands. A spark of light flared, and the crystals embedded themselves into the stone creatures. Viktor removed his hands; a tendril of golden light connected the crystals to his palms. He brought his hands to his own face, connecting the tendril to his eyes.

"Go."

The golem lumbered toward town, gorilla-like in its movements, hand and hammer slapping the ground in time with its pace.

Its companion skittered along by its side.

Viktor returned to the lotus position, eyes closed, seeing the town rapidly approaching through their eyes.

***

The existing plane faded slightly around Salem, and he felt the presence of the Mother within his mind while the world glazed around him. He understood the Mother calling out to him, but the urgency in her voice froze him in place.

"Salem, I need your help. Darkness is coming. There is one who holds the key for survival. One who may stem the flow and restore balance within all the planes of existence."

Salem kneeled down in a show of supplication. Hearing the Mother like this, so serious yet so vulnerable—it was unexpected and unnerving. "Mother, I am here to serve. Tell me what I must do."

"Trust, Salem. You must learn to trust others and especially learn to trust yourself. The key to our survival, you have already met."

"You speak of the Paladin." Salem looked at the ground grimly.

"I speak of my daughter. As the last of the Taker bloodline, I call upon you to fulfill the vows of your ancestors in this time of great need. Will you answer the call, Salem Taker?"

Salem adjusted his legs to kneel in the ceremonial position, the left knee resting on the ground, the right leg bent with his foot flat, both hands palm-down on the earth, and head bowed. "I, Salem Taker, the last of my bloodline, do commit to fulfill the vows of my ancestors in service to Magic and life."

"Rise, my son. What I ask of you is not an easy thing, I

know. Simza follows the ways of the Paladin, but within her is hidden great power. There are those who seek to use her power to usher in the coming darkness. They desire war, feast on it. There is one who seeks her now…" The Mother stopped speaking.

Salem stood and waited for instructions, his mind sobered by the severity of the task. He would gladly serve the Mother, but for her to call for services by the ancient vows… He felt an icy hand clench around his heart.

Minutes passed in silence, the Mother's concentration elsewhere. Something was wrong.

"Simza is in trouble."

CHAPTER 5

Most of the torches illuminating the streets of Reunion Pass had been extinguished with nobody to look after them. The dusty road cutting through the frontier town and the storefronts lining the main street were void of any signs of life. Few had ventured from the safety of the indoors since the bloody confrontation between the Wytch and Sheriff James.

Simza Adenah prowled the vacant street in search of the source of the gunshots which had perforated the relative stillness of the night. She hoped that perhaps they indicated her quarry had not escaped the town. Dim light revealed enough of the Paladin's surroundings to see any signs of movement. Her eyes possessed sharp vision, so navigating the darkened area was of less consequence to Simza than to any others who might be foolish enough to brave the shadows.

She made her way toward Charlie's saloon. It was the last place she had encountered her target and the best location for her to pick up Salem's trail. Simza didn't bother to keep a ready hand on the butt of her pistol. With no sign of attackers, the Paladin knew her hands were faster than any would-be gunfighter she might encounter in the humble town of Reunion Pass. Still, her weapon sat, untied, in its holster, and Simza made sure her finger did not stray too far from the trigger.

Light and laughter poured out from inside the Frontier House of Vice. It sounded to the Paladin like things in Charlie's saloon had returned to their usual, inebriated status quo. Apart from the charred tinder where the swinging doors used to be, nobody would have known of the deadly exchange which had occurred earlier. Simza decided against entering the saloon. She did not want to draw any further attention to herself, and she greatly doubted that anybody within the walls of Charlie's establishment would be sober enough at this hour to offer any usable information.

Simza made her way around the side of the Frontier House of Vice and glanced down the alleyway separating the saloon from the neighboring tailor and cobbler's storefront. Little ambient light came from the sparse, smoldering street torches and booming saloon, so it took the Paladin a few moments to peer through the darkness. An unusual silhouette caught her eye and warranted her immediate attention.

Quickly but cautiously, she moved down the side street between the saloon on her right and the other business on her left. Simza kneeled beside the cooling bodies of three dead men laying in the dust of Reunion Pass. Three more killings in as many hours. *Damn you, Salem Taker*, the Paladin thought before she offered a silent prayer for the souls of the departed men. She visually examined the deceased trio, eyeing a series of simple gunshot wounds.

Simza began to think that perhaps the Wytch she was after might not have been their killer, but whether Salem had ended the lives of these men with his own hands or not, she was certain the Wytch had played some role in their demise.

The Paladin did note that whoever had killed these men had demonstrated a commendable degree of marksmanship. Each man had been shot once cleanly through the heart. Simza rethought her earlier sentiment about the remote likelihood of encountering a gunfighter equal in skill in these parts.

Sighing and discomforted by the thought, Simza Adenah realized her hand had unconsciously come to rest on the grip of her dragon bone.

There was little evidence on which the Paladin could act. A broken lantern lay next to one of the dead men, spreading shades of shattered glass on the ground. All men had guns beside them, useless in defense against their attacker. All the bodies faced the same direction, suggesting they might have been the aggressors or, at the very least, were not taken by surprise.

The man in the middle struck the Paladin's memory; she recognized him as the person who had accused Salem of cheating at cards. This fact at least helped to shed some small sliver of light on what had occurred here.

She did not wish to disrespect the dead, but she felt her duty to hunt down a vile Wytch ultimately superseded a matter of etiquette. Simza gave a quick search of the three dead men's personal effects. She turned up nothing of importance and introspectively chided herself for disturbing a departed soul and coming up empty-handed. Simza offered the men a whispered apology for the offense.

In the midst of her self-imposed admonishment, the Paladin noticed two sets of footprints trailing away from the bodies.

Her guilt doubled for not noticing such a thing before disturbing the bodies of the victims. She pushed the feeling from her mind and followed the tracks. They led her out the back of the alley and away from the town. Simza thought about going back to her room, as she was reluctant to continue hunting her prey with little more than a petticoat and her gun belt, but she was not about to let Salem Taker escape her again. The Paladin followed the trail, and she felt a stirring within her reassuring her that she was on the right path.

On the outskirts of Reunion Pass, where the town turned into prairie, the tracks became far more difficult to follow. Simza squinted and focused her keen eyes on the dust underfoot, but she feared she had reached the end of this lead. She fought to see the tracks shrouded in the darkness, and then everything was pushed from her mind except one thing. Danger.

She sensed something fast approaching on her flank, and she wheeled to face it. In an instant, her dragon bone pistol was clear of its holster and ready to fire. Simza's gaze met that of a massive desert scorpion, vile with wickedly sharp talons, but she quelled any fear trying to take root in her heart. Simza had never seen a beast like this before; there was no way this was a creature of nature. This had to be Wytchcraft.

Could this be a Wytch of the Druid bloodline? They could take animal form. Simza took note the creature's hide, absent of the normal black scorpion's chitin and instead made of earth and sand. A glowing red gem lodged in the creature's head. A Druid Wytch could only take the shape of an animal in its natural form. This thing must be something else. The Paladin raised her gun and fired a shot at the monster.

The bullet slammed into the proverbial bullseye of the red gem and sent a splatter of glowing crystal into the night. The beast let out a visceral hiss but continued charging the Paladin. Simza cocked and fired a second bullet, which struck its mark right in the same place as the first. It slowed the massive creature, but not nearly enough to stop it from barreling toward the woman at break-neck speed. She had the seconds to ready her pistol a third time but not enough to fire before the scorpion reached her. Simza dodged out of the way and sprawled on her back as the beast's powerful, barbed tail struck the earth where she had been standing only moments before.

The scorpion freed its tail and made ready to strike with it. Simza loaded and sent a bullet into the joint between the scorpion's barb and the rest of its tail. The silver bullet hit its mark with expert precision, blasting the scorpion's stinger from the rest of its body. A spew of sand flew forth as the beast waved its stump about.

Simza was not sure if the monster could feel pain, but the loss of the scorpion's stinger seemed to have stunned it momen-tarily. After another load of her dragon bone, the Paladin realized that silver Wytch-hunting bullets were clearly not enough to end this creature. Her left hand shot to the locket around her neck, which bore the crest of the Inquisition. She opened the locket and pulled the bullet from inside. Every Paladin carried one such bullet, given on the day a Paladin was knighted and swore their final vows. The round was anointed and blessed by the Grand Inquisitor him-self, and each bullet had a drop of dragon's blood inside. Its crea-tion was meant to slay any creature not of this earth.

The scorpion had regained its whereabouts and pressed its attack on the Paladin as she loaded her pistol. It hissed at Simza and sent one of its razor pincers careening toward her jugular as she took aim with her gun.

"In his beloved name!" the Paladin roared as she pulled the trigger and shot the scorpion in the head at point-blank range. The beast crumpled to the ground and turned to a heap of mundane dust before her eyes. The prairie stilled. With a fancy spin and flourish, Simza holstered her pistol. Shaking, the pulse of battle still lingering in her blood, she dropped to her knees, closed her eyes, and clasped her hands in prayer.

Simza's devotions were short-lived before her eyes flew open with a sense of renewed danger. Before her stood a gargantuan thing made of the same substance as the scorpion. It looked somewhat human, but one of its enormous hands took the shape of an anvil. In the middle of what would have been its face rested a red, glowing jewel similar to the one on the scorpion. The thing raised its arm and brought it down to strike the Paladin where she knelt. Simza felt death a breath away.

Before the golem's blow could land, the Paladin's feet erupted as a mighty redwood tree sprang from the dust of the prairie and armored Simza in wood. The golem's fist pounded into the tree. It ripped its hand from where it had firmly lodged in the timber and grunted furiously with the sound of grinding stone.

***

"Now, that's no way to treat a lady," Salem Taker said, flashing the golem one of his blinding-white smiles.

The golem lumbered toward the Wytch, bringing both its arms up to strike a crushing blow. Salem stood his ground.

Mother, as your child, I ask of you, imbue me with all the might of your spinning tempest and let the lighting that strikes bolts of argent light through your storm-swept skies bend to my command, so it may serve your blood and your children.

She answered with a thunderous report. The peaceful, starlit sky shattered with the deafening crack of thunder blasting so greatly it shook the very foundation of every building in Reunion

Pass. The golem fell to one knee by the maelstrom kicking up all about it. Salem felt the electric crackle of lighting running throughout the whole of his body. He felt the charge building in his belly, and when it reached an intensity he could no longer contain, he opened his mouth and shot a bolt of lightning straight into the red jewel in the golem's face. The thing drifted into the wind, and only sand and dust remained.

Salem went to the towering redwood and leaned up against it nonchalantly. He could hear the vigorous pounding of the Paladin trapped inside the tree, and he smiled widely.

"Oh, Miss Lark, what shall I ever do with you, you magnificent woman?" Salem said to himself. The Wytch indulged in several very illicit fantasies of exactly what he would like to do with the Paladin, but he was interrupted by a gentle pull at his sleeve.

He looked at the source of the disturbance and about fell over when he saw the boy who worked for O'Malley and had been hounding him since he snuck out of town.

"Excuse me, Mr. Sal, uh, sir?" the boy said meekly.

"What could you possibly want?" he asked. The Wytch was in utter disbelief at the boy's persistence.

"Well, sir, Mr. Pearly's debts."

***

Viktor Chavdar pulled himself out of the mud hole into which he'd been blown. His sight returned to him after seeing the lightning bolt strike the ruby in his golem. He felt like he himself and not his minion had been hit with the blast of energy.

He'd nearly flown into blind rage when he had witnessed the Paladin best his scorpion, but all such feelings of anger were wiped clean now. He cared not that he wallowed in a riverbed, cold and covered in mud. Viktor was not even upset that his creations had failed in their mission to retrieve Simza Adenah. Now, his elation made him almost want to dance under the moon. It was the greatest fortune he'd encountered in longer than he could begin to remember.

Viktor Chavdar now knew exactly where to find Salem Taker.

CHAPTER 6

Although Simza had endured the rigorous training to become a Paladin, losing her family at an early age had left her unschooled in other areas. She should have had a greater understanding of the nature of Wytchcraft by now, but her blood was not pure and she fell short in certain areas. Although she had always been aware of these facts somewhere in her mind, never before had they come to the forefront the way they did now. She felt certain that if Salem Taker hadn't hidden her in the bark of a redwood tree, the last blow the golem let fly might have ended her life. Usually so self-assured, she didn't know how to deal with that thought.

There was something else she didn't know how to deal with either—the heat she felt toward her rescuer. She drew on her sense of indignant outrage to pull her through the awkward silence between them. The strange boy who seemed to be bothering Salem Taker helped too.

"Mr. Pearly's debts won't pay themselves," the boy said into the silence.

"Get me out of this tree," Simza said through clenched teeth.

Salem sighed. "Everybody wants something from me today." His hex tattoos glowed briefly, and the bark around the Paladin lightened in weight.

She struggled out of it gratefully, happy to be free of the Wytch magic binding and surrounding her. The tree pulled away from Simza, but it continued to stand. It towered in the desert plain, and even though it was made through Wytchcraft, the Paladin couldn't help but admire its resolute reality in the desert.

"It won't ever survive out here," she said tartly. The boy stared at Salem with a hard intensity that both Wytch and Paladin found uncomfortable.

"It will survive if Magic wills it to survive," Salem said.

She frowned at him. He shrugged. He was the hand of Magic, and he understood it in his blood. She was a Paladin through her training, but she still felt Magic in her blood as well. "Why did you rescue me?"

"Maybe I'm saving you for myself." He grinned and waggled his eyebrows at her.

Simza fought an urge to giggle at his display. She was here to hunt him, not to flirt with him. "Why did you kill the men on the outskirts of town?" she asked, trying to find her footing again.

Everything she had ever believed had been thrown into question in the last strange battle, and all her once-known strength had drowned attacking the monsters that refused to die. Some force was at work here which went beyond Wytchcraft, and it seemed that only Wytches had the magic to defeat this force. Her usually reliable bullets and the blood of the dragons had proved worthless in taking down the scorpion and the golem.

"You have to pay Mr. Pearly's debts." The boy's voice still lacked any strident note and yet his persistence was implacable.

Salem shook his head. "I didn't kill the men... I would have if it had come to it, but it was the boy, here, who pulled the trigger."

Simza glared at the boy, suddenly suspicious of the timid youth. "Why haven't I seen you around before?"

The boy stared at her stubbornly. Salem grunted, interrupting the stare-down. "I think I'll call him Killshot."

"How do you know he doesn't already have a name?"

"Well, he hasn't seen fit to tell me one, so from now on we'll call you Killshot. Does that work for you?" Salem attempted to reach a hand out to put on the boy's shoulders, but the boy simply stepped out of reach.

"You have to pay for Mr. Pearly's debts," Killshot insisted.

Salem Taker frowned and looked at Simza, who wore the same concerned expression.

"There's something not right here," she speculated.

Salem nodded in agreement, and Simza caught a flicker of possible realization in his eyes as he glanced down at the boy again. "I don't think Killshot is from around here, but I think he's been collecting debts longer than his years would give the lie to. Am I right there, son?"

Killshot nodded slowly in delayed response.

Salem's eyes narrowed. "We aren't talking about coin when you say debt, are we? This goes beyond that. Pearly had another debt, didn't he, son?"

Killshot nodded again as slowly as the first time. Simza observed the boy more closely now, looking for possible signs of Wytchcraft on him. She had only seen a similar case once, though she'd shot the "messenger" before she thought about the delayed gesture. She watched him closer, barely noticing a faint shimmer glide around his body like he was false—something that didn't really belong here.

Salem shared a glance with Simza, who understood their insisted alliance. She couldn't help but feel like she and Salem were in this together, even though she had taken the vow to hunt his kind.

Our kind, a truthful and unwelcome voice offered in her mind.

Simza tried to shake it off and saw that Salem had noticed the telltale signs of conflict in her. How he could tell, she wasn't sure, but she assumed she either failed to hide her nerves or something about Wytches allowed him to see it. It didn't really matter. Either way, Salem had a way of knowing, and she couldn't allow that.

Killshot turned slowly toward Simza and looked at her for several long moments before speaking. "You were going to kill him anyway. You pay his debt."

Simza drew away from the boy and stood with her back straight as she replied, "I owe nothing for hunting a Wytch!"

"You owe his debts," the boy insisted.

Salem chuckled, and Simza whirled toward him. "What are you laughing about?"

Salem straightened his features and feigned a serious look. "Oh, I'm just relieved to be free of the debt."

The boy walked toward Simza. The determination of his footfalls unnerved her. "You will pay Mr. Pearly's debts?"

"No! I won't pay anyone else's debt."

The boy cocked his head, looking at her, though not with the physical eyes in his head. A force beyond him seemed to watch them through his blank, emotionless eyes. Simza's heart sank in realization that the boy was possessed by something greater than himself. Everything he had said until now had been hedged in metaphor, and now something different was poking its head through to their world.

Salem took a step forward and put out his hand; Simza could see his lips moving as he intoned an incantation. Sweat prickled across her brow as she felt Magic's presence in the air.

The presence was so strong, she briefly had the suspicion that he drew the magic from her, and her hand reflexively went for her gun, but she froze the motion before she reached the holster. It was like looking through a heat haze and into a hell-filled abyss. The boy's face became a window, and shapes, flames, and molten rock boiled around each other within him. The shapes grew clearer as mutated tentacles moved awkwardly but quickly toward them. Killshot's face had now vanished, and the tentacles stretched as they came through the abyss of hellish flames.

Heat radiated from the boy, palpable even at the distance they stood from him. As the freakish tentacles moved closer, the boy seemed to shimmer as though a hole to another world sat in the nighttime desert of the plains. The shape of the boy rolled backward, scrolling out and creating a void between the worlds that soon would let one of the monstrous tentacles out into their dimension.

***

Salem grabbed Simza's hand without thinking. Against this larger enemy, she surely would embrace her inherent abilities. He summoned the energy inside him, understanding, either way, that they must slam the doorway shut. Salem raised his left hand and, after he motioned to her, Simza raised her right. He could feel her pulsating with the power of the Mother. Out of the corner of his eye, he saw Simza glowing in the moonlight. He didn't want to use an invocation that the Paladin likely wouldn't know, so he just repeated a simple phrase, hoping the Mother would accept his plea.

"Mother, shut this door. Mother, shut this door. Mother, shut this door."

Simza picked up the chant. Magic moved between their linked fingers, and their arms slowly pulled closer together. The door narrowed. It tried to expand upward, and heat poured from it; their hands were slick with sweat.

Sounds of agony and exultation screamed out of the door. Salem panicked. Sound had joined them on this side of the doorway, and if they couldn't get it closed, it was easy to guess that whatever came out of the doorway next would be yet more unpleasant.

Shut the door, Mother, shut the door, Mother, shut the door...

Their voices rose in unison, and the door squirmed under their control. It was no longer shaped like Killshot but like a tear, then a disentangled starburst.

With a roar like thunder that ended in a profound silence, it slammed shut.

***

Salem and Simza were covered in sweat, and they panted in exhaustion. They could barely stand, both drained emotionally, physically, and magically. Simza's head whirled with the use of the forbidden magic. Her vows were betrayed. But she'd had no choice. To let that doorway open was unthinkable.

The oddly familiar feeling of Magic coursing through her

veins sent a shudder throughout her, and she looked at her hands. The Mother moving through her had felt like coming home, but she couldn't deny the vows she had broken without refuse. Unable to contain the exhaustive contradiction, she started to weep.

She'd betrayed her vows as a Paladin. She'd used Wytch-craft, and not only had she touched Wytch magic, she had enjoyed it.

***

Simza struggled to stand, but Salem caught her before she could collapse on the ground. It was nearly dawn, and Salem picked her up and carried her to the nearby hillside, where a stand of willows signified a likelihood of water. He set her down and followed the refreshing sound of water to a rippling river in the predawn darkness. He took a drink and cupped his hands to wet Simza's lips. They were both burning up with the heat of the dimension into which they'd stared, and it was his fault.

He had nearly opened up a possible terror in his mistaken effort to find out what continued hunting Pearly after his death. What had Dan Pearly been messing with?

He rubbed his hand across the stubble that had grown up on his face while he thought, trying to work out everything he had seen.

Simza had fallen into a deep slumber, and Salem couldn't help but smile when he saw that she had rolled over toward him and curled up against his leg. For the first time since he met her, he felt something other than desire as he looked at the peaceful features lining her face beneath the moonlight.

He recognized a possible affection, something that, if left to its own devices, could turn to love. The blood called to blood.

He smoothed her hair from her face. She had broken out in goose-bumps as her sweat turned cool in the prairie night air. She only wore a petticoat and her bandoliers, so Salem sighed and covered her with his cloak.

Resting his head against the bark behind him, Salem closed his eyes to sleep, but they flew open as a new presence made him uneasy.

Light barely stained the sky in the east, and he could make out a form. The approaching voice didn't sound as young as it had before, and it cracked when the boy spoke. "Hey, mister, can you help me?"

It was Killshot. He was no longer the vague, almost simple boy they had met.

The darkness has let him go, but for how long? asked the suspicious part of Salem's mind—the part which had ensured his survival for this long.

"Please, mister. I need help. I'm lost."

Salem rose to his feet. Simza still slept, pulling his coat over her head. "Killshot, are you…are you okay?"

"I don't know. I don't know anything," the boy said, then paused. "You know me?" He stepped closer, and Salem could see that the boy had been left without anything—not his memory, not whatever had been using him as a window, not even his clothes.

Salem sighed. He'd already given his jacket to the Paladin, and he didn't want to fight her for that. The boy covered himself and walked across the ground with a delicate step; even his boots had been taken from him, and the plains could not have been easy on his feet.

"I don't know you real well," he answered pitifully. "The only name I have for you is Killshot."

The boy nodded. His eyes were wild with fear. The Wytch

wondered what he had seen, what prison he had been kept in. One thing he knew for sure; whatever Dan Pearly had owed, he owed a lot more than coin.

For now, Salem knew, they needed sleep. He wondered if it would be safe to sleep with the boy there, though he was too tired to activate his protections and wards. If something was still using him as a passive vessel and it found them when they were this exhausted, he would be worthless.

***

Killshot noticed Salem appraising him and flushed. "I could stand guard if you're tired. I've been sleeping for a long time, it seems. I swear I'll be a good lookout."

Salem smiled. "I reckon that's the best plan."

Killshot watched the man lie down and try to get comfortable. The river wasn't a bad companion, and it kept him company. The sun already rose over the horizon, and the willow trees shaded them from what looked sure to be a hot day. Killshot couldn't recall his imprisonment, but when he closed his eyes, he saw fire. He was happy just to watch the little currents in the river move around the stones, which had been smoothed by years of the water's caresses. He put his bare feet into the stream, looked behind him, and caught a glimmer of light under the man's eyes. He wasn't quite asleep, and was possibly watching him to make sure it was safe.

Killshot couldn't blame him. He didn't know if he was safe, himself. He knew this man and woman had saved him from something—something he could only call hell. He didn't know how or why they had saved him, and he didn't yet remember how he had come to be trapped there or what had happened during that time;

all he could remember for certain was the flames.

The water ran over his feet, and he tried to remember, but every memory ended with the sensation of his skin crackling and burning. He could only rectify it by thinking of the man and the woman's faces. Turning his gaze to them, he felt the cool water and the dawn breeze against his skin. The man's eyes were shut for real now, and Killshot swore to himself that he would never betray them—not ever. The first thing was to let them get some rest. Then, first thing when they woke up, he would ask them what their names were. Once he knew their names, he would swear to serve them both or die trying.

He sighed. For the first time, he felt like he had an understanding of himself. He watched the sun edge up on the horizon through the leaves. He almost felt like he could rest, too, but he knew he had sworn to be a good lookout, and he wouldn't let anything lure him away from his post.

A loud, thunderous roar carried even over the song of the river—the sound of hooves on the plains.

Killshot turned to wake the man and the woman. They were sound asleep, and he had to jerk on the woman's foot before she stirred and glared at him in shocked anger.

"Ma'am, something is coming."

CHAPTER 7

Salem dreamt of Magic that night. Her ethereal being smiled and invited him into her wealth of power and wisdom. She assured him that looking after Simza was the right thing to do.

The Mother's visage was always joyous and inspired nothing but jubilance, but Magic's form slowly dissipated and pieces of her body shed away. The rosy light around her turned to black. A shadow cast across her face with an expression Salem thought he'd never see; her eyes were filled with fear. Her hand reached out for a desperate grasp. A silent cry came from her as she tried to warn him.

"Salem, Salem!" Killshot yelled at the sleeping Wytch.

Salem's body jerked awake. "What? What is it?"

"Someone is coming."

Salem became aware, and it brought a chill to his bones. He felt the magical reservoir inside him diminish, and what remained was less potent. The voice of the Mother was silenced. He felt sure even Simza could feel it; something suppressed his powers.

"What is it?" Simza asked as the sounding hooves grew louder.

"We've got to go."

Salem grabbed Killshot's and Simza's arms, trying to drag them into a run toward the river, but it was too late. A wagon pulled by a giant, white and black piebald horse cut off their path. A huge dust cloud rose as the wagon rushed to a halt, but that didn't stop the tall, dark, sharply bearded driver from hopping off and approaching them.

"Stay back, now," Salem warned, holding back Killshot and Simza with outstretched arms. "I hope he isn't who I think he is."

The man stopped a few yards away from them. "You know, it will be good fun to kill you, Salem Taker, but I can do nothing yet to harm the daughter of Magic."

"Who are you?"

"Viktor Chavdar, at your service," the man said with a courteous bow. He strode toward them. "Now, come with me."

***

"Enough," Simza said, her dragon bone pistol raised, aiming a silver bullet at Viktor. Her shot rang true, and the bullet pierced the chest of his coat above his heart.

Viktor looked down at the small hole in his chest with the same care one would give a mosquito bite. The wound didn't bleed and Viktor wasn't stunned.

Bewildered, Simza looked over her gun, hoping to find some obvious clue as to why her attack didn't work.

"What kind of Wytch is this?"

"Wytch?" Viktor laughed. "I'm further beyond Wytches than they are beyond humans."

"This is no Wytch," Salem mumbled. "He's a Diabolical."

"What is that supposed to..." Simza paused as she saw the panic in Salem's eyes and the sweat beading on his forehead.

His eyes remained glued to the strange, dark man analyzing his every move. She had never felt such intensity from him.

"Stay where you are," Salem commanded, attempting to keep control, but fear still hid in his words.

"I see you're not going to make this easy on me," Viktor remarked with a shrug. "So be it." Viktor held his palms out to face each other, and around them, a sinister, dark purple glow formed. Ancient symbols darkened around his hands, circling them in a rapid orbit. Viktor slowly kneeled to the floor, chanting, "Putere Fierari este Matisse, Putere Fierari este Matisse."

His chanting continued as he pressed his glowing hands to the dusty ground. The earth shook momentarily, then a sand golem sprouted from the dirt. It vaguely resembled a human's form, though misshapen. Chunks of sand flowed and fell from it.

Two more golems shot up from the ground, then five, then ten. In seconds, hundreds of sand golems surrounded Viktor.

"So many," Simza uttered in disbelief.

"Are those for us?" Killshot asked.

Viktor turned to his followers. "Get the man and the woman. You can kill the young one."

***

As the sand golems slowly trudged toward them, Salem closed his eyes and tried to hold all his strength inside himself. His connection to the Mother had been worn down, but he had to try. He called upon her, fervently trying to drag out a response.

I, Salem Taker, call upon your aid. Now more than ever. Please, lend me your power so it may serve your blood and your children.

The cosmic gleam returned to Salem's eyes, and his remaining magical energy gathered in the palm of his right hand. Flames condensed and cradled by his fingers into a ball. Steaming smog bellowed from the cracks of his mouth, and Salem hurled his fireball at the army of golems.

The inferno ball incinerated any golem in its path, smashing their sandy bodies into glassy chunks. It flew on through intercepting golems, burning its way to Viktor Chavdar.

Viktor lifted his hand to the speeding fireball and the palm emitted a glow. "Projectus," he said, and the fireball disappeared. A second later, a large explosion resounded alongside the river.

"Damn!" Salem shouted as smoke from the explosion engulfed them.

"What do we do?" Simza asked.

"Use the cover of the blast. Come on, let's go!" Salem sprinted for the river, followed closely by Simza and Killshot.

They hit the shallow river, huffing wildly through the water. The golems rolled out of the smoke, steadily making their way to the fleeing group.

Killshot screamed in a panicked frenzy, "We're not going to make it!"

"We'll be okay," Salem yelled. "Look." He gestured behind him.

The golems had stopped at the edge of the river. One of them bravely headed into the water, but its sandy leg immediately diluted, and the golem fell into the current as a giant pile of mush.

The three laughed their relief as they neared the other side of the river. They walked into a small clearing and a wooded area at the base of a mountainous plateau, then ran through the clearing, acting on Salem's cues.

"Head for thc woods. We can lose them there."

"Good thing sand golems can't cross water," Killshot cheered. He looked back to see their mortal folly, but the glee quickly washed from his face.

The sand golems had stopped at the edge of the river and, one by one, fell into the ground. Sand manipulated around the dirt on the other side of the bank, and golems rose into their thick form.

"No, no, no!" Killshot cried.

Salem figured out their next move, eyeing a large pine tree. "Climb. We can hide from them in the trees."

Simza and Killshot followed Salem up the tall tree, scrambling for the thin branches. They hid high among its green needles as the sand golems combed the woods for their prize.

***

On the plateau, a man pulled his brass binoculars from his face. His dark suit was soiled and tucked behind his khaki-colored, tattered cloak. His long-brimmed hat rested, ripped and broken, in parts atop his head. He scratched his wild beard, shedding dust and revealing a wild red beneath its brown layer.

Behind him sat a carriage, rather lavish for his appearance, pulled by two brown horses. Another robed man walked out of the carriage to stand beside him as they gazed at the escaping group.

"Is it him?" the robed man asked.

"Yeah," the bearded man answered. "Looks like he got himself into quite a mess."

"Is Dan with him?"

He shook his head. "Nope, but he is with a young boy and a fine dame. From the look of the firearm she was waving around, she's a Paladin."

"A Paladin? Why would he be with a Paladin?"

"Probably hiding from all them golems, I reckon."

"Golems," the man in the robe repeated, trying to absorb the idea of such an ancient, unseen magic. "That's quite a powerful spell. Who do you think could be behind it?"

"I don't know."

"Why isn't Dan with him?"

The bearded man glanced at his companion. "I don't know."

"Why was our magic connection severed?"

"I don't know that, either."

A wind blew between them, and the robed man hummed in contemplation. "You know what is supposed to have such power—"

"Don't even say it," the bearded man interrupted. "It is inconceivable."

"Still, we need to help him. You remember the First Tenet's code."

The bearded man nodded. "Salem is more important than the Mother's code. We'd help him without it."

"Well, what do we do, Tarlak?"

The bearded man stood, ready to get busy. "Let's get the pickaxes. We got some symbols to carve."

***

Day passed into night while the three still hid in the trees. They were tired, hungry, and their morale was low, yet somehow Killshot felt this might be a good time to vow his allegiance to the others in case the time to show it soon came.

He crawled over to Salem on a sturdy branch. "I realize Miss Lark and yourself have saved my life, and I'd just like to—"

"Shut up." The words strained out of Salem's mouth as he placed his hand over Killshot's lips. "The Diabolical might be able to hear us."

"What is a Diabolical?" Simza asked quietly. "I've never heard of such a thing."

"What? The Grand Inquisitor didn't cover that in your training?" Salem joked slimly. "When the seed of Magic first bloomed in the Mother, it cast a mighty radiant light, but with great light comes greater shade. The shadows the light cast took form and became powerful entities themselves. These creatures we call Diabolicals, and their wills and powers are steeped in evil."

"You're telling me he's as old as Magic?" Simza snapped.

"Hey, I don't even believe it, darlin'," Salem whispered. "I thought they were just tales. Kids' stuff. I never thought I'd actually meet one."

One of the golems screeched as it pointed up the tree. In that instance, the golems converged on the pine, and the sound of hooves could be heard in the distance. The golems pounded their soft bodies against the bark until their collective forms grew larger into one frame. The enormous mass of sand began to consume the entire tree.

"What do we do?" Killshot wailed in desperation.

Salem remained silent, just watching the sand closing in on them. Something hid his connection with the Mother, and he couldn't feel her presence. Plus, dealing with whatever possessed

Killshot the night before still had him drained. He was out of cards to play.

"Well, for now, you can put my jacket on until we find you some clothes."

***

Sensing the worry in Salem, Simza knew she needed to do something. Calling forth Magic was completely foreign to her, and she knew her power was being compromised, but still she needed to do something or they'd all die. Ple*ase, Mother? Magic? Whatever you are. We need your help now!* she yelled in her mind, and her forehead tingled.

***

Salem's gaze moved to a glow coming from Simza's face. A tattoo which had remained invisible until that moment emitted a warm light from Simza's brow. It took the form of a diamond, and Salem recognized it immediately.

"A Hex tattoo?" he said in wonder.

Simza screamed as she released the power she'd conjured in one blast.

The invisible explosion blew nothing back except the golems. The wall of sand encroaching on them was slammed to the ground in one blast as its magical properties were entirely dispelled. In that moment, Salem felt himself revitalized. Magic's presence waved over him again, but Simza didn't look as relieved. Her attack left her exhausted, and she slipped both out of consciousness and from the tree.

"Lark!" Salem yelled. He tried to grab her before she fell but to no avail.

The bed of sand at the base of the tree cushioned her fall, and Salem and Killshot sighed with relief. The remaining sand golems were still approaching, so they scrambled down the tree to rescue Simza.

"Head for the mountain!" Salem instructed.

Killshot hastily took the lead, dashing to the mountainside as fast as his legs could carry him. Salem slumped Simza over his shoulder, and by that time, the golems were nearly upon him. Using his renewed abilities, Salem shot fireball after explosive fireball at his assailants, paving a way to the mountain. The trees were lit up by the flames of numerous exploding bursts. Salem met up with Killshot at the foot of the mountain, his one-time enemy slung over his back, defending them with fatal flying balls of condensed fire. Once Salem beat back the horde, they climbed the rocky terrain and giant boulders.

Salem and Killshot reached a flat shelf, and they pressed their bodies against a wall-like slab of mountain rising straight up. It was impossible to traverse.

"What now?" Killshot said, his words drenched in worry.

Salem didn't answer. He just watched as the countless golems neared the mountain.

"What do we do?" Killshot desperately reiterated.

A light weight struck them both from above, and they looked up to see two ropes dangling from the mountaintop and disappearing beyond its rim.

A voice Salem recognized shouted, "Climb, you fools!"

They did as they were told and headed up the lifelines while Simza clung to Salem over his shoulder. Halfway up to meeting their mysterious rescuer, they heard four voices call out in unison, "Inferno Flames!"

It felt as though the entire planet rumbled. Rocks shook with fury, trees toppled over. The shaking was so violent, Salem and Killshot had to stop climbing and hold tightly to the rope. Then something yanked them up quicker than they had been climbing.

The foot of the mountain cracked, and the earth opened up, swallowing a good number of golems. An enormous ravine formed from nothing, like a mighty fault line had just awakened. From the enormous crack, a faint, orange light could be seen, quickly growing in strength. A blinding wall of flames cut into the night, separating the plateau from the woods. Moronic golems walked straight into the raging wall of fire, turning into beings of glass as they plummeted to their doom.

Viktor, now riding his beautiful white and black steed, rode to the wall of flames as if to examine it. As he neared, the golems halted their advance into the fire and turned, obediently, to their master.

"Yes, yes, yes!" Killshot shrieked with joy as they neared the top of the plateau. Another yank pulled him over the top, and he tumbled to rest face to face with a large, silverback gorilla. It roared in his face, and Killshot screamed his terror. The gorilla threw the rope he held aside, and Killshot went with it.

"Relax, partner," Salem said as he carefully laid Simza on the ground. "The Druid's just provoking you."

Four robed men stood beside a carriage, facing each other in a circle. Below their feet was a circular pentagram etched into the ground, and they chanted, "Pangua Sanfu, Pangua Sanfu."

Viktor looked up at his prey's saviors. "It is not wise for you to stand between them and me!"

The silverback gorilla transformed into Tarlak, who bent over the mountaintop to call down to Viktor. "And you were fool enough to mess with a Wytch, Diabolical!"

"Yes, but you may call me Viktor Chavdar. My plans don't include killing all of you... All I need from you is that Paladin and that Wytch I've been looking for. Then this will all be over."

"Well you can't have them," Tarlak announced haughtily.

"Fine," Viktor called out. "But know this. I will take that as an act of war from the Mother's children and, with the Paladin under your watch, from the Mother's own blood. You have been warned. I will see you all again."

Viktor's golems fell lifeless to the ground, and he rode away, his horse's pace quickening in his determined stride.

"Brother," Salem said, turning graciously to Tarlak and those around him, "of all the Mother's children..." Tarlak's attention drew Salem's thanks to a halt, and he tried to follow the Druid's distant gaze. "Tarlak, what is it?" Salem asked.

"Salem, the Diabolical is not all we need to discuss."

CHAPTER 8

Salem looked down toward the ground, seeing only the hoof prints Viktor's horse had left behind. He shook his head, knowing that whatever Brother Tarlak gazed at, it wasn't the landscape below him. He placed his right hand on Tarlak's arm.

"What do you see, Tarlak? I see nothing worth your rapt attention."

"You cannot see yet. It is not your time, but I will tell you what I can. I see the past, the present, and the future, but it is fluid. It can change in an instant, depending on what we do now. Our future could be bright and progressive, a family united, a feud dissolved, or there could be no future at all—for any of us. It depends on you, Brother Salem."

He turned away from Salem and watched Simza regain consciousness and sit up carefully, watching the others with a hostile glare. Tarlak took a couple long strides toward Simza and offered his hand in aid. "A future of discontent and despair, or even the great black void itself, could ride upon your lovely shoulders, Paladin," he told her.

***

She took his hand tentatively, trusting that he wouldn't try to harm her. Whatever she had conjured earlier still wore at her, and she didn't deny she would lose if she chose to fight the Wytch. He pulled her to her feet. She steadied herself and looked up at the tall Druid. The top of her head only came up as far as his wild, red beard. Her eyes opened wide in shock and concern at his dire prediction.

"Me? Why me?"

"You are a Wytch hunter. It is your duty. You are the last Paladin who still carries the Wytch blood within you, as Salem is the last of his bloodline. You have not killed him because of Mother Magic's intervention, but you must not kill another Wytch, either. The two of you must reunite the Paladin and Wytch Born kin, to become one family again, to fight a far greater enemy. A time of rebirth and unity is near, but only if you personally allow it and work toward it."

"What if I don't wish to…unite with Salem Taker?" Simza blushed a little at what uniting with Salem might mean to her but pushed the thought away.

"If you choose not, you will be sucked into a maelstrom of evil and destruction beyond what this ancient world can bear. It will be destroyed from within; the magma from the Earth's core will spew out of crevasses and deep fissures caused by raging hatred and battle curses and spells. The darkest of magic forbidden by the Mother herself will be used against good, and darkness will prevail."

Tarlak spread his arms, and for a moment, a mirage appeared between them—human bodies aflame and falling endlessly; decapitated heads whirling and bobbing, spurting blood from severed necks; unspeakable creatures with ebony leather wings and claws filled with the remnants of mangled children. All flashed in devastating color and brilliance. Simza caught a glance of mortified stillness on Salem's face, and her heart froze as she watched the gruesome sight predicted by the Wytch.

He slowly closed his arms until his hands clasped, and the vision disappeared.

Simza knew she could not hide the alarm on her face. She was still weak from her interaction with the Mother and the fall from the tree. So much depended on her, and her alone. Her own weakness could be the cause of ultimate disaster, and yet she could barely stand. Her eyes rolled back in her head, and her body began its fainting descent toward the ground.

***

Salem caught her under the arms and lowered her gently to the ground, where he kneeled and cushioned her head upon his knees. He looked up at Tarlak, anger and frustration shooting sparks from his eyes.

"How dare you do that to her?" he screamed. "What gives you the right to put the destruction of all upon her alone? I've never known you to be so cruel. You say she is the last Paladin. How can you possibly know that?"

"I didn't until just now. Magic used me as a vessel…she needed me to inform you of what has to be done," Tarlak answered calmly. "I didn't know until you dropped her at my feet that she was the last Paladin. I didn't know that the vision between my hands could be seen by others until I saw it in your faces. I had no desire to be cruel. What we saw is but one possible outcome. If the two families do not unite—if she refuses to end the feud between the Paladin and Wytch Born…"

"Is that why you're here? To end the feud between families?"

"Not initially. We came seeking you and Dan Pearly to help us rally other Wytches and magic beings…to join us in the coming war. Attacks on us as well as others fighting for good have become more frequent. We were told Dan was with you. Why is he not here?"

Salem frowned. He thought the Mother would have told all Wytches by now so they could mourn for the loss of a Brother. "He's dead. He was recognized as a Wytch and died for it." He shook his head, ashamed. "I tried to stop it, but the Mother didn't answer my pleas for help until it was already too late. She knew he was dead. She took him to the place of resting. Why would she send you to find Dan?"

"She sent us for both of you. Now is the time for discussion. We will eat, we will drink, and we will talk. We must prepare for what is coming." Tarlak motioned the three other Druid Wytches forward. "I will introduce you to our Brothers. This is Atticus, the voice of reason. He is our arbitrator to settle disputes fairly."

A man wearing a brown hooded robe stepped forward. He had long white hair and a flowing white beard. He was not large in stature, under six feet tall, and he bowed and sat on a patch of grass near the pentagram they had carved into the plateau.

"This is Ansgar, our warrior and strategist. He will draw our battle lines and train those who would help us fight the enemy.

The Diabolical was only the beginning."

A large, clean-shaven man with short brown hair and heavily muscled arms bowed at Salem and turned to sit beside Atticus. He wore black with worn boots and a linen shirt, covered with a brown, hooded cloak.

"What, no robes?" Salem grinned.

"Robes are rather difficult to fight in," Ansgar said gruffly.

Ignoring this exchange, Tarlak continued. "This is Morvyn, master sailor. Not all of our battles will be fought on land. The sea will bend to his will."

Morvyn went to sit with the other two. Tarlak nodded toward Killshot, who stood riveted to his spot beside Salem. No doubt the previous vision had frightened him, and Salem could only assume how much more frightened he was of the Druid who had greeted him as a gorilla.

"Who is this young man, and why the devil is he naked?" he asked.

"This is Killshot, a skilled marksman. He protected me against those who would harm me. He was just recently possessed by something…difficult to explain, but he seems fine now, just somewhat bare. Whether he'll stay unaffected remains unknown. For now, he has no other place to go. I will allow him to stay with us unless he becomes strange again," Sal said, looking pointedly toward the boy.

"All right, we'll accept that for the time being. Young man, there is a crate of supplies in the back of the carriage. You will also find some items of clothing you can rummage through. Bring the crate back once you have preserved your modesty," Tarlak told Killshot.

The boy hesitated and looked at Salem, who nodded. He

walked to the carriage to do as he was told. Tarlak made a sweeping motion for Salem to join the others on the grass.

***

Simza had opened her eyes again and had heard most of the introduction. She stood up with little help from Salem, and they returned to sit with the others, who now formed a perfect circle. A small fire appeared in the center of the patch.

"I did not wish the boy to be part of this discussion, especially if he can be easily possessed by something unknown to us. He will sit in the carriage and sleep until I summon him." Tarlak turned to Salem. "You know me, Salem, as a Brother, but that is only figuratively speaking, as you are the last of your bloodline. You are the direct son of Adam Taker, the man who married your mother before she loved the Paladin's father."

"My name is Simza Adenah," she said quietly.

"Yes, your father was Caldar Adenah, whom your mother loved, but he took you and left her. You were not allowed to follow your Romni heritage for fear that your mother would take you away from him. The Caldarari clan is of his lineage."

Simza sat quietly, taking it all in. She was now learning more about her own background than she'd ever learned from her father. Once, she would not have believed these words from a Wytch, but now, she understood the severity of the erupting world. She heard the truth in every word.

***

"Why am I the Favored Son?" Salem interrupted. Tarlak's words cut into him. He didn't want to believe what Tarlak implied;

he didn't want to believe the Mother had held something from him.

"I've not heard such a thing."

"It's what she called me."

"I don't know of the title, Salem, but you are part of it all, as well. Magic was married to your father, Adam Taker, but he was killed when you were very young. She never married another. Although she physically had many lovers, she gave her whole heart only to your father. Most of her children have different fathers, but you are the only legitimate son, perhaps the favored last of the Taker bloodline."

"Simza is my blood, then?" Salem didn't like the possibility; his stomach churned, but he would hear Tarlak speak.

"The Mother has lived many lives since her time as a human. She is not immortal, as you know, but the First Tenet continues to survive her in a new life. Magic has taken many physical forms over the centuries—different bodies with one soul. Because you are both her children, you haven't aged as humans do. Nor do you share the same biology—just the Mother's Wytch Born blood. Simza has more of her father's blood in her than Magic's. Perhaps that is why you can contact Magic more regularly." Tarlak sighed, exhaustion worn on his face. "That is enough for today. I no longer feel the need to impart my hidden wisdom. Now we rest. We must decide what we will do next."

Tarlak spoke, Killshot approached the group, dragging a large wicker crate. Salem rose to help him carry the food closer to the fire.

CHAPTER 9

Simza could not recall ever feeling so utterly exhausted. Not only was her body sore from all the fighting with strange sand monsters, but her spirit—her power—was drained. She supposed it was a result of the day. Upon discovering her bloodline crossed with Salem Taker's—her being told she was Magic's daughter—the night turned into a hazed cloud in her head. Now, she felt the weight of the knowledge, though she still had trouble believing it.

The powerful warmth in her blood when she chanted with Salem to close the portal had excited but exhausted her all the same. It was a miracle she was still standing. She barely remembered the words, and part of her hated herself for using such magic, but the flowing power was enticing…relaxing.

What bothered her the most, however, was that for the second time in her life, she felt a nagging ache of doubt. Why had she not been able to kill Salem when she had a clear opportunity? If she had done her job, she wouldn't be surrounded by Wytches and their prophecy requiring her to leave behind all she'd been trained to do.

Every moment after first calling upon Magic ebbed that desire to follow everything the Grand Inquisitor trusted her to do. Always strong, determined, and confident in her powers, Simza worried that now she couldn't, or even more disturbing, shouldn't kill Salem Taker.

She had to get away—to be alone to think—to clear her head and sleep. Rather than go back to the others, Simza started in the direction of the mountain's base. She had wandered out this way once before and had found a peaceful clearing amidst beautiful trees and foliage. Trees always seemed to fortify her, to help her gather her thoughts and strength. Before she could decide which way to go, she found herself in the clearing. With a huge, exasperated sigh, Simza lay back on the soft moss, closed her eyes, and clutched her locket, feeling the engraved crest of the Inquisition as she fell into a troubled sleep.

***

While Killshot loaded the food and other supplies, Salem paced, half-mumbling and half-yelling.

"This is ludicrous! How is it possible that a Paladin is the one who decides the fate of this world and everyone in it?" Before Tarlak could answer, Salem turned and faced him with a deadly calm. "You claimed you did not know any of this and that the Mother used you as a vessel, but earlier today, Magic appeared to me and specifically warned me of a terrible war in all dimensions. She said before any type of understanding or peace agreement is made, many lives would be lost. The way the Mother told it, it very well could have had something to do with your vision. However, what I find strange is that Magic made no mention of Simza being responsible for whether or not there is a war. In fact, it sounded to me like war was inevitable."

Tarlak looked at Salem with something close to pity. "All I know is what I received during that vision, and I told all of you everything. I'm sorry if you doubt me, Brother Salem, but that is your right." Tarlak went back to eating his food and did not speak again.

As Salem watched the men eat, he made a decision to keep a closer eye on the Druids. He had considered himself honored to have heard from the Mother in his own vision, and Tarlak's claim that Simza held the future of all didn't make sense.

Tarlak may have been like a brother to him, but why did the Mother not tell the Druid of Dan's death, and how did Tarlak know so much about the history of Salem's and Simza's childhoods? Salem had decided to believe Tarlak at the time, but now he had the distinct feeling all was not as it appeared.

***

Simza kneeled in the middle of a field surrounded by carnage, the scent of death all around her. No human or animal sounds broke the deathly silence. She found no signs of life at all. The barren land expanded as far as she could see, and she felt for the crest of the Inquisition, but it was not there.

She awoke in exasperated breaths and swollen tears. Words tumbled from her lips before she could halt the chill trembling throughout her body or realize the desolation no longer surrounded her.

"This is all my fault. I could have prevented this."

The calm of life formed around her and came into focus, and she steadied herself. *It's just a dream*, she told herself. It was only the lingering words from that redheaded druid. *Curse him!* She spit on the ground, despising her willingness to believe what Tarlak had showed her. The vision he'd conjured was most definitely some sort of magic, meant to distract her from her objective—to kill Salem Taker.

The more she thought about it, the more convinced she was that this was all a trick. Then, in her mind's eye, she saw her father's face clear as ever. Simza composed herself. More determined and with a clearer head, she set off back in the direction of the Frontier House.

***

Viktor knew how to find Salem without following the Paladin, but he knew she was part of his master's plan. Not only was she a distraction to Taker, but he didn't like loose ends or potential threats, and this girl was definitely proving to be one of them, if not both. He sensed a lot of Wytch power when she was around, too, which drew his curiosity.

While the Paladin had been having her nightmare, Viktor created what would surely be much worse than whatever imagined terrors had made her scream. Viktor found the thorniest tree and once again took out the red gems, placed them in two perfect knots in the trunk, sat down, and began chanting.

***

With her eyes on the Frontier House and her hand on her loaded pistol, Simza slowed down to decide what strategy would be best. She called on the ancients for support.

Ancient Ones, please hear my call. In the name of the Grand Inquisitor, I ask that you come to my aid in my quest to rid this world

of the Wytch, Salem Taker. Please hear my plea and aid me in aveng-
ing the death of my father, Caldar Adenah.

Simza went into the Frontier House and waited patiently for
an answer or a sign.

The sky went black. It was if night instantly descended upon
Reunion Pass. Then came the wind—a wild, thrashing wind like
nothing Simza had ever experienced. She fell down to the ground in
an attempt to shield herself from whatever destructive force was at
hand.

She buried her face and curled inward; a horrible screeching
sound permeated through the bursts of wind, followed by an earsplit-
ting flapping she couldn't identify.

What in the name of the Universe is happening?

Simza had never felt such confused fear until she dared to
look up and saw two eyes staring at her, blood-red and filled with
pure hatred.

"Mother Magic, I, your daughter, Simza Adenah, call upon
you for help at this vital moment. Please tell me what to do so I can
prevent death and destruction and do whatever I must to protect our
kind." The words flew from the Paladin's lips before she could even
think about what she was saying. She couldn't take them back now,
and a part of her didn't want to.

Protect our kind, a voice repeated in her head. Simza felt
warmth emanating from her forehead, and with that, a surge of power
propelled her to turn and run toward the place she'd last seen Salem
and the Druids.

***

Salem was with Tarlak and the others when they saw the beast
flying toward them, its red glare aimed at something on the ground

below it.

Viktor, Salem thought. *And Simza!*

He did not even stop to ponder why she may have left. He jumped up, ready to run toward the clearing. Before he could take a step, he heard a strange humming chant coming from behind him. When he turned, Ansgar transformed into an enormous, prehistoric vulture with black scaly wings and dagger-sharp talons. They all watched in amazement as what was once Ansgar now rose into the dark sky and aimed itself directly at the gleaming red eyes. Confident that the Druid had the situation under control, Salem took off down the mountain toward the clearing.

With the deafening sounds of grinding, flapping of wings, and the inhuman resonance of screeching and screaming following him, Salem ran. Finally spotting Simza running toward him, he caught up, grabbed her in one arm, and headed for the protection of the forest.

Once she caught her breath, Simza turned on him. "What are you doing, Salem Taker? I can take care of myself. I certainly don't need you rescuing me like some damsel."

Salem looked her directly in the eyes. He fought the pull of lust and attraction he felt even now in the midst of danger. "Lark, there is no time for your tantrums. We must protect ourselves if we are to prevent the predicted destruction to come."

They both looked up as a blood-curdling shriek came from above. It suddenly seemed to be raining blood all around them—a deep purple, blackish blood.

The giant creature with the gleaming red eyes dropped from the sky with an earthshattering impact. Ansgar had succeeded in defeating Victor's beast.

But I am sure this is only the beginning, Salem thought darkly.

He turned to look at Simza, but she stared trancelike at someone standing next to the beast. From a few yards farther away, Salem heard Viktor scream in defeat, uttering words neither of them recognized.

***

Simza tried to make herself look away, but then she saw them. Those deep, violet eyes. A shiver which felt more like an electric shock went through her whole being. She had seen those eyes before, but they'd belonged to someone else.

CHAPTER 10

Under the cold, black sky, the defeated beast lay in a purple pool, its once red eyes now closed forever. At its side, amidst the lashing wind, a golem slowly rose to its feet from a crouching position, never taking its violet eyes off Simza. In contrast to its long, wide, stiff body, its head was human-like and very familiar.

Can it really be him? Simza thought in complete disbelief, gazing at the same glow she'd seen in Viktor's eyes.

***

Sensing the danger and without wasting more time, Salem called upon Magic.

"Magic, as your child, I ask of you, as lightning strikes the rotting redwood trees, driving through them and blowing their trunks apart, let that timeless energy flow through my hands, so it may destroy your enemies."

A bright white glow beamed from the Hex tattoos on Salem's arms, confirming that his call was answered.

***

The golem now stood over seven feet tall. After a slow nod, it walked toward Simza. Its distinctive and familiar stride, the head of black hair, and its eyes—even in Viktor's violet shade—made Simza's heart stand still.

It is *him*, she thought.

Salem screamed as he blasted the golem with lightning strikes, which, even though they slowed it down, did not prevent it from approaching the group.

"Stop! It's my father!" Simza yelled, earning the surprised looks of Tarlak, Morvyn, Atticus, and Killshot, who had just arrived.

It had been so long since she'd last seen her dearest Caldar, but she would recognize him anywhere, even inside a golem. *He must be trapped*, she thought.

Salem kept hitting the golem with lightning bolts, ignoring Simza's order, while the other two Wytches assumed battle positions.

The Wytches wouldn't listen. Simza knew who could make them listen, and she suppressed her pride. Realizing that her last hope was Magic, Simza called upon her, desperate and in a daze.

"Magic, you have to stop them! They don't know what they're doing!" Simza knew almost right away that Magic would not answer that call. Caldar was heavily outnumbered by the

Wytches, but Simza felt obligated to try again, no matter how help-less and exhausted she felt. "Mother, as your daughter, I call upon you with all my strength. Build a wall around my father. Help me protect him from harm so I can protect our kind."

Simza's diamond-shaped Hex tattoo flickered faintly on her brow. *Maybe it worked this time*, she thought.

When the golem was nearly within arm's reach, Simza held out her arm, but a last-minute blast repelled him away. "No!" she screamed and raised her arms palms-out toward Salem, throwing a transparent energy wave his way and knocking him down. When she threw another at Atticus, the waves seemed to have suddenly grown too weak to inflict any kind of damage.

"Lark, what are you doing?" Salem immediately got back on his feet but received no answer.

***

Killshot, who had observed everything from a safe dis-tance, raised his gun at Simza but quickly realized that his arm was shaking. He couldn't understand if his inability to aim straight was because he had no energy left in him or because something pre-vented him from shooting at Simza. He panicked and struggled to keep aim.

***

"Stop attacking your own kind, my good woman. We are on your side." Atticus had to yell to be heard, since the wind had picked up.

Simza looked up to the sky and noticed Ansgar, still in his vulture form, rapidly descending straight onto the golem. When the long-necked scavenger approached the end of his dive, his sharp claws open and ready to grasp the tall creature by the shoulders, Simza drew her pistol and fired at him. Ansgar jolted and flew right over her head, then disappeared into the deep forest.

With a look of horror, Killshot ran toward Simza and threw her to the ground, grabbing the pistol from her hand and throwing it into a nearby hedge.

"And keep her there!" Salem yelled, then turned to Morvyn. "Let's do it your way, shall we?"

Morvyn nodded. Then Salem called upon Magic once again. "Mother, I, Salem Taker, ask of you, as great torrents of water fall and splash against rocks, let endless and powerful currents flood my veins, so it may serve your blood and your children."

Just as the golem threw whatever it found in its path at the Wytches, a large boulder crashing into Tarlak's shoulder, Salem's call was answered.

Swiftly, he raised his arms and pointed his palms to the sky, sending vigorous streams of water at the golem. Simza's pleas for them to stop attacking what she claimed to be her father were in vain. When the water reached the golem's head, Morvyn whispered an incantation unknown to the others and, arms facing the dark sky, turned the stream into a ceaseless waterfall three times the golem's size. Yet despite the tremendous torrent pouring down on it, and even when only two bright violet circles could be seen behind the thick blanket of water, the creature stood its ground and pressed its attack.

Tarlak, in great pain after the blow he had received, pointed at Viktor, who had been trying to remain distant in the background. "Brothers, remember who the true enemy is. Aim for the Diabolical." And they did.

With the strong winds aiding their effort, Salem and Morvyn moved their arms in unison and guided the waterfall away from the golem and closer to Viktor, then tilted it. When the violent stream reached Viktor, immobilizing him on the ground, Tarlak assumed the form of the silverback gorilla and ran toward his foe, holding his injured limb close to his chest.

***

The golem had reached its destination and stood looming over Simza and Killshot.

"Let me go!" Simza tried to fight Killshot off her, but the boy was actually remarkably strong for his age and build.

The conjured creature rose its clenched fists above them, hovering over the struggling duo.

***

Viktor struggled to keep his creation alive against the never-ending stream pouring down on him when the silverback gorilla grasped his neck and screeched in his face. Having served its purpose, the waterfall eased and dissolved until all that remained was a thin gray mist in the air. Before Viktor could utter a new incantation, the gorilla opened his mouth wide to screech again, exposed his large canines, and closed its jaws on Viktor's neck. At the same time, the golem shined a blinding violet light, then crumbled into pieces on top of Killshot and Simza. Killshot shoved himself over Simza, catching the shards with his back.

When the gorilla momentarily turned his head to see what had happened, Viktor seized the opportunity to push him off, then ran as fast as he could.

"Don't let him get away!" Salem screamed, and the gorilla chased after the Diabolical.

Viktor tripped over a rock, and the gorilla dove forward, but Viktor vanished, leaving the animal to land hard upon the empty ground. The Diabolical had escaped.

Everything was cold and still in the darkest area of the astral plane when Viktor arrived. Breathing through his mouth and with a hand over his bleeding wound, he entered an empty, unlit room. He had failed to capture Salem Taker and could no longer fight for the cause. The Wytch had already gathered too many allies to be faced alone.

Viktor had sensed that the Paladin's will was still weak, and he thought that maybe there was still time to turn her against Salem Taker—but he was not sure. The bond between the Wytch and the Paladin continued to grow.

Viktor opened his eyes wide and raised his eyebrows high, then lifted his free arm to shoulder-height, palm down, humming and whispering, calling upon the power of the shadows. Soon enough, a ceremonial pentagram appeared in the center of the room, each of its corners beaming a violet light.

Viktor sat down in the lotus position and floated inside the circle, letting the blood drip down from his wound. Then he spoke loud and clear. "Ancient One, I call upon you by my true name. I, Viktor Chavdar, your first True Servant and the last of the Chavdar line, ask of you, as the Moon becomes crimson under the Earth's perfect shadow, let the blood I am offering you be enough to do what cannot be undone, so that we may make new the world in your image."

Viktor's palms warmed up without hurting him even when he felt his flesh burn. He closed his eyes and kept to his position until he finally received his response. This time he had succeeded. Viktor smiled a wicked smile and as he did so, a menacing gray cloud formed over Reunion Pass.

The Wytches had formed a circle to assess their injuries. Even though Killshot had aimed his gun at Simza and taken her down, she still lay on the ground, weeping in his arms. When Salem ran up to them, demanding an explanation for her behavior, Killshot held onto her protectively and motioned him to go away. Simza was not ready to face the Wytches' anger and confusion yet.

"What were you thinking back there? You could have killed us! What about Ansgar?" Salem asked, but Simza would still not look at him or respond. Before Salem could do anything else, he heard Magic call upon him, bringing him swiftly into the astral plane.

"Magic, do you know what that was about?" Salem asked Magic's ghostly form.

She stood in silence for a while, then spoke oddly, as if in a trance. "My child, something is amiss in both our dimensions. Events beyond our control have been set in motion. A long, sleeping, dark power has awoken. It has been centuries since the last time this malevolent force was called upon. I know it will fail again, as it did then, but this will not be without a cost. My child, as your Mother, I bring upon you the Essence of my Spirit. Kneel." When Salem did as she ordered, Magic slowly raised a finger and brought it up to the Wytch's head. "I mark on your forehead the symbol of our last harbinger of hope, in both the physical world and the astral plane. Only you can call upon it, as the very few before you have done. Use it wisely. It is all up to you now. Go. There are things I must do."

After her last words, Magic came out of the trance and motioned for him to leave her alone. Salem returned to the physical plane, and his mind settled without hesitation as a calm overcame him. The gray cloud over Reunion Pass dispersed.

***

At the Frontier House of Vice, the intoxicated voices of dispute, the songs of the out-of-tune piano, and the sound of dancing heels against the wooden floor had been replaced by absolute stillness and quiet. Local drunks, prostitutes, miners, railroad workers, and merchants lay motionless on the saloon's slippery floor, on the long stairs, under the broken tables, and even on top of the wagon-wheel chandelier. Some of them still had their guns untouched in their holsters. The torn playing cards and the scattered bills told only a small part of the story.

Outside was no better. Merchant carriages had been turned upside down, their goods ruined in the wet, viscous sand, drenched in brandy and rye whiskey which had poured out of dozens of broken bottles. No standing or undamaged barrel, or any other wooden object, existed anywhere in town. Broken houses emitted smoke from giant holes on their rooftops and wells had overflowed. The signposts were no longer there. Reunion Pass was no more.

The eternal creature, summoned by the Diabolical and which now observed its work with pride from a distance, had made sure of that.

CHAPTER 11

In the moments before its destruction, Reunion Pass had no reason to suspect what was coming. The streets were filled with exuberant characters and busy workers. They managed to make the cold, autumn night feel warm and joyful, and the Frontier House of Vice welcomed its patrons with dim lights and strong brew.

As the drinks flowed into the customers and out to the street, a subtle clip-clop sounded in the background of the cacophony and steadily grew louder until it overtook the surrounding area.

The galloping of Viktor's white and black horse echoed throughout the town. He rode with a fiery determination on his face despite the fact that he wasn't sure where he was going. The Wytches were rallying together, and Magic somehow still fought with them. They would be hard to fight, and with the Paladin and her unknown power beside them, he wasn't willing to test the extent of his strength. He felt it within the Paladin. She resembled a threat he couldn't identify. In the astral plane, he had made a plea to help him do what could not be done on his own, but he'd only received instructions, instead. The gray cloud in the sky had directed him back to Reunion Pass, and it disappeared when he arrived, confirming the location of his orders. There, in the small town, all would become clear.

Viktor reeled his horse to a dead stop when he noticed a sharp pain in his arm. He looked around and saw a small pool of his blood on the ground, dripping from a wound that had formed. The blood began to move; it ran down the dirt road and off the beaten path beneath his horse's hooves. Viktor slowly rode down the path and stopped in front of the Frontier House of Vice.

He dismounted and looked around at the commotion in the street. He disregarded the drunken slurs and hooting, and moved off the dirt road toward a river. By the riverbed, he found what he had been looking for—his pool of blood had stopped right next to the remains of Dan Pearly's body. Decay had yet to set in, but the effects of what had occurred to him showed through. The unearthed corpse bared the presence in a fading veil. Viktor put his hand over Dan's forehead and recited an incantation as instructed.

"Uti hoc corpus penes temet ipsum."

Dan's body glowed, and the remaining light in his body escaped while an ocean of shadows seeped in. The corpse shifted rapidly and contorted as the new evil made itself comfortable within the walls of his hollow carcass. The dark creature which now inhabited Dan's body held an ominous aura, sucking in any surrounding light and creating a field of emptiness around itself.

The creature floated up to its feet and stared at Viktor. Viktor extended his hand. "We have been waiting for the time you would return to us. Welcome back to the shadows."

The creature replied to Viktor, not in any earthly tongue but in a language conceived before words. Viktor could not make out what the creature had said, but it appeared that the creature understood him.

"I have brought you back, Conqueror. Consider this town a tribute to you. I know it has been a long time since you walked on the Earth, so this will be a good place to...reacquaint your-self...with how things work here."

The Conqueror nodded. He made another comment in his native tongue, then moved toward Reunion Pass. Viktor watched as the creature seemed to glide back to the beaten path. Within moments of its arrival, he heard the cheers and laughter replaced by the screams of death and despair. It sounded all too grizzly that even he felt he better not look at what had become of the town. Instead, he smiled, ready for the moment he would fulfill his duty and destroy the Taker bloodline—and all the Wytch Born.

Viktor mounted his horse and made a quick exit. He turned once and looked back at Reunion Pass to see the smoke rising and the creature, which seemed to have more than doubled in size, almost a blur as it moved swiftly from one person to another, leaving carnage in its wake. Viktor knew time was all that remained until his victory over Salem. In time, Salem would come to face the creature Viktor had unleashed, and whether the Paladin was on Salem's side or the Conqueror's, their lives would both end to make room for another in their place. He turned away from the destruction and rode away to watch the next move from a safe distance.

Once he was far enough away that the screams in the distance sounded like whimpers, Viktor stopped his horse and walked it to a clearing in the woods. He sat down and dragged a knife across the back of his arm. He watched the fresh blood drip and form a small pool. The blood then spread out into the form of a pentagram and dried into the dirt, its dark paint now a stain in the ground.

"I, Viktor Chavdar, your first True Servant and the last of the Chavdar line, ask of you, as the moon becomes crimson under the Earth's perfect shadow, form the path I should take to rid this world of Salem Taker. Guide me to the most prosperous path and provide me with the strength of those who lived before me."

The dirt inside the pentagram disintegrated and became fluid. It swirled until it solidified and revealed Simza. The image on the ground moved, and Viktor watched Simza intently from his place in the woods.

**

While the rest of the Wytches stayed together and discussed the task at hand, Simza decided to break away from the group for breath. She felt eyes on her back after the outcome of her last expedition but was relieved no one followed her.

She hiked up to the peak of the mountain where they'd made camp and sat there, looking down on all the Wytches. Simza's mind raced with the recent events, and it disoriented her after a while.

She tried to calm her mind and think rationally. She tried to think the way she had before she got dragged into this mess with the Wytches. Before, things were simple. She'd become a Paladin because of the harm Wytches had caused this world—because of the harm they'd caused her. She was trained to hunt them down and make the world safer. Wars like this were the very definition of her job. A war between the Wytches, the Diabolical, and whatever else lay lurking made it easy enough to pick a side, which was why she needed to remain with the Wytches for now. But when neither side took into account the countless innocent human lives that would be lost in the crosshairs, neither party was the righteous one.

That was what she was brought up to believe, and her recent experiences had reinforced that fact. However, now she felt conflicted. The Wytches hadn't listened to her when she said not to attack the golem she'd thought was her father. That fell right in line with what she knew about Wytches. They did what benefitted their own kind, disregarding all others. They were dangerous... arrogant.

However, they had also protected and helped her when she still grappled with her newly awoken Wytch powers. But were they doing that out of the kindness of their hearts, or by this misguided notion that a trace amount of Wytch blood lived inside her? She doubted that. They knew she was a Paladin, by blood and by heart—a trained assassin who wanted to rid their kind from existence. So why would they welcome her into the fold so easily?

The sound of approaching footsteps interrupted Simza's concentration. In one motion, she spun around and stiffened her stance to face whoever trespassed on her thoughts. She reached into her pocket for her gun.

"That won't be necessary. I mean you no harm." From out of the shadows, Viktor stepped out. He kept his distance from Simza, who remained coiled and ready.

"Really? Because last I checked, you wanted to kill all Wytches." Simza slowly stepped forward, forcing Viktor to step back to maintain his distance. She wanted to give Viktor no misconceptions about who was in control of this situation—and exactly with whom he was dealing. That was the Paladin she needed to be…the Paladin she still was.

"Yes, my dear…and as I recall, you are a Paladin. So what do we have to quarrel about? The enemy of my enemy is my friend." Viktor's bravado made Simza uneasy. He had to be up to something, but it would be an awful risk to expose himself like he did now.

"Explain to me how you could possibly be a friend. You worship an even darker and more twisted form of magic than the Wytches. As a Paladin, I don't just oppose Wytches. I oppose all who endanger the innocent. Innocence is my only ally," Simza said.

"Well, let me prove my friendship and offer the answer to the question which plagues you. You want to know why the Wytches were so quick to protect you and help you?" Viktor grinned when Simza cringed, and he took a brave step forward.

"How did you—"

"It's as clear as the eyes on your face, my dear. You're conflicted. How could you not be? But let me tell you that your instinct is correct. Don't throw out all you have ever known about Wytches just because of a few instances of perceived kindness." Viktor smiled genuinely for the first time.

"And how would you explain this, then?"

"Simple, my dear. You have Wytch blood in you."

"What does that have to do with anything?"

He smiled like she had provided the question he wanted to answer. "A Wytch cannot stand idly by while another Wytch is in danger, or their life is forfeit, and they will see their connection to Magic severed forever. They weren't helping you out of kindness.

They were helping you because they were forced to. They're selfish, Sizma. They will only help you out of obligation. They won't lay down their life in exchange for yours. The moment they feel they can do nothing to save you, they will leave you to your death." Viktor stepped back toward the forest but didn't break eye contact with Sizma.

"I don't need their help, and even if I did, does it matter if it comes from obligation rather than kindness? I'll still be alive to complete my mission when this is over." Simza held her dragon bone gun by her side. She found herself conflicted with the idea of siding with the Diabolical, even if he was right.

"You won't see the end of this, Sizma. They will see to that. They've been dealing with this law all their lives. They know its limits and they know where they can slip through. When it's time to fight, they'll make sure they are in no position to save you. You will fall at the hands of these Wytches." Viktor's form faded away as he walked into the woods, out of Sizma's sight. "Just like your father."

Simza raised her gun and pulled the trigger, but no bullet was prepared for the shot. She sat back down and dropped her gun on the ground in front of her. The Diabolical may not have been a side she wanted to choose, but he was right about the Wytches.

Just as she felt her anger swell, her hands glowed bright white.

CHAPTER 12

Viktor waited until he had walked deep into the woods and out of Simza's sight to whistle for his steed. He only had to whistle once, and the horse galloped to his master's side, coming to a full stop. Viktor patted the horse's neck.

"What a shame," he said. He removed the saddle and the rest of the tack. The horse did not move. He placed his hand on the horse's forehead. "Omne quod vivit, sic oportet eum occidi."

The horse collapsed instantly, letting out a final, painful exhale. Viktor kneeled to feel the neck for the horse's pulse. Nothing.

"Omnes dies rursum vivat."

The horse's coat paled, the black fading like death had welcomed itself into the corpse. Viktor slowly disappeared into an overwhelming red smoke. He swam through the fluid air and into the horse's carcass through its nostrils. Then the horse stood, its coat a gleaming white, glowing with life.

***

Simza snuck back into camp after considering her options and hearing the Wytches return to the peak. She knew she had to hide her glowing hands, or the others would ask questions she could not answer. She put her hands in her pockets and ran to Salem's tent. Luckily, no one was there, and she could grab the pair of gloves she always kept in her saddlebags.

"You better hurry. The council is gathering," said Salem, causing Simza to jump. "What? Hurry up. Trust me, you don't want to make them wait."

"The council? Gathering?"

"The Thirteen are here. We've got to make some important decisions, and they've graciously decided to allow you to attend. It is one of the highest honors someone like you…"

"Someone like me? You mean a Paladin?"

Salem shook his head hurriedly, and she figured he barely considered what she had said. "No, I mean someone who has not been brought up as one of us. Never mind. Get ready quickly. They're lighting the fire."

"I'm ready. Lead the way."

"You're going to go like that?" said Salem with a furrowed brow.

"Like what?" Simza glanced down at her gloves then back at Salem.

"You need to wash up. This is a serious meeting. The Thirteen only gather once a millennia."

She waved her hand at him. "Then get out and let me get ready."

Salem opened his mouth as if he was about to protest but walked out of the tent instead, his head down and a frown painted across his face.

Simza took off the gloves. Her hands had returned to their original color. "Well, that's some improvement." She searched through the tent for a small mirror but found none, so she grabbed a steel dish and used it to inspect her reflection.

She was in a sorry state. But what could she do? She'd been through a lot and was exhausted. Finding a brush, she decided that combing her hair was the least she could do for whomever she had to meet.

When she walked out of the tent, the sun was almost gone. The Thirteen sat in complete silence around a large pit with a blazing fire. The only sound was the crackling of the flames. It was as if all the creatures on Earth had disappeared to give this group the privacy they demanded. Simza scanned the group before she dared walk closer. As she'd learned in her training as a Wytch hunter, the Thirteen were the elders of the thirteen Wytch tribes left in this world. There had been a time when their numbers rivaled the humans, but it was the quest of every Paladin to make sure their numbers dwindled, and they had been very successful. It was surreal. She knew if she killed these thirteen, right now, it would be a most devastating blow to the Wytch society. If she only had bullets… But her mission in life had blurred. She needed answers, and she could possibly get them tonight.

She recognized a few of the Wytches. Tarlak, Atticus, Ansgar, and Morvyn were there, and of course, Salem. It was hard for her to imagine Salem as the leader of any group, but she was learning that their world was very different from hers.

All the Wytches had closed their eyes as if meditating. Simza didn't know where to go but noticed Salem had left her an empty place next to him. She stepped carefully toward them, hoping to remain quiet and avoid attention.

Though she didn't make a sound, they each opened their eyes at the same time and stared at Simza, who sat down as fast as she could next to Salem.

Salem offered his hand. Not knowing what else to do, she took it, and he squeezed. Somehow, she felt calmed by his simple gesture. The devilish grin he threw her way was the final act to put her completely at ease, and it still felt strange that he could affect her so.

Everyone's eyes bored into hers. Not being one to back down, she stared back. Politely, of course; she was outnumbered here. Their magic was powerful, and they were not to be trusted.

After what seemed like years, Tarlak broke the silence. "Welcome, Brothers and Sisters. You have traveled long and far to join us, but there was no way to avoid it. Before the sun rises, we have to decide the path we will take."

"We cannot run away from those who wish to destroy us," said Ansgar. "If we do, we will find ourselves with no place to hide. They will have destroyed us already. We must gather all our strength and fight." His fiery eyes reflected the dancing flames.

"We can always go into the oceans. They will leave us alone there," suggested Morvyn.

"That's because no one wants to live there," laughed Ansgar. The other Wytches chuckled along.

An ancient woman raised her cane above her head. Simza figured she had great power, for the Wytches fell silent and offered her their absolute attention. Salem leaned toward Simza and whispered, as if he knew what she was thinking, "That's Carabin, the eldest of us all."

"We are creatures of the Earth, Morvyn," Carabin said. Her

voice did not match the frail body which contained it. It was clear and melodic like the voices of the sirens from the old Paladin tales. Simza was mesmerized. "We will not run away and we will not become fish."

Everyone laughed except Morvyn, but eventually, he cracked a smile.

Carabin frowned, and everyone became very still. "Human towns are being raided and Wytches are murdered every day. Their methods of tracking us down are improving. It is a massacre, of which I fail to understand the purpose, but the ways of the world have always been a mystery. We must allow the Mother to guide us through these trials."

"We can't do it alone," Atticus said while he looked at Simza. "We need the Paladins to join us in the fight."

Simza laughed aloud. She hadn't meant to. The elders were not pleased by her outburst, but even they had to admit the idea was rather ridiculous. "I don't see how that's possible," Simza said, trying to recover the little dignity she had left.

"There was a time when our kin were allies," said Carabin.

Everyone nodded, including Salem.

"Yes, I've heard that story before," said Simza. She looked down as a draft of cool air brushed against her palm where Salem's hand had let go.

Salem gave her a dirty look. "You're being disrespectful," he hissed.

She shooed him away with her hand. "Perhaps we were allies at one time, long ago, before any of us were born." She turned to look at Carabin. "This is not our fight."

"Just because the Wytches are being persecuted now does not mean Paladins will not be next. The Diabolicals will not discriminate. They will kill anything in their path. They wish to rid the Earth of anything not under their domain," said Atticus.

"Atticus is right," said Tarlak. "Our clans must unite against the common foe."

"They haven't killed any Paladins yet, and they wouldn't be able to if they tried," said Simza, though her confidence in the Paladins wasn't as strong as her tone suggested.

"You are not well informed, young one," said Carabin. "Look into the fire. Allow the Mother to show you what is happening to your people."

The flames seemed to grow to twice their size. Simza was a little hesitant to look too closely. If there was one thing she feared, it was fire. She had no power over the flames. But as she got close to it, she realized the blue flames weren't hot, and she stared into them.

She thought she could see her hometown. She saw her neighbors, her school, and the Inquisition where her arduous training had taken place. She thought she could see her instructor, Sire Katin, now old and withered but still powerful. He'd become her father figure after her own had been murdered.

The flames turned a deeper blue, and her hands began to throb.

"Don't look away, Simza. Watch," Salem ordered.

She looked at the flames again and saw golems in different shapes massacring the people of her hometown. She watched her teacher ambushed by ten golems at the same time, and they quickly overpowered him, tearing him to shreds. She had to look away.

"No, this is a lie. You have put me under a spell. You are Wytches," said Simza, bringing her throbbing hands to her face.

Salem put his arm around her. "This is no lie, Simza. This is what is happening at this moment. We must act."

"I don't know what to do."

"You must talk to your people and ask them to join us. They will listen to you," said Tarlak.

"But I don't even know where to go…who to talk to…" Simza felt lost. What she had seen in the flames destroyed her resolve once again. She hated the Wytches. They killed her father, and now they wanted to kill the Paladins. That was what she wanted to think, but now they showed her the Diabolicals' rage on her people. She didn't know what to believe, and she had battled the thought enough that she felt weak, inside and out.

"Salem knows where the Paladin council resides," said Carabin.

"I do?" He looked bewildered, his face pale against the soft, blue flame.

Carabin looked at Salem long and hard. "You've had visions."

Salem didn't speak, but the Thirteen rose and all walked together away from the fire. Carabin led them and she turned, facing Salem once more as the others walked ahead into the night.

"You must meditate and ask for the Mother to guide you. Something is wrong in the astral plane. I cannot find her. The Diabolicals have murdered many of our Wytches searching for you, and we must know why." She glanced at Simza and narrowed her gaze. "You are Magic's first and strongest blood. You will determine our fate."

CHAPTER 13

Magic's ghostly form solidified and ran down the opposing wall as sludge.

"Think you can run off again, do you?" screeched the slender form which had thrown her.

Magic lusted for the regenerative and incorporeal nature of the astral plane, where she could recover her abilities and physical attacks would do her no damage. She gathered herself into a puddle, streaks of chunky cyan and gold betraying her weakening essence.

"Think you can warn your Wytches?"

A simple chair crashed into Magic, splashing her essence and tearing thought from thought. But Magic embraced it, for she had made contact with Tarlak, finally. He would spread the true prophecy, and her beloved daughter Simza would bring it to fruition.

117

Over the past two days, her captor had hunched over Magic's tomes and groveled before dark spirits, beseeching them to obey the will of the Diabolical, Viktor, that all may feast on souls this night.

So caught up in these rituals, her captor had not noticed when Magic slithered through the boarded-up window and let the wind carry her to the mountain. Her captive had, several times, underestimated the Mother's power and evasive attempts, which often allowed her to lend aide to her children. But her escape was quickly remedied and prompted an afternoon of instruction on the consequences of disobedience.

An end table and second chair crashed down upon her, splintering themselves and her resolve, for it was difficult to stand up to one's enemies when shards of furniture percolated one's essence. It was difficult to even string two thoughts together. Who had captured her again? And how?

She remembered being in Reunion Pass. It had not been Dan Pearly's time to die, and yet die he had, his spirit shuffled away despite her having empowered Salem Taker to save them both. And now she felt Dan Pearly crying out while something wretched and insatiable made its home in his corpse. Magic's essence roiled at the thought of her child being used so.

A vase pressed and twisted at the edges of her essence, squeezing away bits of personality and centuries of knowledge. It took all Magic's will to draw back to her what was squeezed away. That was the point of this—for Magic to spend all her energy surviving and not fighting. She knew this much.

Releasing her ethereal nature, Magic condensed into human form. Toes and fingers wriggled out of the sludge first, followed by arms, legs, and a torso. A gold-trimmed cyan smock materialized decently before her head had finished sprouting up out of her shoulders. Newly grown eyes struggled to take in the small attic room. The scents of musk and vinegar disoriented her. It had been centuries since she had smelled anything, and centuries more since she had smelled anything near this revolting.

"So you've given up," said her captor. With a snap of her captor's fingers, heavy shackles pounded across the floor and clamped around Magic's ankles.

Magic stared at her captor, familiarity seeping in. Dark, dull, slowly curving hair framed stoic features and delicate lips. The scent of brine and a stifled rage hung about her like thunder in a stormy sea. "Branwen?"

"But don't I do a lovely 'Magic'?" she asked, taking a bow and standing up as, in all appearances, the ghostly manifestation of Magic.

"Why are you doing this, Branwen? Why start this war? You'll put the world in peril."

"Have you ever wondered why Wytches exist?"

"What does it matter?" The shackles were cold and heavy against her skin. Never in her existence had such a human device contained her.

"You were named the Mother, Magic. You must have been told."

Magic faltered. "That was a long time ago. Because the world needed protection."

"And why do the Diabolicals exist, and why the Paladins?"

Magic stared at Branwen, believing centuries of self-prescribed isolation had driven her insane.

"Why do we exist? What are we here for?"

"To watch over the world, to guide it," said Magic, citing her personal belief, though she did not truly know.

Branwen giggled. "That's not why."

Magic pressed her back against the wall. Branwen had either gone insane or been fooled into believing an insane doctrine about existence and purpose. Either way, Magic was done listening. "Simza Adenah will stop the war. It is prophesied."

"Stop deciding how the world should be and stop calling it prophecy!" Branwen clutched her own arms, the hurt of an old wound running through her. "There's no sense letting you hope, old friend. Your darling daughter is out of time—or she will be, soon enough."

"The Druid Wytches protect her."

"Oh, Simza." Branwen kneeled before Magic, feigned terror on her face. "I've just come from town. An insane man with golems is destroying everything. Oh, you think the golem is your father? You're right, those Wytches aren't to be trusted. You should go alone."

"Why would she trust you over them?"

"Because I'm her close friend and landlord." A smirk slathered Branwen's face. "You should have paid more attention to your pawns."

"She'll see through you."

"You best pray she doesn't, else my master will make the boy dispatch her."

"I never took you as one for masters," said Magic with a furious glare.

Branwen slammed a tome upon the table, but then turned back around with the sweetest smile, a new secret glistening in her eyes. "Salem's been oh so sweet…so ready to accept the mantle of 'Favored Son.' Ha! Favored Son, indeed."

"What do you mean?" asked Magic, afraid to hear the answer.

"'Magic' has been whispering in his ear, playing with his powers. He will be the destruction of it all."

Magic lurched forward in her chains. "Why Salem?"

"You've always been fond of the Taker line. Disgustingly fond. Why is that?"

Magic looked down, shame and fury scalding her cheeks. Salem was barely her blood, one of many lives she'd transitioned through, but he was as much her blood as Simza.

"When Salem Taker is blamed for the razing of Reunion Pass, the war on Wytches will begin in earnest, and he will be the center of it all, beside Simza Adenah."

"Salem wouldn't do that," snapped Magic, lifting her chin.

"He will, as Simza will, too. Once all other souls in this town are stripped from their bodies, you will see."

"You don't have the power." Magic knew this much, but she believed her insane friend would commit this dark act if she could.

Branwen ignored her and instead threw her another grin, but this one held disappointment and feigned pity. "You took Dan Pearly to the astral plane."

"Before you took my place." She grimaced, the spite like poison on her tongue.

"It should have occurred sooner. Before you buried him among others."

"What of it? He is a Son."

"But he loved a mortal. He has no place in our realm."

"What did you do to Daniel Pearly?" Magic's hand shook. She felt helpless, like secrets hid from her only to reveal themselves as torture for her to bear.

"The others agreed, so I brought him back to the physical realm." She raised an eyebrow. "The Conqueror came too."

"Whatever dark master you have bound yourself to will only turn on you in the end. You must know this."

Branwen's smile dropped and she deftly left the attic; a swift flick of her wrist sent a gush of wind to slam the door.

Magic ran her fingers through her hair, massaging her scalp. It had been a long time since she'd fully taken human form, and what a mistake that had been. But the little luxuries of easing a headache and feeling soft hair between her fingers gave her comfort.

Just within reach, either by kindness or happenstance, Branwen had left a woolen blanket crumpled upon the floor. Magic pulled the thick wrap over her shoulders and tucked it under her toes.

Branwen's plan hinged on Simza's lack of faith in Wytches. Magic needed only to ease Simza's rage over the loss of her father, and the child would come to her senses. Branwen may have shackled her physical form and drained her of the energy to return to the astral plane, but there were other ways of travel available to those born so closely to Time. Her disappearances only drove Branwen to barricade the room with charms, and she wouldn't have much longer before the woman created one strong enough to hold her inside as the shackles now held her in place.

Magic fought sleep. Despite being physically and magically depleted, her mind wouldn't settle. A war involving Wytches, Paladins, and Diabolicals would devastate the land. What possible gain could Branwen and her master seek from such destruction?

Outside, Magic could hear the screaming townsfolk and their ineffectual gunshots. The building shook. Dust sprinkled down from the ceiling. Magic laid down her head and bade sleep take her. All turmoil faded away.

She found herself walking along an old and misted path. Giant figures and half-formed beings lurked in the distance, but she paid them no mind.

"Simza Adenah," called Magic.

The path solidified as loose dirt and rubble. The lord of dreams had been neglecting his duties.

"Sleep now, daughter, that I may speak with you."

In a clearing ahead, Simza Adenah lay propped against a crumbling cornerstone. The diamond Hex tattoo on her forehead glowed.

Magic kneeled at her side and whispered in her ear with a quick voice, knowing she had little time before Simza's mind would wake her. "Caldar Adenah died by a Diabolical's hand. Don't trust the boy who serves you. Salem Taker is not my Favored Son. Save Reunion Pass."

***

Simza awoke, surrounded by the four Druid Wytches.

"What happened?" asked Tarlak.

"I was just testing out an idea." She glanced at remnants of the great oak she must have destroyed. "I must've fainted, but then…" She paused. "Magic."

"She came to you?" Morvyn said, shoulders taut. "Why would the First Tenet honor you with her words?"

"What did she say, child?" asked Tarlak, stepping in front of Morvyn.

"That my father was killed by a Diabolical, not a Wytch." Simza struggled with the strange dream, almost hating that she willingly revealed it to Tarlak. "And that Reunion Pass is in grave danger."

"Salem is meditating in the Crimson Glade," said Ansgar. "I'll retrieve him." His Hex tattoo glowed. His form melted and reformed into that of a giant, black-winged vulture.

"Wait, there's no time!" said Simza. The secret about Salem burned at her lips. This was not the time to test their loyalty to him as compared to her. She knew Morvyn wouldn't take her side. Tarlak might. But she'd need all four of the Druid Wytches by her side if Reunion Pass was to be saved. That was all that mattered.

"Hey, Killshot!" Atticus called.

"This isn't a fight for humans," said Tarlak as Killshot came in to view, sprinting. "Besides, he's recently possessed, and such darkness lingers."

Killshot skidded to a halt in the clearing, barefoot. "What's wrong?"

"The town is in danger," said Tarlak. "Inform Salem in the Crimson Glade."

Morvyn flicked him in the forehead, transferring a momentary glow. "Now you can go."

Killshot nodded and took off sprinting.

"We can take the wind," said Morvyn. "But what about her?"

Simza bit her tongue. Despite Morvyn's clear bias against her, he had a point.

Giant talons gripped under her arms and ripped her away from the ground. Simza shouted through the roar of the wind but didn't fight for fear of being dropped. She looked up at Ansgar, who held her securely. Though a fall from this height would be instant death, Simza trusted this Brother. She smiled a little. She could only have faith if she wanted to save Reunion Pass, and they had readily accepted the task. It was a warm and secure feeling, having faith in the Wytches. Magic's visit had given her more than words. She believed the Diabolical had killed her father, and she could not find it in herself to believe anything different. She didn't have to have been raised a Wytch to recognize the truth in Magic's words—her mother's words. She looked straight toward Reunion Pass. For the first time since her father's death, Simza felt free.

Ansgar landed with enough grace to not injure Simza. She picked herself up from the ground and brushed dirt from her front. "Where are the others?"

Morvyn, Atticus, and Tarlak appeared with a flurry of dust and debris. A clot of dirt smacked into Simza's torso.

"Oops," said Morvyn. Atticus cuffed him. Simza looked down at her dress. Definitely ruined.

Having transformed back into human form, Ansgar asked, "Where are the townspeople?"

Though the edge of town was never crowded, it shouldn't have been deserted.

They watched for movement in alleys, windows, and roof-tops, but saw nothing and heard nothing. Tarlak motioned ahead, and in the middle of the road between the Frontier House of Vice and a shattered cart, Dan Pearly stood before them.

"So glad you're not dead, Dan-o!" called out Ansgar.

Tarlak held out an arm to block Ansgar from approaching their still and silent Brother.

A dark aura lingered and twisted about Dan. His head tipped precariously to the left. Simza instinctively reached down to her holster.

"Still fighting like a Paladin," remarked Morvyn.

"Atticus, check the buildings," Tarlak ordered. Tarlak's Hex tattoo glowed, and he transformed into a gorilla.

Deep, echoing laughter ripped from Dan's open mouth.

Ansgar transformed into a giant vulture mid-leap. Atticus ran to the Frontier House, his long white beard waving behind him. Morvyn sat. He closed his eyes and chanted in quiet, foreign syllables Simza couldn't hope to understand.

Tarlak had given her no instruction, but with the Druids backing her up, attacking the former Dan Pearly head-on seemed a logical course. She felt her forehead grow warm and the Mother's presence grew strong.

"Mother, grant me the power to end the creature which disrespects the body of our Brother, Dan Pearly, for my name is Simza Adenah, your daughter." It wasn't quite the same as what she'd seen Salem do, but it had the same elements, and she hoped Magic would accept it.

Her hands glowed white, and she grinned at the prospect of turning this dark creature into a charred remnant as she had the great oak. Only this time, she wouldn't feel guilty about it.

Dan Pearly's glossed eyes fixed on her approach. It unnerved her enough to slow her charge, but the building magic in her hands needed a target. She slammed her palms against Dan Pearly's chest and let loose a storm of lightning.

Steam and static rolled off his chest. The laughter pouring from him continued, though he did not breathe and his chest did not heave.

The gorilla charged from the left, fists raised and howling. Dan Pearly pointed and unleashed lightning, crumpling Tarlak, who transformed back into a human, unconscious.

Unable to find shelter, Ansgar fell to the same attack. Water burst forth from the ground to soften his landing.

"Delicious power, my dear," said the dry and brutal voice of the creature that must have existed within Dan. He smirked and pointed at Morvyn. Simza paled. A lightning attack could do more than knock out a water-user like Morvyn.

Simza grabbed Dan's hand and drew the lightning back into herself. The impact drained her and she fell to her knees.

"Now, Dan, you never did know how to treat the ladies," called a familiar voice.

Simza looked up to see Salem with Killshot at his side. With uncanny speed, Atticus snagged both Simza and Morvyn and dropped them off in the alley next to Mathilda's Boarding House.

Simza recognized Killshot's rapid fire and the explosion of Salem's fiery magic. Atticus stood, and Simza noticed his feet glowing. He ran out into the battle and picked up Tarlak and Ansgar. At the mouth of the alley, a lightning bolt caught him in the back. His eyes rolled up and he fell in a heap with Tarlak and Ansgar below him.

"Tend to them," said Morvyn with a focused eye on Simza. "I'll rejoin the fight."

"No," said Simza. "I can take a hit from Wytchcraft. He'd fry you."

Morvyn nodded and looked away. "Hit him hard for our Brothers," he said, almost challengingly. "For Dan Pearly."

The words gave her more pride than she'd ever felt with a task from the Grand Inquisitor. "I swear it," she said, sprinting back into the open.

CHAPTER 14

The land turned to dust as they followed the thing that was Dan Pearly out of Reunion Pass and into the prairie. Ahead of Simza, Salem stopped and wiped his brow with the back of his hand. They'd travelled in silence from Reunion Pass, and she was glad. Memories of the fight were still raw in her head, and she found herself swimming around in the recent past just to escape the stretching desert before them. The thirst and burning skin from the unrelenting sun were reason to jump through moments of time.

Salem had been adamant when he demanded the others stay behind after Dan's sudden, mysterious retreat. The Wytches didn't argue, but only eyed Simza with threatened stares that questioned her purpose, her power. The remnants of the surging energy swept through her and into the breeze. She shuddered, clenching her fists as if they would glow again, this time to consume her completely.

Salem kneeled down, his eyes scanning the rough ground. "Dan must've headed this way, not more than a half hour or so ago." He looked over at Simza, eyes narrowing as he regarded her. "I can feel how close he is."

Simza couldn't help but pity Salem. "It's not Dan, you know."

The wind picked up, hot and stale, blowing up a whirlwind of dust. The place was as dead as Dan Pearly, and Simza couldn't help feeling that while they hunted him down, death followed behind them. Salem rose to his feet and half-smiled at her.

"Might be true, but I know Dan's in there somewhere. You ever hear about Wind Voices? They're strong out here in this desert. You can actually hear them."

Before she could answer, the wind picked up and howled a lonely voice around her, sending a stream of dust that caught her eye. Squinting, she tried to keep Salem's gaze, hoping to see the glint of a joke in his eyes.

"Sure, I heard about them. Folk say the lost souls whisper in the wind...howl against your windows as you sleep at night. Kick up a sandstorm with their anguish and pain." She shrugged. "Just superstitions, nothing more. Only you Wytches cling to superstitions."

Wind whipped around Salem, but he stood firm. The sand swirled at his feet, whistling by him. For a moment, it seemed like Salem was the wind, as Simza felt the whispers flow through him like voices in a shared mind. It reminded Simza of the battle with Dan's host back at Reunion Pass. Yet images flashed up at her, Dan standing against them, watching a wind bellow around him and scream to him as though he'd called it. The dead, lost souls, desperate to cling to the living.

Wind Voices.

And she'd felt a surge within her when she ran out into the fight again, a growing ball of energy at her center, moving up through her veins and into her hands that reached out toward Dan, glowing brighter than ever. It wasn't power that had come from Magic, but something else. Something darker. Whatever it was, it pulled something from Dan, sucking out his power until the explosion threw them all back. Through the growing wind, Simza had watched Dan leap from the town, heading out as though he was carried by the gust itself, already a voice on the wind. The Wytches had gathered around Simza, fearful looks thrown her way as though she had summoned the dead. Inside, she could feel a coldness, a trickle of something she'd taken from Dan. It was still there, a creature deep within, scratching at her insides to get out.

"You Paladins not the superstitious kind?" Salem said, bringing her back to the present as though he'd reached into the past and dragged her up from drowning. "Truth is said to exist in some superstitions."

"Superstitions have their place. If you want to believe in lost souls whispering in the wind, feel free. A good gun at your side is all you need against the dead."

Salem threw her a challenging glare. "But it wasn't a gun you used, was it, Lark?"

He stepped toward her, taking her by surprise. She hated hearing the silly name he gave her now, taunting her with a ridiculous gleam in his eyes. Grabbing her hands, he turned them over, studying them. With a sigh that Simza sensed as disappointment, he let her hands go, and she dropped them to her sides, not curious as to what he'd been looking for. They stared at each other, their faces inches apart.

She felt something, then—a slight spark between them. His eyes seemed to wash over her, and she was lost in them, listening to the sad sound of the dead blowing around them, pushing them closer together to cling to the life that still existed.

"You don't trust me as much as I don't trust you," Simza said, breaking the spell. She couldn't ignore the enmity between Wytches and Paladins. Salem was no different. "And we'll never trust each other. Not really. You and your kind can spin tales about saving us all from the Diabolicals, but at the very heart of your being, you hate us."

His mouth set in a tight line, Salem turned away from her. "The world will burn if Paladin and Wytch don't unite. You don't believe in superstitions or prophecy, but look at the town we've both ended up in. Look at where our destinies have led us." He turned back to her, a glint in his eye.

"I went to Reunion Pass to kill you and your kind, not unite with them." Though she said it, she could feel the conflicting emotions. Things were not straightforward. Not now. Under Salem's gaze, she suddenly felt vulnerable. Naked. All she wanted to do was get away from him. She didn't know why she had agreed to hunt down Dan Pearly with this man, this Wytch. Every moment alone with Salem Taker confused her.

"We should get going," Simza said, walking ahead of him without waiting for a reply. "Before sundown."

They continued across the desert, caught in their own dreams and worries. No monsters lurked around them. Just the wind kicking up the dust clouds. In the distance, a lone horse galloped across the horizon, and Simza smiled at it. If the Wytch wanted to talk about superstition, she knew a few tales. Maybe it would lighten the mood, which had soured into an itching silence.

"Paladins believe that when we see a lone horse cross our paths, death is close at hand."

"I don't believe in superstitions," Salem mocked, glancing over his shoulder with a grin. "And I didn't think Paladins did, either."

She snorted. "Think you're so clever, don't you, Wytch?"

"Happen to think that a lot, Lark." He turned away to look at the horse disappearing across a rocky plain. "Perhaps death is coming to someone. Reckon it's already come and gone."

"Keep talking like that, Salem Taker. Maybe I'll just reunite you with Dan Pearly's troubled soul. Add you to the Wind Voices, let you whistle around out here in the desert for all eternity."

Salem feigned offense. "And I thought you were starting to like me."

Casting her eyes down to the dust, Simza remained silent. The truth was, she did feel something growing toward Salem. Right now, she wasn't too sure what that was. Sometimes it was hate. It was mostly hate when he called her Lark, but she knew he did that just to get her wound up. Then, other times, she couldn't help but feel awe toward him. There was something about him. She shook her head to rid herself of the thought. There would be no union between them. Then she felt herself blush, bit her lip in anger, and focused instead on the rocky horizon. It would be half a day's walk toward the rocks. If that was where Dan had gone, it would make a good place for him to ambush them, hidden away in the boulders. And, they were heading right toward his trap. The wind blew harder as they marched on, almost as though the dead really called out to lure them in.

Come join us in the wind, come and step beyond...

"So tell me something, Lark. You know any good songs we could sing? Gonna be a long walk, I reckon." Salem laughed, and she just sniffed and kept walking.

By the time they reached the crop of rocks, the sun had fallen, spilling red across the horizon like blood from a fresh kill. The rocks were still warm from the day, but the air quickly cooled as night rushed in to smother the light. Far too many hiding places among the rocks jutted up like giant teeth, crooked and chipped. In the distance, Simza heard a horse neigh and thought again about death. The wind had finally died down, and for that she was glad.

No more Wind Voices. No more voices of the dead.

Salem held his hand up to halt her. Ahead of them, smoke rose into the sky from behind a jagged grouping of rocks and the smell of a campfire drifted to Simza. Did a dead thing like Dan Pearly need the warmth of a fire? Closing her eyes, Simza tried to feel Magic within her, but there was nothing. As they edged around the rock, they caught a glimpse of a figure with his back to them. A fire flickered in front of the figure, sending embers up into the sky like fireflies greeting the darkness.

They made their way toward the fire, stepping as quietly as they could. Simza stood back and watched Salem enter the circle of the fire's warmth. Nothing implying life emanated from the figure, nor did anything that felt like darkness.

"Dan Pearly," Salem said, his voice wavering slightly with emotion. "I command what has possessed Dan Pearly to show itself."

The figure at the fire slumped to the side and fell from the low rock on which it sat. Salem rushed over to it, and Simza followed. He turned the body over, and a grinning skull stared up at them. Bones snapped, as though aged, as Salem turned him over and examined him further, little surprise visible on his tight face. The clothes were the ones Dan had been wearing when he was alive, but nothing else resembled Dan's living self. Pushing the skeleton away, Salem went to the fire and crouched by it, warming his hands.

Simza watched him for some time, sensing his sadness, seeing the slight movement of his shoulders as though he were crying. She didn't know if Wytches cried, but she still felt empathy for him. She went to him and rested her hand on his shoulder, frowning when she noticed a slight glow on her hand.

"I was too late," Salem said. "He's been taken by the wind." ·

As though in response, a wind whistled through the rocks, chilling Simza. "There's nothing more we can do. We should get back to Reunion Pass."

She turned to look at the skeleton, having the feeling that the thing had led them out here for some purpose. There was a growing sense of unease, of something lurking in the shadows. Salem stood and turned to face her with glassy eyes.

"We need to bury him. At least give him that."

Simza reached out with her fingertips and touched the tears on Salem's face. He didn't flinch away. The confusion within her eased for a moment, then returned as the wind grew in anger with the voices of the dead.

The skeleton moved toward them, a red fire burning within the black sockets of its eyes. Its deathly grin hollowed as it moved. Fleshless fingers reached out like little hooks, looking to sink into flesh. Within the skeleton's eyes, Simza saw the soul of death and destruction. She saw endless deserts and a sea of Diabolicals. Then within her, she felt that strange energy she'd taken from Dan Pearly back at Reunion Pass and raised her glowing hands. There was a sharp pain, nausea, and a burst of power leapt from Simza and into the skeletal demon. The skeleton shook as it was bathed in brilliant light, and the night became day for just a moment.

Simza closed her eyes against it, feeling the wind in her face, screaming at her now.

When she opened her eyes, it was night again, and in front of her sat a pile of bones. Holding her hands up in front of her face, she studied them as they shook incessantly.

"I don't know where this power is coming from," she whispered into the now calm night.

The flames of the campfire licked out at the sky, blowing embers around her. The sky was now pitch black, a full moon glowing red.

Salem dropped to his knees and pulled up bits of bone, gathering them close to his chest. "There's a different type of magic going on here," he muttered. "I can feel it in the air, within the wind, and now within you." The concern on his face churned bile in Simza's stomach.

"I didn't ask for this power."

"But you have it." Salem moved closer to the fire, dropped the pile of bones in front of it, and pulled out a small knife from a strap at his boot. With the orange flames reflecting in his eyes, he carved symbols on the bones. Simza recognized the ancient symbols, ones dating back before the Wytches and Paladins. From a time before Magic was born into the world. Such symbols were to be used with care. Even Paladins knew this.

"The Necromancers use those symbols," Simza said. "I came across a tribe of them in the Gundrin Hills, talking to the dead."

"Wytches may whisper to the dead. Sometimes you can learn a lot if you find the right spirit to commune with."

Simza crossed her arms and stared curiously at the bones. "It's against Magic."

"Magic isn't here, is she?" Betrayal lined his words, but Simza didn't address it.

She couldn't argue with that, though it was odd for Salem to disobey the Mother, whom he held in such high regard. She couldn't feel Magic and hadn't for a while now, either, so she didn't question his rebellion. Instead, she felt the strange, dark power that had flooded through her. At least it was now out of her, and she felt a lightening of her spirit again.

Salem continued carving as Simza watched. Loss inspired different things, and Salem seemed to have a plan. Kneeling next to him, she studied the jagged symbols he inscribed. Picking up a rib bone, she turned it over in her hand.

"Give me your knife," she said. "Your carving is horrendous."

Salem raised his eyebrow in surprise. "You know the language of the dead, Lark?"

"We were taught the symbols as children, as wards against the dead. I've never used them to communicate before, though." From distant memories, she carved the symbols on each bone, losing herself in the art. "The dead are often full of lies. Never trust the spirits."

Finishing, she handed the knife back to Salem.

"Quite the carver of bone, Lark." He picked the bones up and threw them into the air, watching where each one landed. Under his breath, he called for Dan Pearly to step forward and give guidance. The bones landed in the sand in a chaotic scattering, but Salem studied them as though reading a book. For a long time, he was silent, lost in the words of the dead.

Finally, he looked up. "The bones talk of a child born of enemies who will be the Deliverer."

"Deliverer?"

"In the ancient tongue it's 'Amalatuu.'"

It would be that word. What else could it be? "The Paladin word is different than your Wytch word. To us, Amalatuu translates as 'Uniter.'" Rising to her feet, she brushed sand from her hands and looked back across the dark desert toward Reunion Pass. "We should get back to town."

Salem remained seated by the fire, staring into the flames. "It's a day's walk. The desert is cold at night. Reckon we'd best stay here and camp by the fire. We can keep it burning through the night. Fire's good to keep the dead away."

Simza shivered, feeling the cold drawing in. The Wytch had a point, but she didn't fancy spending the night out here alone with Salem Taker. Not after hearing a prophecy of a child born of enemies. For a moment before the skeleton had come back to life, she had felt an unnerving closeness to Salem.

Salem gathered up the bones, carrying the bundle like it were a precious child. In silence, he buried the bones of Dan Pearly in the sand, away from the warmth of the fire. She wondered if Dan would find his way or be lost out there in the desert, a Wind Voice.

Shuddering, Simza helped the Wytch bury his old friend as a horse neighed again in the distance.

CHAPTER 15

Tarlak raised his head beside the fire and watched the others. The boy lay sleeping on the ground, twisted awkwardly but snoring softly. Atticus, Ansgar, and Morvyn completed the dreaming circle, their robes wrapped tightly about them in the night air. They all waited, presumably for the night to end and for Salem and the Paladin to return. But Tarlak was through waiting.

"Mother," he prayed, "as you send the winds to part the clouds, revealing the light of the sun and the beauty of the earth's truth, so I ask you to part this veil of mystery across our purpose. I ask you to reveal something to me, a course for us to take. Anything."

He knew the last part of that prayer was only his own desperation showing through, but he couldn't help himself. They all knew what had to be done, that the approaching danger would destroy their worlds and take their souls with it. They knew that, if they did not do what needed doing, their existence would forever be in the hands of evil. But they had no direction.

Tarlak felt his own energy flowing through him, focusing it in the center of himself as he searched for Magic's hidden word, some sign that she had heard him. But there was nothing. Lately, that was all the Mother had given him.

The wind whistled across Reunion Pass, howling through the empty buildings and winding its way with terrible purpose. The group had decided it was best to camp outside, not to use any of the dwellings previously occupied by the souls who had been destroyed in the town. Keeping their distance from the dead not only eased their discomfort, but it was safer. Smarter. Especially now. The dead existed among them everywhere, and Tarlak sensed a change within the energy of the dead. They felt more visceral than he cared to acknowledge—more present in space and time than they should ever be.

The wind whipped at the crackling fire, brushing his robes and momentarily sifting through his beard, sending chills through him that he knew did not come from the cold. Then he heard it— the soft, low moan of voices, a million souls reverberating with their songs. One only had to take the time to listen, and their message would be revealed.

The Wind Voices. Though a wave of anxiety clenched his insides, Tarlak closed his eyes and brought forth his awareness, sifting through the sound. *He has seen the bones. The bones see Amalatuu. Child of war. Child of peace. Union of the blood. Ancestral enemies.*

Tarlak's eyes snapped open. It had been so long since he'd heard the Wind Voices, since they'd come to him with their messages. But he knew enough of the prophecies and of his own brethren to feel the meaning behind the words, and he cursed Salem's foolishness. He knew without a doubt that he had used bone magic out in the pass, wherever he may be with the stubborn Paladin who still refused the knowledge inside her. He also knew why Salem had taken that chance, why he'd chosen to commune with the remains of the dead and take action wholly against the Mother and all that Magic embodied.

The Mother wasn't there, and so Salem had taken the only other option in finding direction. Tarlak had used the bones himself, ages ago, but that had been in a different time and place—when the danger of this world had not lapped at their heels with insatiable hunger.

The wind picked up, howling around their little encampment and shrieking in furious gusts. The flames of their fire rose, whipping with the wind and swirling in shapes and forms unnatural in their very essence. Tarlak stared at it, seeing the visions of chaos and eternity rise and fall among the embers. The ground beneath him vibrated, growling in hunger, and the flames shot up and coalesced into a form that struck the Wytch with a terror he'd never known before.

Glowing eyes surveyed their camp, falling on each of the sleeping Wytches in turn. Hulking shoulders hunched within the flames; a massive, horned head rose up, tongues of flame flickering in and out of its gaping maw. Tarlak froze as he stared at the fiery apparition, recognizing it completely and unable to do anything about its disastrous presence. The eyes turned within the fire, fixed him with a malicious, sickly amused stare, and it laughed thunderously in the flames. The figure pointed a hooked claw at Tarlak, and the earth's vibration rose to ear-splitting groans.

The ground beneath him trembled, the deafening roar making Tarlak's head feel like it was being split open and turned inside-out. Buildings around them crumbled in the quaking chaos, and thunder cracked in the sky without clouds to bring rain.

Tarlak blinked, and all was quiet around him once more. The buildings still stood, and the stars within the studded sky shone down on him in pity. The fire remained nothing more than a crackling warmth, illuminating the still-sleeping faces of his brother Wytches and the boy whose secrets remained buried far too deep.

The Wytch's heart pounded in his ears in stark contrast to the sudden silence around him. The vision in the fire had come to him unbidden, uncalled. *Mother, help us*, he thought. Something was coming.

***

He moved. He hunted. He called his Diabolicals to him and fed them the blood of centuries. The fires of his being raged within his age-old form, and he felt the stone of his sleeping eternity crack and crumble, releasing him from the bonds of timeless banishment. She had called him with the hidden darkness thriving in her, and now he searched for her, answering her call.

The void had temporarily been opened to him by the Diabolical servant, and he reached out with his unholy vision to find her. The opening would not last long, he knew, but time was no deterrent to him. He'd been frozen in it since the world had birthed time, since time had formed the world, one and the same. This sliver of opportunity was all he needed.

Across the expanse of thousands of worlds, of existence passing before his hungry glare in the blink of the eye, he found her. She lay beside the carved bones, a calling he knew had been left by the same servant of his in this world. He briefly thought of the reward he would bestow on the son of his, wherever he may be. Yes, there would be payment for the soul who had served him in the only way it knew how.

The image of her sleeping form among the cliffs consumed his focus, and he flew to her, raging against the bonds of time. Those bones had spoken of a child born of enemies—but he was the enemy of all, was he not? Amalatuu. The word stung at his memory, but only for a fleeting moment. How little these creatures knew. He laughed at the word, roaring as he recognized the hinting of possibility. But he commanded far more than they knew, far more than eternity could take from him. Amalatuu. He laughed, and worlds shattered.

She shimmered before him with the new, dark essence she struggled to contain, and he made himself known to her.

"Paladin," he hissed, collecting all of himself to stand in a form before her. She would recognize that title—she had accepted the meaning of it into her heart. He used what she thought she knew of herself. She did not open her eyes, but he knew she felt him. The veil was only torn enough for this to seem a dream, but he would make it real enough for her.

"My power calls to you," he told her. "Why do you struggle against it? The world has tossed you aside, thrown you into the chasm of your own soul, and I can bring you back. I will raise you above the confines of this world. I will take you with me as we ravage all planes where life exists. I will make you mine."

She did not stir, but her chest heaved in heavy breath. Though she could not answer him, not here and now, he knew she heard his call.

"You fight the weakness within yourself. Let it go. Embrace me. I am all you need."

A tear trickled down the side of her sleeping face, her brow furrowed in pain and longing. Yes. She heard him. He would not be ignored.

"Come to me," he said. Roaring, he floated toward the ground where she slept, glancing quickly at the tiny other life beside her—the Wytch who thought himself the Favored Son. The only threat to his rule over the daughter of Magic. But he would win her now.

He hovered over her, the thin veil between them shimmering as he strained against it to reach her. He would make her his, her powers an extension of his own, and their rule an unquenchable fire. He had enough force here to extend a flame of himself, the tiny wisp of his power, and he brushed himself against her burning lips. Her breath drew out of her and into him, filling his being on this plane of dreams. He consumed her, lapping at her life, and the hint of a whimper flickered from her sleeping form, contorted in the nightmare he brought for her. A dark, shimmering light glowed in her chest, the darkness swirling there as he had seen it. He fed her his power, and the swirling essence pulsed, reaching out to him in want.

That was all time would allow. The veil was closing. He removed himself, biding his time until another of his servants opened one of the many doors to this world. He left her. She would follow him.

***

Simza awoke with a start, beads of sweat stinging her eyes as she opened them. When she sat up, she felt her face streaked with tears. She raised trembling fingers to her lips, and when she touched them, they burned as if a nameless fever consumed her.

The sun poked out from behind the cliffs in the distance, and she remembered only the terror of what surely must have been a dream. Something had called to her, and she found herself trembling—whether in despair or longing, she didn't know. Simza wasn't sure she could separate the two.

She turned to look at Salem, who, to her surprise, was already awake and staring at her, tossing handfuls of the sand at their feet into the almost dead fire.

"Bad dreams, Lark?" he asked with a smirk, but his eyes burned through her only with focus.

He noticed something was wrong, she knew. She felt her heart skipping within her chest, felt a weight there that had not seemed to exist before she'd fallen asleep. "No," she said firmly, her voice coming out far surer of itself than she felt.

Amalatuu. Uniter. The words echoed through her head. The thought chewed at her. She'd thought when they'd read the bones that the message had been for them—about them. Salem Taker was her enemy, was he not? The same enemy who had slept beside her in the night, who had seen the same message from the bones and had not done a single thing to force that prophecy into fruition. Not yet.

"Good," Salem said, and stood as the last wisps of smoke from the smothered fire petered out into the air. "Bad dreams are a warning. We've had plenty of those."

Simza stood, slapping the dust from her clothes, and winced as something painful pulsed in her heart. She heard Salem gathering his things, and she turned to see him staring at her with something like confusion and wariness.

"Dan's buried," he said. "No more walking games for my Brother, I think." He stared off at the expanse before them in the direction of Reunion Pass. "Time to get back to the others." He took off walking ahead of her, his shoulders set squarely but without their usual brash swagger.

Had he dreamed of something, here, too?

"Do try to keep up," he called over his shoulder.

CHAPTER 16

Killshot woke with a sharp breath. At first, he knew only that he lay on the ground, and he hadn't been quite himself for some time. He felt as though he hadn't really slept for days, if not weeks, up until this moment, and that this sleep had somehow restored him, though he wasn't sure what was missing, or how it was restored. It was dark, though he felt the warmth of the fire behind him before he saw the glow, and he sensed the others sleeping on the earth around him.

He tried to remember how he came to be in this place, but his mind felt sluggish, like a rusty machine slowly warming up. He recognized his surroundings slightly, but he couldn't remember coming on his own—like he had endured a long dream he couldn't piece together. They had called him "Killshot," like he didn't otherwise have a name. He would have told them, he was sure, but somehow he never mentioned his name was Michael.

Memories and nightmarish reminders flooded through him so quickly he couldn't place them or decipher their meaning. It was as if he'd been detached from his body or trapped within his own head—much like the feeling that comes with a severe illness—for a long time. He felt the cool wind buffeting his face and the heat of the fire's flames growing as they whipped upward.

The space around the campfire grew unnaturally bright. Laying on his stomach, Michael shifted his body slightly so he could look over his shoulder. He froze in terror at the form that rose from the flames. The vast shape, its head crowned with horns, let its ember-filled eyes wander over the camp. Michael didn't move even to so much as breathe and hoped that the thing couldn't tell he was awake. He had felt the heat of this unholy fire before; its flames had flickered behind his eyes and cast their lurid light inside his mind. He saw the figure of another man silhouetted against the ghastly shape, to which it stretched out its taloned hand as thunder rumbled overhead and the ground shook below them as if in answer. Then all was still, and the fire was a fire once more.

Michael shut his eyes and lay still when he saw the silhouetted figure of a man turn around in the direction of the sleepers. He hoped his heavy breathing, the only thing he was unable to still, wouldn't give away that he no longer slept. Had this man been as afraid of the thing in the fire as he had, or had he summoned it by some dark magic? His heart pounded against his chest so hard that he hoped the others couldn't feel its beating through the ground. Whatever the case, he knew the creature which had taken shape from the flames and the fire that had consumed his mind once before were one and the same.

Michael's only other thought was that he had to find the man and the woman. His memories of the day before he'd slept were a foggy dream, but he knew that they had somehow helped him and that he had sworn to help them in return. He dared not move while the man was awake, however.

Michael had even more dream-like memories of that man and the others sleeping around him, changing themselves into fantastic creatures before his eyes. Druids, the man and the woman had called them. The man who had helped him clearly trusted them, the woman less so, but he couldn't be sure what part they played in all this—what part he played if he still traveled with them.

The eastern sky grew a pale pink tinged with orange to announce dawn before the man by the fire slumped down where he sat. Michael waited to make sure he had fallen asleep. He crawled on his stomach, pulling himself with his arms and then on his hands and knees once he was away from the other sleeping men. Only when he was several feet from them did he rise to his feet to run. He didn't know where the man and woman had gone, but he would search the entire prairie to find them if he had to. He reached a hand down to his side for the pistol he carried, reassured by its weight on his leg. He shuddered as the distant sound of three successive bangs echoed through his mind but pushed the memory aside, re-holstered the pistol, and ran again.

***

Dawn broke while Salem and Simza returned to the place where Tarlak and the others had camped. Although the Paladin had insisted she was all right, Salem knew better. Nothing could have disguised the fact that the woman walking behind him, attempting to keep pace with his long stride while taking painfully careful steps, had been touched by some strange and fearful darkness. The only question was where it came from. He would have asked the Mother for guidance, or at least a clue of where to start looking, but he knew she wouldn't answer, and her silence troubled him all the more.

Salem didn't look back, pretending to be solely focused on retracing their steps across the plain—but in truth, he listened to every footfall behind him, which gradually slowed and grew even more distant.

"You know," he said at last, "it would be one thing if you were the only one liable to die for the sake of your pride, but from a gambling man to a fellow temptress of fate, you've been shown the stakes here, and they're a slight bit higher than just—"

Salem cut himself off, for when he turned, he saw Simza had stopped a yard or so behind him. She stood wavering on her feet like a person overcome by heat, although the sun had barely slipped above the horizon and the air was still cool. He rushed toward her as she began to fall and caught her in his arms before she hit the ground.

"Don't you see what a fool you are?" Salem asked in frustration. Sweat beaded on her brow, but her feverish eyes seemed lucid as she met his gaze, which looked a more brilliant green in her flushed face. "Sooner or later, Dame Lark," he continued, though he felt his own head growing warmer, "you'll have to choose a side in this fight, because I think you'll find it's too much for you to face all of us alone."

"How can I? I can't trust any of you, no matter what side I'm told to take." Her voice tensed and her fists clenched against her breast, arms pinned close to herself in Salem's grip.

"At the risk of sounding sentimental," Salem said, not releasing her but only tightening his hold as he saw how weak she really was, "might I suggest you follow your heart?"

Before Simza could reply, Salem heard the sound of hooves racing toward them.

***

Michael had found the white horse wandering on the prairie without saddle or bridle, but it looked well fed with a beautiful, glossy coat and was as tame and gentle as if Michael had raised it from a foal himself. It allowed him to climb onto its back and responded with almost human-like intelligence to his direction as Michael steered it with the pressure of his legs, riding bareback and clutching the horse's long mane. He couldn't help but wonder why it wandered alone in the open, but he had seen no brand on it, and it had almost seemed to call to him when it trotted across the plain and waited for his response.

They raced across the prairie as the sun crested the horizon. Michael's senses were still unusually heightened, and the wind rushing past him felt like an almost tangible substance. It seemed as though he could hear some pattern in the murmur of the wind. He couldn't forget his thoughts, however, and the urgency of finding the man and the woman he sought.

Eventually, two small figures appeared in the distance, one following slowly behind the other. Michael's heart leaped as he saw them, and he felt a great relief sweep over him. Whatever they had done before to help free him from the flames gave him reassurance that they would also know how to deal with the strange and frightening apparition which had appeared in the fire during the night. Although his memories of the day before were vague, he seemed to recall that they both possessed great powers. Strange powers, but used for good, it seemed, to protect others like himself, the way his mother always used to say his father had done.

When he saw the smaller, more delicate of the figures totter and begin to fall, only to be caught by the other, Michael's throat seized up and tightened. Was he too late? So much time had passed before he had been able to leave the camp, surrounded by the men who could change into beasts. Had something already happened? But as he came closer, he realized the man and woman were talking, even as he had to support her to keep her from collapsing, and she seemed about to speak when Michael rode up, pressing both feet against the horse's ribs to slow it to a trot before stopping in front of them.

The man looked up at him, one eyebrow cocked. The look on his face seemed to settle somewhere between exasperation and amusement. "What in the blazes—what are you now, a sharpshooter *and* a horse thief, Killshot?" he said.

Michael stared at the man dumbly for a second, his mouth slightly open, but then he remembered the man had been calling him by that name. Now wasn't the time to correct him, and anyway, it mattered very little what anyone called him. Few people called him anything at all. He opened his mouth fully to speak, then realized he had no idea what to say. Describing the thing which had appeared in the fire would make him sound mad, but he knew what he'd seen, and that it was real. Besides, it seemed that the kind of things these two saw every day could drive a normal man mad.

"I found it, sir," he said instead.

"Of course you did," Salem said. "And just call me Salem, for pity's sake."

"I came lookin' for you, Salem, sir," Killshot said, sliding off the back of the horse, his feet landing softly on the ground. "I saw something in the night, something awful. It was a shape in the fire, like some demon that grew up huge from the flames and towered over everything, and…" He trailed off.

Salem looked at him, and now, his face didn't bear a hint of amusement. He looked both grave and completely focused on

Killshot's words. "Go on," he said.

"I seen it before," Killshot said at last. "It was…it was like that same fire burning inside me before you and the lady helped me, sir."

Salem let out a long breath that ended in a low whistle. "Well," he said, "you've suddenly become a lot more personal in your topics of conversation, Killshot. In fact, it's quite the bit of information, as little as you've said lately."

"I don't think I've been myself for a while now, sir," Killshot said.

"Indeed."

"And one of them fellows, sir," Killshot continued, "the ones who could turn into all sorts of creatures. He saw it too. The Druid. He was sitting right in front of the fire when it happened, like he was watching it all. I don't know that you can trust them, Salem, sir. I—"

Killshot stopped at the sound of a small whimper. He looked down. The woman, still supported in Salem's arms, stared at him, and he realized she had probably been staring at him the whole time. It was a look of fear, he realized, and he found that it hurt him, because he couldn't understand what would have given her any reason to fear him.

"It's him," she began, her voice breaking as if in pain. Beads of sweat glistened on her face, which drew up tight with anguish. "It's him who can't be trusted. She told me, in my sleep, before…she said…"

The woman couldn't finish whatever she'd been about to say before her head fell back and she sagged further in Salem's arms, her breathing ragged and heavy.

"What happened to her, sir?" Killshot asked. He felt a great weight in his chest, like he was somehow responsible for this because he hadn't come in time.

"Something she won't admit to, but it's serious. Now help me."

Together, they lifted the woman onto the horse's back as the patient creature stood still to allow them. Killshot patted its muzzle before they took off in the direction of the Wytches' camp, the horse following obediently behind without even needing to be led. Killshot thought it was the most beautiful animal he had ever seen as, in the early morning light, its great, dark eyes even seemed to glow with the slightest hint of violet.

CHAPTER 17

Viktor walked between the boy and the Wytch, carrying the Paladin on his back, thinking hard. The Conqueror, his master, had given a part of himself to the Paladin and still lingered somewhere in the boy, though the darkness undeniably continued growing in the woman. He had never been so close to this power, and the feeling of it on top of him felt like an unquenchable thirst; the Conqueror wanted her, he knew, but Viktor didn't understand what she had done to earn such a gift as this. He thought the privilege would have been given to him. He had longed for the right to bear such power and cursed his inability to complete his task to take Salem Taker's life and Simza's loyalty. Too late to fix that now; instead, he obeyed his oath to remain close to the duo until called upon once more.

He looked sideways at the boy, who had drawn closer to him as they walked and now rested a hand on his sleek white neck.

The boy looked at him, and when Viktor dropped his head to break eye contact, the boy stopped walking. "The horse needs water, sir," he told Taker. "Do you have any?"

Taker grudgingly handed him a half-empty skin, and the boy poured a little into his hand and held it for Viktor, who drank it begrudgingly and turned his head away. The annoyance he felt pouring off Taker greatly amused him, so he turned to the boy again, who offered more water which he splashed onto the sand. Worried about the Paladin, was he? Viktor snorted. The Paladin's vows would overcome her feelings soon enough, he was sure of it. She would kill the last of the Taker line, and then Viktor would take the Wytch's body and use it to much greater effect than Taker himself ever had. He may not have earned the un-promised gifts of the Conqueror, but he knew this promise still stood.

He wondered if the fool knew what he'd done, calling on the bones like that, setting the Wind Voices back to whispering their madness in everyone's ears. They weren't trustworthy, those voices, but very few realized that—many did not realize it until it was far too late to seek warmer and wiser counsel. He nudged his head against the boy, extending the barest tendril of power to brush against him at the same time, ignoring the taste of stone-ash it left in his mouth. A little bit of emboldening wouldn't be amiss, and he thought Taker could use a bit of a dent in his already shaky confidence. If he had to be a steed, rejected of all pride listening to the orders of these two, he would have his way with their sanity.

It didn't take long. The Wytch started asking the boy questions again, or at least demanding answers. "Why do you think Simza said you're not trustworthy, Killshot?"

The boy stiffened, much to Salem's surprise. "My name is Michael, sir."

"I didn't know that." Salem seemed taken aback. "You

didn't tell me, you know."

Michael shook his head. "I wasn't myself. And I don't know why she said that, sir. That thing…the fire I remember being inside of me, maybe that was it. It's gone now, though, right? If I can feel it in her, can we get it out?"

Salem pulled the horse to a halt, irritation flaring into anger. "I don't know if it's left you yet, boy. Not if you can feel it."

Viktor relished the look of fear in Salem's eyes. He couldn't know what lived within the Paladin; the Wytch truly underestimated the danger they were all in now.

"You said one of the Druids saw it, too. Feel anything in them? Did it take one of them?"

***

Michael started the horse walking again; the horse seemed more than happy to comply and even nudged him with its head again, which made him feel quite a bit better. It was like he could feel confidence flowing into him from the horse, clearing the remnants of the fog of confusion which still clouded his thoughts in some places. He had to think about Salem's words for a while before he could answer, unsure exactly what he felt. "It didn't take a Druid that I saw, sir. But I can feel it in the lady here, like a banked fire burning away at a piece of wood. Even the horse doesn't seem to like carrying her."

***

Salem moved to stop the horse's forward movement by the simple virtue of just standing in front of it this time. Simza had passed out again trying to attribute her suspicions about the boy to someone else. The Mother? Mentally, he reached for the connection he should feel and again felt nothing. And again, he wondered about being named the Favored Son. Surely, she would have had more reason for giving him such an unheard of name if he had greater purpose than to suffer through her silence. Something didn't feel right, but why would she mislead him? Why did she not speak to the Druids anymore either, and why give different, conflicting stories to different people in ways that would cause harm and not good? Weren't they all supposed to be working together to reunite the Romni?

The horse snapped at him, startling him out of his introspection. "Well, you are a troubled beast, aren't you?" he said. "Beautiful, but troubled. Okay then, Michael, hold him still. I need to check Simza. If she's truly possessed by something, we shouldn't go a step farther until I know what we're dealing with."

Michael traded places with him. "He likes me," the boy said, somewhat defensively. "He let me ride him. He helped me escape from the camp."

"You didn't escape. You snuck away," Salem corrected him. "And if you described that thing correctly, the Druids are no danger to us. That thing is not something a Wytch would work with, trust me."

"I do." The simple statement made him start. "I do," Michael repeated, blinking at him. "You and the lady said you'd protect me, sir, and I swore to serve you. I didn't trust the others. Why would that thing in the fire come to the one with the red beard?"

"I don't know, but it wouldn't be because Tarlak was working with him—I've known him a long time," Salem admitted. "He'd no more touch that kind of magic than I would."

"What kind of magic is that?"

"Elemental darkness," Salem told him absently. He

reached for what power of his own he could gather now, brushing it over Simza, looking for something he hoped he wouldn't find. "Reaching for it would be like sticking your hand into an offal pit to look for gems—anything you do manage to find is going to be tainted, and you'll be tainted as well." The magic he used recoiled suddenly, snapping back at him like a broken bowstring, and he flinched away from it. "It's…it's calling her."

"Like it called me, sir."

Salem shook his head stiffly. "It doesn't want to possess her the way it did you. It wants her loyalty. We have to get back to the others. I can't do it alone. Not without…" He paused before he could reveal a possible weakness. "Maybe between the five of us, we can drive it away, hold it back—something." He looked Michael in the eye, not hiding the grim wariness he knew haunted his expression. "You've my word as a Wytch that no matter what is going on, I won't let the others harm you. But I want your word in return that you won't let anyone harm Simza—not even me."

Michael nodded. "That's fair, sir," he said. "You've my word."

"Good. Now we have to get back as quickly as possible. Lead the horse. I'm going to stay back here and make sure Simza doesn't fall off, since we'll be moving faster."

***

Viktor considered balking at this, then decided he'd go along with being led. What he really wanted to do was kill Taker, the boy, and the Paladin too, then go back to the camp himself in Taker's body and kill the Druids. He wished it was that easy, but the Conqueror needed her, and it would take her to kill Taker before their powers could do whatever the Conqueror demanded next.

Viktor wished he had earned his master's favor to at least know the final destination of this journey, to know what use it was to wield the powers of the two Wytches—but he couldn't ask, and he wouldn't dare challenge the Conqueror's plan.

It had been revealed, recently, that Branwen had fault in her hold on the First Tenet. She'd been tasked with capturing and holding Magic, keeping her imprisoned and imitating her to spread confusion and conflict like some discordant goddess of old, and, until recently, Magic somehow slipped through for moments of providing her Wytches help. He knew the First Tenet would be withheld, but he did not know she had been captive since his arrival. Viktor's job was to kill Taker and take possession of his body while Magic could do nothing to protect it. The Conqueror provided Viktor the gift to take on the bindings of the Taker bloodline as well, and to earn the gifts offered to the only remaining children of Magic. Together, their efforts would widen the schism between the splintered factions of the Romni, dragging both sides into a vicious war, which would put an end to them all. Viktor knew what he would earn—power, which was all he wanted and all he ever had wanted. He didn't know of Branwen's reward, but he suspected revenge played a large part, although he still didn't know the cause of her vengeance. He'd avoided her as much as possible; all this time, the plan had been so slowly unfolding, and while he concerned himself with the possibilities, he also wondered what would encourage her to remain loyal—what vengeance she required to ensure her oath kept with their master. He didn't trust her, no matter what the Conqueror promised. If he had his way, he'd have killed her in the beginning.

Their master wouldn't have liked that, however, so Viktor kept his distance and enjoyed himself in carrying out his part of the plan. After the war, he'd be able to rule like a god anywhere he so chose, flush with Taker's power and with no one left to stand against him.

Except Branwen, of course. Which was a truly disturbing thought, though he may kill her, then.

***

Simza slowly woke to the jarring movement of the horse over whose back she draped, but self-protective instinct kept her from opening her eyes. The horse felt oddly familiar somehow. She could hear Salem talking with Killshot and felt the sun beating down on her back with uncomfortable heat.

It still wasn't nearly as uncomfortable as the burning she felt inside her now, though. Inside her breast. In her hands. On her lips. And in her mind and heart, a desperate ache of longing for something nameless and horrible that she wanted to embrace and reject at the same time. It only further fueled the confusion, which had already been churning inside her. Confusion over her duty, over Magic and the Wytches, over her strange feeling of connection with Salem Taker in spite of the fact that she still felt she needed to kill him and leave his body to rot on the ground somewhere.

And then she remembered something Viktor Chavdar had told her. He'd been attempting to manipulate her into helping him, she knew that, but he'd said the Wytches were only helping and protecting her because she was also part Wytch herself, and they couldn't allow harm to come to another of their kind. That rang true when compared to what she'd been taught about Wytches as a Paladin—that they would always come to the aid of another Wytch, whether they were known to each other or not. So her

Wytch blood, the supposed blood of Magic inside her, was her protection against the Wytches. They didn't dare touch her, no matter what. Simza smiled to herself. Whichever side she ended up on, it was a good thing to know.

CHAPTER 18

$\int$ mall puffs of smoke from the campfire embers drifted slowly across Tarlak's cheek before drifting into his nose, causing him to cough. Pulling himself up onto his elbows, he wiped his eyes with the back of his hand, his head heavy from so little sleep. Visions of the hooked claw in the fire danced in his mind. He knew it was the darkest of all magic, something he had only read about in the ancient scriptures. Elemental darkness could penetrate even the strongest souls, possessing them, manipulating them until it got what it so desired. How could it have been unleashed? Who could have opened the void to such madness? Feeling his heart quicken, he clutched his chest to steady its rhythm. He scanned the sleeping bodies, counting all except the boy. No great loss there.

He tossed sticks on the fire and watched them smoke, a flame reaching to lick the sides of the wood. The reawakened fire crackled and spit, causing a stir in the other Wytches. Atticus and

Morvyn checked themselves for residual injuries from the battle the day before.

Tarlak scanned the town's expanse for a possible place they would find supplies. He avoided eye contact with the others, who now walked toward him with questions on their minds. He felt it hanging above them like a rain cloud about to burst. The answers they so desperately sought were not answers he could give. He knew they would wait until he said something, but not even he could know the result of Salem and the Paladin's chase after Dan Pearly. He would not tell them of the demon, either—not until he knew more.

Squatting against a large piece of what remained of a wall, he rested his back against the rubble. Closing his eyes, he replayed a dream of Magic coming to him; she was vague, unwilling, or unable to give certain details. It was one thing to be commanded to build an army but to then have to unite Salem and Simza, and as a result Wytches and Paladins? Did Magic know more than what she was willing to give? He grimaced. Until he understood, he would have to protect the others from the same uncertainty.

Snapping twigs in the distance jolted him back to reality. Killshot ambled away from his place beside a white horse and slowed until he walked at the rear.

Salem angled his head in acknowledgement, then quickly turned to the horse's back when they approached him and the others.

"Quickly, help me, Michael. Get yourself together."

Tarlak moved toward Salem, pushing the boy out of the way. He wondered about the name Michael, but Simza's limp body on the back of the horse caught his immediate attention. He gently lifted her down and carried her toward the fire. Her cheek softly rubbed against his as he lay her down. Her eyes flashed open, and she narrowed a glazed stare at him.

"You," she murmured softly.

Tarlak rolled his cape and placed it under her head. He faced Salem. "What's wrong with her?"

Salem sat beside the fire, exhaustion creasing his face. "Simza will not tell me what happened, only that she does not know who to trust. But she might be possessed, Tarlak. If so, it's the same thing that was in the boy."

Tarlak moved toward Michael, who backed himself up against the horse's chest. He pressed against the white stallion and the horse stood firm, unbothered by the boy's body pressed into its own.

"Where did you get this horse, boy?" Tarlak's gaze bored into Michael's nervous eyes.

"Found him wandering the prairie, sir," he stammered.

Tarlak frowned at the creature; it looked healthier than any wild stallion somehow separated from a herd, though its tame nature drew his curiosity as well.

The horse let out a strained whinny. Michael tried soothing the horse, looking to Salem for help, and Tarlak almost smiled at the display of childish dependence. The boy was a sharp shot, Salem had told him, yet he still had the mind of a boy.

Tarlak laughed. "Make yourself useful, boy, and head to the other end of town with your horse. We need supplies—whatever you can rustle up."

"Are you sure that's wise?" Salem asked. "What good could exist here?"

"Who would hurt the boy? We need supplies, Salem. The other end of town might not have suffered the same fate." He turned to the boy again. "Still got your gun?"

Michael patted his holster. "Yes, sir."

"If you get into trouble, fire a shot and we will come rescue you, but I think you'll be just fine."

Michael looked at Salem, who nodded a confirmation, then mounted the horse, and they trotted across the clearing.

***

The sun was midway up in the sky as Michael galloped through Reunion Pass, the cool wind rushing through his hair and underneath his shirt, billowing it out behind him.

He passed the place where his father and the other coal miners stayed when his mother had disappeared. He didn't remember the day his father didn't come home, but all he knew to do was work for the only woman who offered to take him in.

He leaned back a little, slowing the horse to a trot as he passed the path to the mine where his father had worked every day. No one knew what made the mine collapse, but Michael had sworn never to look back and allow himself the pain he wanted to feel.

Rounding the final bend in the road, he came down the last hill toward the back of the general store. The horse stopped just beside the loading dock, allowing Michael to step down easily.

Looking over his shoulder, he walked up the ramp. "Stay here. I'll be back soon, boy." Shaking his head, he turned back to the store, swearing the horse had just nodded at him. The back door to the store squeaked softly as he pushed it open—one of the first buildings he found that hadn't crumbled into the dirt. Fallen shelves lay scattered on the shop floor. Michael clamored over them until he reached the counter. Scratching his chin, he tried to remember what had happened to the town, but all he saw were flashes of fire, causing him to inhale sharply. Reaching behind the counter, he found what remained of flour and a sack of potatoes.

He grabbed a wooden crate from the floor and gathered whatever else he could find, knowing in his heart that all he wanted to do was make the lady happy and hold up his end of his promise to Salem.

***

Viktor scratched his nose on the wooden railing. His patience ran thin. Flicking his head back up, his ears pricked up in the wind. The sound was so faint—naked to the human ear. Walking to the main street, he surveyed the carnage now littering the town; he couldn't help but feel a little proud of what the Conqueror had done with his offering of the town. Viktor made his way east, stopping every few paces to listen to the wind yet only hearing sounds of doors clacking backward and forward in the breeze.

Ahead, Viktor could see only one building still standing proud and strong amongst the devastated town. A lone woman stood on the front porch, her gray hair pulled back in a tight bun, small spectacles resting on the end of her nose. Viktor felt a sudden heat coming from the dirt beneath his hooves—a protective spell placed around the house, though it was not meant to keep him out.

He walked closer and grinned inside as the town-known Mathilda O'Malley stood up straight in acknowledgment.

"The poor creature never stood a chance," she taunted him with a wave of her hand.

Viktor breathed a black smoke through his nostrils and enveloped himself with it. The dark smog surrounded the horse's body, and he slowly left it in the tar stream spitting from the horse's nose.

He stretched his arms out in front of him, smelling the air that now held the stench of his decaying horse. "Don't mock me,

Branwen. We have more important matters to tend to."

CHAPTER 19

Magic lay in the shadows under the small attic window. Branwen had opened it a couple inches for ventilation the last time she was up there. She could hear voices directly below the window on the porch. She couldn't tell what they were saying, but she knew Branwen spoke to a man. It didn't matter who it was as long as he kept the woman occupied long enough for Magic to do what she needed. She put her body into a deep trance and allowed her spirit to enter the astral plane. Her blood called to blood, so she found Simza and Salem among the ruins of Reunion Pass easily. As Magic approached, she saw Simza sitting up, staring into the fire while the Druids lounged around her. A deep, elemental darkness hid and smothered her soul. That dire situation would have to be rectified, but not then, and not by Magic alone.

Salem lay on the ground away from the fire, staring up into nothingness, battling with the apparent abandonment of his mother.

Magic lay down beside him and whispered into his ear. She could not read his thoughts while he was still in the physical plane, but she could read the distinct sorrow of loss in his aura.

"I have not abandoned you, my son. Do not despair. I have been kept from you. Please enter the astral plane. We must hurry."

Magic waited for Salem to feel her presence and accept her words. He glanced at Simza for a moment, then turned away from the fire once more and closed his eyes.

***

Salem saw Magic's spirit shackled to a shadowy wall behind her. He ran to her, but he knew he could do nothing here. The sight of her reminded him of an only recent truth. He didn't only look at Magic, the Mother over Wytches, but at his own mother, and Simza's mother from another life.

"Who did this to you?"

"I'm in the attic of the boarding house where Simza lived. Her landlord isn't who she seems. Her real name is Branwen, and she has been deceiving you. You must gather the Druids and come to the boarding house."

Salem searched for the woman's physical presence, but she wasn't there. "Why can't you leave? You cannot be bound by shackles."

"I have no magic here, Salem. Branwen is empowered by something stronger than the Wytch Born...stronger than me. Something of the deepest evil has possessed Simza, and she might fight you, but you must bring her with you."

"Can we free her? I cannot identify the source of the elemental darkness."

"I don't know who or what possesses Simza. That may be

true of Branwen as well, because she was not once against us. If that's the case, you can't fight her alone."

***

Salem returned to his body, and Magic returned to hers. She pressed her ear to the open window and listened. Both voices were still deep in discussion. She smiled. If she could only get free, she could protect both her son and her daughter. They must be kept alive to fulfill their destinies, to bring the two clans together and win the coming war.

***

Simza stared into the fire, not paying attention to anything around her. She didn't know what to feel, but she felt more hatred toward the Wytches as time passed, and it pained her. Whatever filled her wanted something, and she felt that longing, but she wasn't sure she wanted to give in to it. She also wasn't sure she wanted to resist it.

Salem gently pulled her to her feet, shaking her from the internal fire rising inside her.

"It looks like your boarding house is still standing," he said. "Maybe Mathilda will let us stay the night while we decide what to do. You probably would like to go home, too. It's been a long day."

Simza looked up at him, slightly confused. The burning in her didn't seem to object to the change of venue, so she followed behind Salem as the Druids followed her. She looked around the group for Killshot and wondered where he was, as well as the horse.

She had seen them only a moment earlier, though she didn't remember much after they reached the camp.

When they reached the boarding house, Tarlak, Atticus, and Ansgar split off and sneaked around front. She watched them curiously, and a threatening feeling told her Salem might have lied about their purpose there.

She followed Salem and Morvyn around back. Salem pressed his forefinger against his lips to warn her to be quiet. She didn't understand, but the look on his face told her it would be safer to not make any noise. Reminding herself a Wytch couldn't ever harm her, she obeyed and followed the simple request. As she climbed, the darkness within her tried to make her stop, but she wanted to know what the Wytches sought in the boarding house, so she fought it. When they reached her door on the second floor, Salem put a hand over her mouth and whispered in her ear.

"Magic is being held captive in the attic. That's why she hasn't been able to help us."

The darkness in her took over, and she pulled away from Salem. She opened her mouth to scream, but Morvyn slid beside her and put a watery hand over her mouth. The water filled her mouth as though she were underwater, and she coughed unsuccessfully into his hand. He pushed her up the stairs while she tried to twist away from him. Her own anger drove the darkness away for a moment, and she felt alive again, fighting less every step she took. Morvyn pushed her through the attic door. She could see a woman over by the window, and she ran to her without thinking. She recognized the presence of Magic, her mother. She hadn't seen her in the flesh since she was a little girl, and she stopped before she reached her, conflicted with hatred and suppressed desire to see her mother again.

***

Magic watched Salem look around for something to release her shackles after his magic failed to destroy the enchantment on the metal. He found an old, rusted chest against a far wall. He didn't find bolt cutters, mumbling aloud in his search, but he did find a hack saw. He brought it over to the window and whispered a few words over it. Magic hoped the veil didn't restrain his magic as well. Then, its teeth turned to diamonds, and he sawed at her chains, eating through them like butter. In a moment, she was free. Morvyn stood at the door should Branwen come up the stairs, but she didn't. Magic listened at the open window, staying in the shadows. The voices below grew louder, joined by the voices of Tarlak and Ansgar.

Turning toward Simza again, she stared into her conflicted daughter's eyes. Simza had never felt so weak, she knew, but her daughter's strength managed to suppress the darkness still. She wished she could take some of her suffering.

"I can feel its darkness, now. It is rising in you, my daughter. Come. Let us help you," Magic said.

She moved closer to Simza, who had walked away and headed toward the stairway door. As Magic came forward, Simza ran. As she tried to push past Morvyn, who was still on watch, the Druid put his hand on her shoulder and held her, his eyes wide for a moment before hardening again.

"She's burning hot," he said gravely.

***

Simza's memories flew and she remembered what the Wytches had said about her father. She looked at Magic again and wondered if her mother truly wished to help her. The Wytches brought her here to Magic. To save her from the darkness. She opened her mouth as the realization of the possibility of their alliance stood in front of her, but her question diminished, and the burning spread into her mind as the darkness swallowed her. She felt its presence—his presence—stronger than ever. His voice whispered in her mind, calling for her soul. He was no longer interested in her as an ally, now, as he had said many times. Now, the darkness enveloped her, demanding complete control. Simza's soul fought back. The creature she felt was not her ally. Magic's eyes pleaded for her to resist, and she felt the love shower her like a magic of its own.

Wytches didn't kill her father, nor were they her enemy. Not this time. Nothing she thought could have rejected that now— not while a danger fought to control her and the Wytches sought to save her as they offered their own power to meld with hers. They surrounded her, and she desperately fought against all she had rejected for so long. She had the strength to fight off the thing in her. Feeling the same power from them in herself, she no longer doubted the Wytch blood in her. She could feel it, pushing against the bonds of darkness, trying to force it out of her body, which now glowed as if on fire.

You are mine, Simza Adenah. You are now a daughter of darkness. Do not resist me. Our power together will have no boundaries. Take me into your soul, daughter! She heard called to her, commanding her to submit to total possession. Her hair caught fire and yet was not consumed by it.

Morvyn stopped her in her tracks by embracing her tightly. His body became an all-encompassing bath of icy water which covered her and seeped into her skin. Her hair ceased to burn, her skin cooled, her heart felt the strength of the Druid enter and add his power to her own. Salem and Magic joined the two of them at the doorway. Mother embraced Simza, as did Salem. They now added their power to hers to defeat the darkness.

"Remember the prophecy of the bones, Simza," Salem said. Desperation stiffened his words. "It spoke of a child born of enemies who will be the Deliverer, the Uniter. That is you, Simza. You are born of Wytches and Paladins. You are the Amalatuu. Unite with us. Deliver the world from the darkness within you. We can defeat the ancient evil together." Salem held her, adding more of his power to hers.

A roar of fury came from Simza's mouth, shaking the rafters of the attic. She belched fire and sulfur which erupted in plumes. The flames made an attempt to set the dry oaken beams above them on fire, but Morvyn quenched them and focused on the growing flames. Tongues of fire burst into existence on Simza's skin, which was now dry and cracked. The fire burned hotter than a furnace in an effort to consume everyone, but the Mother had erected a protective shield that now surrounded the four of them.

***

The Conqueror fought to regain his control over Simza, but her growing strength, and the strength of the Wytches around her, was directed at the small part of his essence in her. He couldn't take her now, and he knew he would need to offer more of himself if he wanted Simza, for now his essence was being forced out of her through her mouth, her nose, her ears, even the pores in her skin.

The Conqueror burst out of Simza's mouth and out through the roof, sending the oak rafters tumbling to the floor. He would destroy more than Reunion Pass, and for now, he would let them think they'd won her soul. But he would have Simza Adenah before she united Wytches with the Paladins.

CHAPTER 20

Tarlak scanned their surroundings with a careful eye. The front of the boarding house, well-kept and inviting with flower pots on the porch, stood in sharp contrast to the smoking wasteland of Reunion Pass. A tumbleweed rolled down the street, bouncing to the rhythm of the breeze. No other movement disturbed the town, which was completely devoid of life.

After the strange creature escaped through the roof and into the sky, Viktor and the woman disappeared before the Druids could attack. He felt the Mother now and knew they had successfully saved her, but he couldn't deny that saving the Mother did not give him joy. In fact, it seemed too easy.

Atticus kneeled to examine the horse's corpse lying at the steps of the boarding house. Blackened as if burned, the outline of the horse was barely recognizable. He lifted his eyes to observe the street once again, moving his head to look more closely. Tarlak stood to one side, eyes fixed on the far horizon.

Ansgar kneeled on the other side, eyes roving across the desolate street. "This was the boy's horse," he said, fingering the amulet around his neck.

"Where is he?" asked Atticus.

"At the end of the street in one of the buildings." Tarlak didn't remove his eyes from the far blue mountains.

"We are too exposed here," said Ansgar. "Let's get the boy and rejoin the others. I don't like the feel of this place."

Tarlak nodded. He could feel the powerful, defensive barrier behind them dissipate, a deadly protection spell on the boarding house now nothing but a lingering reminder of what was once there. An electrical feeling hovered in the air like the precursor to a coming storm. This was magic at its darkest.

"Atticus, stay here and wait for the others. We'll get the boy," Tarlak said. Gesturing for Ansgar to follow, they started up the street.

***

A shadow passed over Atticus, diverting his attention from his companion's forward progress. A black shape cut lazy circles across the sky. The bird swooped down and landed on the eaves of the boarding house. A loud caw announced the presence of a raven to the desolate town. Atticus glanced at the bird, then returned his attention to his companions. The violet eyes of the raven sparkled in the desert sun.

Tarlak and Ansgar disappeared from view, returning a few moments later with Michael in tow, laden with several canvas bags.

The raven glided to the sand behind Atticus, dropping a

piece of bone onto the remains of the horse. A swirling hole appeared, swallowing the bone shard. The raven took flight, landing opposite the boarding house in a dead tree on the edge of town.

Atticus felt the swirl of energy—a clear indication of the discharge of magic. He turned to study the boarding house, but nothing seemed disturbed. The horse's remains lay unchanged and the ground around it undisturbed. A tiny pit formed in the sand next to the dead horse. No wind stirred, but the pit began to churn. A coal-colored diamond shape emerged from the spot where the bone shard had disappeared. The blackened body of the horse swallowed into the widening hole, coalescing into a great serpent decorated with a diamond pattern of red on black, smoke rising from the beast's nostrils.

Atticus sensed a malevolent presence behind him. With magic building in his right hand, he turned to confront this new enemy. The snake struck out, sinking razor-sharp fangs into Atticus' raised hand. A shockwave of magic erupted as the two made contact.

***

Tarlak felt the magic as they returned to Atticus. Atticus shook his right arm while his left hand glowed with the build-up of additional magic. They sprinted toward their friend. Michael dropped the bags of supplies, un-holstering his pistol. Ansgar unsheathed a throwing knife from his belt, imbuing it with power, the runes carved in the blade glowing white-hot.

The snake released its grip on Atticus' hand, slithered around his feet, and coiled for another strike to his head. Atticus clutched his hand in agony. He sank to his knees, red-tinged sweat pouring down his forehead. He opened his mouth to speak—nothing emerged but a puff of black smoke. The other Druids watched as their friend fell to the ground, unmoving.

The serpent unlatched from the back of Atticus' head and wound into a tight spiral on the fallen Druid's back. It raised its head as Ansgar approached, fangs bared and nostrils smoking. A gunshot barked in the silence, a red hole now punctured between the violet eyes of the serpent. The snaked reared back and let out a menacing hiss. Its head swayed back and forth as another bullet ripped into its neck. They watched in horrid fascination as the two bullet wounds healed over without a spot of blood spilled or movement altered.

Ansgar threw the knife as the serpent struck out toward the trio. The knife entered the serpent's open maw, transforming the head of the snake into black smoke. They watched the passage of the knife as the snake's body evaporated and the knife emerged from the beast's tail, embedding itself in the ground next to the downed Atticus. Then the snake disappeared into the ether.

"Atticus!" yelled Tarlak as he kneeled at his friend's side. He rolled the body over, exposing the snowy beard lying in sharp contrast to the blackened skin of the dead Druid. He withdrew a vial from his pouch and poured it into Atticus' open mouth. Tarlak stared into his unblinking eyes. Gathering the earthen elemental energy, he placed his right hand over Atticus' chest. A single drop of blood exited the dead man's eye, leaving a red trail across his dusty cheek.

"What happened?" came Morvyn's voice. The other half of their group rounded the boarding house. Morvyn and Salem reached the downed Druid, magic blossoming in their hands to help. Simza and the Mother clutched each other. Tarlak noticed the flash of fire power emanating from within Simza's aura.

"A conjured serpent attacked Atticus," Ansgar replied in an agitated tone.

"How could one serpent overpower the three of you?" Morvyn asked angrily.

"We were collecting the boy from down the street. We rushed back when we saw the attack, but it was too late."

Morvyn glared at Michael. "You were told to find supplies. Where were you?" he demanded.

"I was getting supplies," the boy replied defensively, gesturing at the canvas pile farther up the street. "I'm sor—"

"Save it!" Morvyn cut him off with a sharp wave of his hand.

"Morvyn," Tarlak began.

"No, I won't hear excuses. Atticus is dead because of this boy."

"This is not Michael's fault," said Salem, stepping in front of Michael.

"There is a darkness in him. He will lead us all to our deaths," Morvyn said, his eyes burning with anger.

"The darkness is gone now. He was trying to help us by finding food," said Salem.

"I say the sooner we get rid of him, the better off we'll all be," Morvyn said, staring at Michael.

"Michael, go gather the supplies. Morvyn and Ansgar, prepare Atticus for travel. We will return to the mountains and give our Brother a proper burial ceremony," said Tarlak.

"Come, Michael. I'll help," said Salem.

Tarlak, Ansgar, and Morvyn formed a triangle around Atticus' body and began chanting.

"Tigherna draíochta, tigherna an bháis, a chaomhnú ár gcara agus a chosaint a chorp."

A soft, white glow surrounded the body of their fallen comrade.

Salem and Michael carried the canvas bags back to the group, Michael maintaining his place behind the protective barrier of Salem Taker. They watched as the Druids fashioned a travois to transport Atticus' body into the mountains.

The group departed the ruined town to the sound of a raven's laughter.

***

A pair of amber eyes watched the group march out of town, ears pricked and body tensed for danger. The coyote materialized from its hiding place in an alley behind the once-inviting Frontier House of Vice. The creature skulked through the alleyway separating the Frontier House and the general store, emerging into the street.

Lifting its snout, the animal smelled the air and sneezed. It loped over to where the man had died and began digging. The brown-eyed coyote snatched the bone shard out of the newly created hole and snapped it in two pieces. Shaking its head, it raced out of the human habitation.

***

On a hillside, miles from Reunion Pass, amber eyes opened to stare at the twisted twigs and branches of the spirit lodge. The fire burned to coals, but the smell of white sage permeated the confines of the structure.

The white men had brought their magic but left his people alone. Now, though, an evil entity invaded their land. The bone shard, which had created the deadly serpent, reeked of the blackest magic.

Dismantling the spirit lodge, Ahtunowhiho offered a blessing to the four directions and began his journey homeward. A calling of the tribal councils was necessary.

CHAPTER 21

D eep in Bredon Woods, in a stone hut camouflaged behind braided, leafy vines and heavy brush, the eight leaders of the Paladin Council sat cross-legged in a circle on a raised platform made of blessed timber. One space was empty—one for the Caldarari line. Select hunters from each remaining tribe sat around them on woven rugs, their dragon bone pistols holstered. A falconer stood by the iron door, his black and white peregrine falcon perched on his gloved arm. The wind whipped outside the hut in angry bursts of high-pitched whistles, carrying whispers of generations past, but did not extinguish the many candelabras lit within. The Council had not met for a decade; there had been no need, as peace abounded across the region thanks to the Paladin hunters who kept the Wytch Born contained.

"What is it, Ahtunowhiho, that makes you call this meeting in such haste?" Katar, the Grand Inquisitor and leader of the

Draugoi, the strongest tribe, asked.

"Our tribe is a peaceful one," Ahtunowhiho informed the Paladin Council in a hushed tone. "But we cannot stand idly by while the Wytch Born bring destruction to our land." He raised the still-smoldering bone shard above his head. All watched him as he stood, walked to the center of the circle, and dropped it into a deep silver cauldron with mystic markings. Red flames shot into the air, followed by a lingering hiss. Candles flickered, and then the bone was no more.

As was often the case when terrible evil was near, no one spoke.

Finally, Katar said, "Why would you bring such evil magic into our temple?"

"Its power is no longer able to cause harm. I blessed it with the four directions. I brought it only to show you that we are all in danger. Reunion Pass and its inhabitants are all dead, killed by an unearthly and vile force."

"This cannot be, Ahtunowhiho. Reunion Pass is outside the Wytch's territory."

"I do not think this is Wytch-made destruction. It is something greater." He took a deep breath and continued. "Dare I say it reeks of Diabolicals. There are many signs, this bone shard just one."

"How can that be? The Diabolicals were expelled from the natural world centuries ago, according to the Great Book."

"I do not know, Katar. The Great Book also speaks of the Diabolicals waging a great war: 'And then the Dark Shadows shall rise again and tear a rift so large in the fabric of the natural world that no human shall survive.'"

"We are all aware of the prophecy, but it was not expected so soon."

"There is something else related to the prophecy. I have also learned that one of our own is involved. Caldar Adenah's daughter, Simza. She has been seen with the Druid Wytches."

Katar, who rarely raised his voice, bellowed, "She took a vow to hunt Wytches, not consort with them. If the Diabolicals are rising, they will be seeking all sources of power, even ones which have been dormant by the Council's command. We should have denied Caldar's daughter a place among us long ago. She must answer for this." He motioned for the falconer, but before he could approach the Council, a young hunter stood and cleared his voice to speak.

"This must be important, Wolfeye, else you would not break decorum and speak when not asked," Katar said.

"My humblest apologies, Father, but I would like to volunteer to bring Simza to the Council."

Katar, knowing the history between the two, shook his head. "Impossible," he said. "Sit down."

Wolfeye did not sit. Instead, he broadened his mighty shoulders as he held both palms up in a gesture indicating he had more to say.

"My motives are purely for the future of the Paladins, Grand Inquisitor. I know Simza, how she thinks, how she moves. If anyone can find her, I can. I am your fastest rider, and my senses are as keen as the falcon's. Besides, she won't have a choice but to come back with me. I'll make sure of that."

Katar raised his hands to the dome, which held a mosaic of The Ancient Ones. He closed his eyes and prayed for guidance.

"Ancient Ones, we serve you," the Paladin hunters repeated when Katar had finished. A great wind shook the hut.

When it passed, Katar made his decision. "You may go,

Wolfeye. But hasten. If what Ahtunowhiho says is true, we have many preparations to make before the war."

***

Salem and Simza sat with the Mother, helping her regain her strength through a nettle-infused drink and rest. They talked little, yet there were so many questions to ask. Magic explained her imprisonment as Branwen's captor and tried to explain to Salem that Branwen had impersonated her.

"She wanted to tempt you by falsely calling you the Favored Son," she said. "Yet, as I appear before you now, I tell you that her words could not have been truer. You are the Favored Son."

"But what does that mean?" Salem asked.

"You will know when the time has come. As for you, daughter." Simza looked up when the Mother addressed her. "You have to choose whether or not to accept your bloodline and the magic that comes with it, for my magic will not flow through the hands of one who does not want it."

Simza could not answer her. She had felt Magic's power—it was an unsettling yet familiar feeling that awakened a part of her she hadn't known existed, or if she had, she had long forgotten it. Her mind was awash with confusion. All her alliances in the past, as a Wytch Born hunter, as a Paladin, came into question. How she could reconcile the contradictions was a mystery to her. Her body experienced a heavy fatigue, and she was certain she could not make any decisions until she, too, recovered from all that had happened.

It was decided that it was too late to make the journey to the burial place; the party would march at sunrise. They would take turns guarding Atticus' body in the cart next to the porch. The others settled in to rest, the Mother lying alone, the Druid Wytches on the opposite side. Michael, Simza, and Salem sat on the steps and watched the sun slowly edge behind the mountains, ribbons of orange and red intertwined across the sky. The strong winds from hours before had dissipated and the Earth was silent; not even a cricket made a sound.

"Why are you so quiet, Simza?" Salem asked.

"There are too many unknowns to speak of," she said. "I need time to think about the implications of uniting. Right now, I should take out my pistol and kill every one of you resting on this porch."

Salem folded his hands into light fists.

Simza laughed. "Relax. I said I should, not that I would. Even I recognize the law of reciprocity. You have saved me more than once now and brought me to the Mother. I could not live with myself if I took advantage of that."

Salem folded his arms over his head and leaned back, his eyes focused on hers. "You're wise for a Paladin." They sat there considering each other for some time until a falcon startled the both of them by landing on the railing of the porch. "Don't move," Salem whispered.

Simza nodded but slowly wrapped her fingers around the pistol.

"You should listen to him," a familiar voice demanded.

Simza scanned the moonlit street but didn't immediately see anyone. "Announce yourself," she said in her deep, fighting voice.

A figure on a black stallion moved out of the shadows. She recognized the animal first. Her neck stiffened. Her mind froze. She gathered her senses and spat at the man. "Wolfeye. How the hell did you find me?" she asked, her hands far from steady on the pistol.

"Holster your weapon, Simza. You know you would never shoot me."

"Try me." She glared at him.

Wolfeye dismounted and walked toward her. He was an alarmingly tall man with a long, ink-colored braid down his back. He was dark as the night, but the moonlight bounced off his one yellow eye like a sunbeam. He reminded Simza of a slick panther, not a wolf.

She glanced at Salem, who stepped beside her.

"I come not for you, Wytch, though I ought to destroy the lot of you," Wolfeye growled, eyeing the sleeping Druid Wytches. "Get on Blackspire, Simza."

"I'm not going anywhere with you," Simza said.

"The Council has requested your presence, and I have orders to bring you back with me. Conscious or unconscious. It's your choice," he said. "Besides, as you know, the vows one takes before the Council are supreme."

Simza had the sinking feeling that she was in big trouble.

Wolfeye came closer. He was a giant compared to Simza and Salem, both tall in their own right. He could take them both with one throw of his fist, yet Salem moved in front of Simza despite his towering size. "The lady said she wasn't going with you," he said. "So you should leave."

Wolfeye did not laugh. "Your opinion, whoever you are— and it's best you don't tell me—has no bearing on me." Before Salem could protest, Wolfeye made a fist and punched him with such might that he was knocked unconscious.

"Now look at what you did," Simza said. "This is the exact reason I left you. You can't control your anger."

"You have bigger things to deal with than my anger," he said. "The Council is requesting your presence, and you can either come with me willingly, or I will kill all your friends right now."

Simza turned. The Druid Wytches were asleep, but the Mother was gone. She silently thanked Salem for possibly having warned Magic. "They aren't my friends," she said, turning back to Wolfeye.

"Save it for the Council," he said and picked her up. She did not fight him. It was pointless.

***

Standing before the Council, now in a semi-circle, Simza felt the heat of her blood under her skin, her hands burning with Magic. She wanted to take off her gloves and kill Wolfeye with one fistful of fire, but then she would certainly be shot by the very same silver bullets she used to kill Wytches.

"Explain yourself, Caldar's daughter, Simza Adenah."

Her mouth dried. She couldn't find the words to explain everything she had learned over the last few weeks. She didn't know what the Council would do if she acknowledged she had Wytch blood in her, that her quest to avenge her father's blood had revealed her true name, her connection with all she thought she despised. She had to pick her words carefully. If what the Thirteen had said had any truth, she was the chosen one to unite the Paladins and the Wytch Born. This was her chance. But what could she say?

***

Salem was close to finding the Council's meeting place. He could feel it, a resounding buzz deep in his inner ear, or was that because of Wolfeye's punch? He wasn't sure. The woods confused him. Every moss-veiled trail he went down turned up empty. He searched for a hidden stone hut which had appeared clearly in his dreams, but now the image wavered. It wasn't until now that he realized the insignificant dream was what the Thirteen had claimed as his vision of the Council. The details were so elusive, every leafy canopy empty.

He chewed on a stem of wood sorrel to alleviate his thirst as he thought about the Thirteen. They could not have been serious when they said he knew where the Paladin Council was. His dreams didn't come with directions. But one image kept him going—Simza leaving with Wolfeye. Fire grew behind his eyes. He suspected he was jealous, and this fact alone disturbed him. Simza was the key to unification, but she was also something beyond that. What that something was eluded Salem, and he did not like how uncomfortable it made him feel. He knew that Wolfeye had power over her. In the short time since they'd met, he had never seen her lose herself like she did when Wolfeye appeared. He had the sense that she was in more than just physical danger, certain that the Paladin Council would not look favorably at her close connection to the Wytches. He had to find her before they changed her mind completely.

Just then, he noticed a seated coyote ahead on the trail before a rather large mound. He heard horses braying in the distance, too. Salem stopped and bent down to place his ear to the ground. He felt the vibration of voices traveling on the roots of trees under him, and he called upon Magic, hoping she could hear him in her weakened state.

Mother, as your child, I ask of you, imbue me with all the stealth of a slithering snake, make my movements invisible to all creatures of the earth.

He waited, then felt Magic's power reach him. He moved toward the coyote, who sniffed at the air but did not move. The closer he came to the mound, the more it began to take form as a dwelling. His heart beat as fast as a butterfly's wings in flight, yet the coyote stood still. Salem saw a subtle outline of a door behind the coyote, and he inched toward it, mere centimeters between them. The coyote stood, its ears twitching on high alert. Salem pushed aside several leafy vines and located a handle. He took a deep breath, turned the knob, and slithered inside. Just as he stepped in, the coyote growled. He slammed the door shut and when he turned, a hundred Paladin eyes and raised pistols were aimed at him.

***

Viktor looked into the fire. It was all coming together now, the plan to begin the Great War that would lead to his ultimate prize—the power of Salem Taker and Simza Adenah. Salem would certainly be killed by the Paladin hunter, and his body would be Viktor's. His patience was paying off. He was, however, worried about the Druid Wytches. He had successfully taken down one, but there were still three to go. They were missing Salem and the Mother now. The Mother's whereabouts were another issue, but here was an opportunity.

He created a ceremonial circle and drew a pentagram in the sand within it. He placed five ruby stones in each tip and began to chant.

CHAPTER 22

Simza was unsure how her decisions had changed in leading her to stand before the Council like this. She had known that this moment would come from the first time she'd neglected her chance to kill Salem. She had betrayed her vows, and the Ancient Ones would know—and then the Inquisitor of the Paladins would know. She looked at the faces staring at her, faces she knew, the faces of the ones who had trained her, taught her, loved her, and all she saw staring back was their disapproval. Simza had already been judged, but there were a few whose eyes showed a hopeful compassion amidst the crowd of judgment. Gyron—who had taught her to track and who had been the first one to ever treat her like an adult—and Kerome—who had taught her histories and many of her other studies—stood out to her in the light of the fire.

Gyron had taken her out tracking when she had barely been a teenager and one night had shared his wine with her. She had ended up falling over in his lap and professing her love for him while singing the Paladins' Marching Song. He had told her to go to bed with a firm kiss on her forehead. He had never underestimated her, and he always loved her like a sister. His eyes were bright now, waiting for her to speak, to defend herself and offer a rational explanation for her actions with the Wytches.

Kerome had known her since she was young and had taught her to read and write. He was an old man now; his eyes were moist with unshed tears. He smiled hopefully at her, encouraging her to speak.

All she could think about was that she would kill for a drink of water. Standing before the Council now, her entente with Magic and her feelings for Salem seemed foolish, and all words that came to mind seemed even more foolish. She stood in the circle of mostly men, and she felt like a little girl once more. She had been brought before them for discipline a few times in the past, but nothing anywhere near as serious as this. She remembered the results of the last time, when she was ordered to be lashed after losing her first dragon bone gun. The one she bore at her hip now was her second. They were valuable weapons, and part of the oath was to protect those weapons second only to their lives.

She had had no explanation for where her first gun had gone, and she had even less explanation now. Perhaps someone had stolen it, or she had been careless, as the Council had asserted. She still thought it was an act of revenge from someone she had scorned. A punishment from someone who wouldn't take no for an answer.

She wished she were innocent now, but not only had she not killed Salem when she'd had the chance, she had also saved his life on more than one occasion.

"What do you want to know?" she asked, her voice parched

in her dry throat.

"We would like to know why a Wytch you had the opportunity to kill became your travel companion, and why you neglected your oath and your duty." Katar wore a mask over his face, as the Grand Inquisitor usually did. This kept her from making eye contact with her questioner. It was part of the protocol when a serious discipline hearing had been called. She had seen his white and gold mask once before, at another trial—an old man accused of the same crime of which she was now being asked to speak. He had been found guilty of betraying his oaths and burned.

"There wasn't a chance," she lied.

"Speak the truth here, child," he said. "Or you will be reminded of how we find the truth from those who would lie."

"It seemed wrong to kill him," she lied again, not wanting to mention that Magic had stayed her hand. "He saved my life."

"A Wytch's trick to lure you under his spell. It seems he was successful," Katar said. A murmur filled the room.

"No, not a trick. My choice," she asserted. She couldn't let Salem take the blame for this. She had no inkling of why she couldn't kill him the first moment she'd laid eyes on him, but she knew it wasn't a trick of his. It was her Wytch Born blood rising within her after so long of hiding beneath the Paladin's hate.

"Explain yourself!" Katar commanded. "We will have a full and detailed account, from your first encounter with the Wytch to this moment."

The mask was larger than a human face with a starburst of gold as a crown. She knew the voice of the man behind the mask, but she couldn't see the eyes. She couldn't plead with someone she had once called friend to understand. She had violated her oaths and found her voice so pinched from her dry throat that she could barely use it at all.

She was spared the need to speak when one of the Order's alarms was triggered—a Wytch was nearby. She was unceremoniously shoved aside as the Council flew into battle mode. Simza knew this was her chance to escape, perhaps the only chance she would get. They still thought of her as one of them and had forgotten about her when they were threatened. Once the real questioning began, they would not be likely to forget her. Then it occurred to her that she had the taint of Magic on her now. Perhaps it was she who had triggered the alarm. If their wards sensed a Wytch, they would alert the Inquisitor. Perhaps in her fear she had reached out to Magic without realizing it. It had happened before.

They drew their dragon bone guns in unison and listened to the wards. She should be able to hear the wards and what message they sent—a Paladin heard them the first time they said their vows.

Then the truth came crashing home to her. She couldn't hear the wards anymore—she couldn't hear them because she was no longer a Paladin. She was prepared for the Council to turn their guns on her when the door opened and Salem stood in the doorway. The guns turned in unison to point at him; he didn't have a chance.

Simza called out, "Wait!" But only a few heads turned in her direction. They were only waiting to see which of them would have the honor of killing the encroaching Wytch. She pushed her way through the throng and put herself between the guns and Salem. The guns were so close that one pressed against her forehead. The Paladins looked at each other with the knowing of betrayal in their eyes.

"You have no justification for your betrayals, Simza. You have knowingly broken your vows and have been harboring a known Wytch all this time." The Grand Inquisitor himself spoke the words.

Simza didn't wait for him to say anything else. All her life, she had been in awe of the man, but her feet voted with her heart, and she quickly pushed Salem out of the hut and stood guarding the doorway.

It was then that she opened herself to Magic for the first time with her whole heart. With the admission of betraying her vows came the admission of her love as well. Magic formed a shield for her, and as she stood in the doorway, a hundred dragon guns firing at her, not a bullet touched her. She walked away, closing the door behind her. The door would not hold the Inquisitors at bay, but the shield would last long enough for her and Salem to escape.

She heard him coming and turned to Salem him in the moonlight. He took her hand in his, and they ran deep into the woods. For the moment, it wasn't a Wytch and Paladin; only two souls met, two souls fled.

The deep conflict which had been increasingly on her conscious mind returned to the forefront of her thoughts. Simza laughed aloud. She had no idea what she was anymore, but she wasn't a Paladin. She tore off the locket she wore with the Inquisitor's seal and tossed it heedlessly into the bushes, and the dragon bone pistol followed. She felt like a young girl, free for the first time since her duality had forced her into a life of hunting her own kind.

Salem laughed at her exuberance, then hushed her. "What are you trying to do? Leave a trail for every member of the Council to follow us by?"

"I'm free. I'm not a Paladin anymore. I defied my vows and now I'm just a woman," she whispered as they rested against a tree for a moment.

"You are embracing your Wytch heritage?" he asked.

She shook her head. "No." She smiled at him. "I'm just a woman."

"You'll never be *just* anything, Lark," he said, pulling her into his arms, and without warning, he kissed her.

She had betrayed her vows for this man and for the words of Magic. Without thinking of anything except the moment under the trees, she kissed him back. It lasted for a long time, and they pulled apart from each other, each scanning the other's face, fearing more betrayal and seeing only the rawness of the other's heart. Throwing herself back into his arms, she kissed him first this time, trying to show all the words she couldn't explain, all the ways she felt in the language of lovers. He kissed her back just as urgently, as though their words had been stopped up and now must express themselves through their lips in another way.

They were startled by the cry of a nightjar nearby and let go of their kiss with a guilty jump. Separating, they laughed at their skittishness, each of them self-conscious and unsure—each praying the other wouldn't say something to break the unspoken words that had passed between them.

Salem's unusual outbreak of shyness made him miss the red dot that appeared on Simza's forehead. He glanced at her and saw that, just above her eyebrows, a glowing red dot formed. Her left foot began to glow, then her right hand.

"What—" she started, then stared at her glowing hand before looking up at Salem in alarm. Her left hand shone red now as well. He frowned. Her right foot filled with light too.

***

Salem had never seen anything like this before. He called on the power of Magic to try to find some method to defend his

Lark, but he didn't understand what was happening to her. His attempts to find a handhold on the evil attacking her felt like trying to scrabble up the blank face of a cliff.

A violet line shot from her forehead to her left foot, and then to her right hand. He knew what was happening now as the light formed a shape but was too late to do anything to stop it. Diabolical magic created a pentagram on Simza. He grabbed her and held her to him, but as the last violet line reconnected to the red dot, glowing like a fire-lit ruby on her forehead, she fell from his arms as if she were made of sand.

***

Viktor didn't usually indulge in a good caper, but as he saw Simza's body start to form in the ruby pentagram, he couldn't help but dance around. Branwen stood in silence behind him, still unsatisfied with the action he took to collect her. He'd spent the better part of the night performing rituals on the pentagram he'd laid out, invoking the dragons and the Ancients they later became, shedding the blood of a warrior to compel and bind her. It was working. The dead body of the warrior lay nearby. He had been a powerful man with a lot of blood. The rubies were flawless, and all of Viktor's hard work was paying off.

Simza's beautiful eyes opened, filled with rage. He could see that she was confused and frightened, but so powerful was her beauty that her rage dominated those smaller emotions. He calmed himself and kneeled carefully beside the pentagram, adjusting his robe to ensure that not even a hem of cloth would enter the magic circle containing her. He was sure it didn't matter; the rubies had fused with her flesh and held her helpless before him.

"Hello, Simza. How I have longed to bring you to me," he

said, his violet eyes glimmering.

Simza would find it hard to think, impossible to move. Even if she reached out to the Mother, her thoughts would do nothing to find her. He knew this.

"You're going to regret this," Simza promised him, her face nearly as scarlet as the ruby.

Viktor was happy to see it. The pentagram and the Diabolical binding worked well with rage. The trap only fastened tighter the more the victim struggled.

***

Simza thought of her last moments in the forest. She had been so happy, and then this. She thought of her happiness, her memory of her victory over the Paladins, keeping them from killing Salem, the sense of freedom from her vows. Then she remembered something else. She had channeled Magic for a shield to protect them when she had saved Salem from the Council's bullets.

She stopped struggling. It was getting her nowhere. She had to think. She knew magic was targeted somehow. But she had been a Paladin. Channeling Magic, throwing her locket and gun away...maybe what Viktor didn't know was enough to find a way out of the prison he had built to summon her.

She calmed her mind and recalled the feeling of Magic, the love she'd sent out, the peace she'd filled her with, the feeling of Salem kissing her, and felt a loosening of her bonds.

***

Viktor frowned. Something was wrong. She was finding peace from some deep reservoir inside her and using it to gain a bit of freedom, nothing like the conflicting Paladin he'd last seen before the Conqueror demanded their retreat. Then, he noticed she no longer wore the locket of the Inquisition and her holster was barren of the dragon bone pistol.

He had been depending on her connection and the vows she had made to the Ancient Ones to bind her for the Conqueror, who needed to take her completely. He had a sense of unease as he looked at her; she had changed, and in changing, challenged his summoning.

Viktor tried to sense what the change was, but all he could tell was that some peculiar start of something bigger now took place in the woman. She was neither Wytch nor Paladin—definitely not Diabolical—and yet she was all these things. While he felt he had stopped something dire from happening, he also felt certain that he'd been too late in his spell-casting, and that an impossible setback had occurred while he accomplished his great working.

Anger filled him, and violet fire arced between his hands as he strengthened the pentagram and tried to decide what to do. He might have no choice but to drive a dagger into her heart while she lay helpless and bound. But that would go against the Conqueror's wishes. If he killed her, he might suffer a worse fate.

CHAPTER 23

Salem stood silently, staring at the empty space in front of him. His hands clenched and unclenched, and his breathing was uneven, chest heaving as he fought to control the panic enveloping him. His eyes blurred over, and he was forced to blink, bringing them back into focus. With a shake of his head, he obliged himself to turn away from the spot where Simza had been standing. Looking around, he saw that he was completely and utterly alone.

He thought about sitting down against the trunk of the tree to collect his thoughts and try to work out what could have happened to her, but he knew he hadn't the time. The Paladin Council, fired up by his sudden appearance and what they would consider Simza's betrayal, would already be on his trail. He would be a fool to assume they weren't adept at tracking. They could be upon him at any moment, and he had to keep moving.

He forced his feet to move, running lightly through the trees, feet making no more sound than a light rustle against the fallen leaves scattered on the ground. He summoned her name to mind, and, using the bond of Wytches forged by centuries of unification under Magic, began to track her. He picked up a vague glimmer of her whereabouts. It was hazy and gritty and kept slipping out of his grasp. Salem knew he would not find her easily. Still, it was something.

It was all connected. The sand golems, the ruby-eyed snake, the Diabolical, the horned figure Michael saw emerging from the fire, and the darkness he had so briefly sensed in Simza. The Diabolicals wanted Simza; it had to be her Wytch blood. She was the only one who could unite the Wytches and Paladins, the only one who could prevent the disaster Magic sensed. Tarlak's vision had been but one small look into the devastation that would tear the world asunder if Simza didn't succeed. And if he couldn't get her back… His breath caught in his throat and anxiety lay heavy on his heart. If he couldn't get her back, it would mean more than a darkness to swallow the world.

Unbidden, thoughts of her came sweeping through, wave over wave of intense emotions. Her hair illuminated in the hazy twilight, creating a halo around her, lighting her face with the touch of angels. Her lips pressed softly against his as their breath mingled in the night air. In that brief moment, right before she was taken, he had surrendered himself to her, and he had known, irrevocably, that she had done the same to him. He could still feel her fingertips gently pressing against his cheek as she tilted her head back and told him, soundlessly, all the things she felt for him. If he couldn't get her back…

He sensed movement in the distance behind him. Far off still, it seemed, but close enough that his intuition picked up on it.

Clearing his head, he forced himself to move faster, attempting to put some more distance between himself and his pursuers. He ran faster than he ever had before, and it wasn't long before his breathing became labored and he felt the burning weight of exhaustion and overexertion pressing heavily against his chest. But despite how fast he ran, he could still sense the pursuers behind him, closing the gap. He began to lag, unable to keep the intense pace he had set. Soon now, they would be on him, and no amount of magic would be enough to help.

Just as desperation started to take hold, everything went still. He could no longer feel his pursuers. Only the silence of the moonlit forest remained and the sound of his harsh and ragged breath. He slowed to a stop and forced his breathing to steady. He stood perfectly still, listening for any sign of his pursuers, but still he felt nothing. Standing in silence, he could hear the slight crackling of dried leaves as the wind scattered them across the ground. Tree trunks creaked and groaned as the wind made a feeble attempt to uproot them. Branches scraped and tapped against one another in the treetops above. The wind whistled through the trees, and his own breathing provided a steady, pulsing beat, keeping tempo for the symphony of the near silent forest.

His body relaxed out of the tense hunter's stance he had unknowingly taken. He blew out a breath and slowly walked forward.

"Don't move another inch."

Freezing in place, Salem looked around. He still couldn't sense the presence of another human being, and the darkness of the night concealed the man from his sight. "It doesn't seem fair. You know exactly where I am, and yet I've no idea where, or who, you are."

A low chuckle came from between the trees to his left—so quietly that Salem was sure he wouldn't have heard it if he wasn't listening for it specifically. He heard the whisper of leaves and the soft patter of hooves as the man made his way out of the cover of the trees. The man's face was shrouded beneath the hood of his cloak, but there was no mistaking the dragon bone pistol he held or the massive black war stallion on which he rode.

"I have to admit, I'm a little impressed. Not many people can manage to sneak up on me like that."

Wolfeye threw back the hood of his cloak and grinned at Salem. "You can't have met many Paladins, then."

"How did you do it?"

Wolfeye burst out laughing. "You don't really think a Paladin would betray his secrets to a Wytch, do you? No. You're smarter than that. You're hoping to distract me so you can call on your Magic and attempt a daring and heroic escape."

Salem threw him a look of chagrin, mostly because he was right. It had been too much to hope the Paladin would be side-tracked by his own vanity and allow Salem a chance to make a run for it, but he had to try. "What happens now?"

"I kill you."

"That's great, I guess. Only one problem I can see with it, though."

A small smile spread across Wolfeye's face. "What would that be?"

"Simza's been captured, and since I'm the only one who has any information about where she could be, or who might have her, if you kill me, you're losing any chance you have of finding her." Salem regretted speaking of Simza like bait, but he silently swore he'd never let the Paladin find her and continued. "And, since the Council is probably extremely interested in finding her, you might want to hold off on the killing me part."

Wolfeye stared at him, his eyes dark and intense in the faint and shaky glow of the moonbeams filtering through the trees.

"You're right," he said after a moment. "The...Council...is very interested in having Simza back."

The way he said it made Salem grit his teeth and clench his hands into fists as a sudden burst of jealousy swept over him. He was sure of it, now. Something had happened between this Wolfeye and Simza. Clenching his hands tightly enough to leave little crescent-shaped indentations on his palms, he stared back at Wolfeye. It would be so easy for him to summon Magic and make a run for it, but as they had been standing there, Salem realized that if Simza's situation was really as dire as he thought, he'd need help.

"You'll just have to take me back with you then, won't you?"

The small smile playing on Wolfeye's lips spread into another grin. In the pale wavering light of the moon, his eyes took on a feral glint. He nodded to Salem and held out a rope of finely linked chains. At the end of the chain was a collar wrought from iron and laced with silver runes. The runes, marking it as Romni-crafted, glittered in the darkness. Wolfeye motioned for Salem to put it on and said, "Let's go see the Council."

***

The walk back to the Council seemed to take much longer than his panicked flight into the forest earlier in the night. And no small wonder, Salem thought, since he was chained like a wild animal. The collar burned against his skin, chafing and rubbing his neck raw as Wolfeye dragged him along behind his war horse. Salem could feel the blood trickling down his neck, running over his shoulders and down his back as the silver runes dug into his flesh and slowly burned it away.

He knew it wouldn't kill him. The collar itself was made of thick bands of iron—only the runes were silver. But just that small touch of silver, wrought by the Paladins and imbued with the same strange essence they used to craft their silver bullets, was enough to make him feel an immense amount of pain. He endured it silently, eyes glazed over with pain as his feet dragged across the ground. Every so often, he would stumble when Wolfeye quickened his pace. The man seemed to take some sort of perverse delight in watching Salem struggle to keep up. Salem counted himself lucky that Wolfeye was forced to maintain a fairly slow pace in the forest; moving too quickly would be dangerous as they picked their way through the trees.

The pitch black of night just began to lift as they emerged from the forest. The sun, not yet risen in the east, lightened the sky, creating a misty glow on the horizon which blended into the darkness, barely discernable. As they walked toward the small city that was home to the Paladins, Salem saw torches blinking in the distance, moving closer. He swayed and stumbled. He had lost a lot of blood from the collar, and he knew he wouldn't be able to walk on his own for much longer.

His vision doubled and clouded, and he collapsed. Wolfeye continued on, dragging Salem's limp body behind his horse. The collar dug painfully into Salem's neck and the world went black.

He woke up to the sound of a fire crackling. He could feel beads of sweat dripping down his face and lifted his arms to push back the blanket. Opening his eyes, Salem sat up. Sharp pain shot through his body, searing a path up his spine and exploding in his skull, pounding and hammering against his temple. A moan escaped him, and his head fell back against the pillow. Someone lifted a cup to his lips, letting the liquid trickle into his mouth and down his throat. It tasted chalky, and he vaguely realized it was medicine.

After a while, the pounding had subsided to a dull throb, and he was able to sit up again. After taking a few deep breaths to make sure the pain wouldn't come back, he opened his eyes. He was in a small room, tucked into a bed in the corner. A fire blazed in a small hearth on the wall opposite him. The floorboards were covered in dust and marked with footprints. In the corner next to the door, a small man with graying, wiry hair sat on a stool, watching Salem intently.

Salem opened his mouth to speak, but instead coughed and sputtered, his throat burning as he tried to talk. The collar had choked him when he fell unconscious, and his throat was raw. "Water?" he managed to say.

The old man pointed to a jug on the dusty table next to the bed, and Salem reached over to pick it up, wincing as his bruised body twisted. As he lifted the jug to his lips, the old man stood and left the room, closing the door behind him. Salem heard the faint click of the lock, followed by the man's footsteps fading down the hall.

He drank slowly, letting the liquid in the jug soothe his throat. It wasn't just water. It tasted slightly sweet, and he realized again that someone had put something in the jug to help ease his pain. He silently thanked whoever it may have been, since it was likely the only kindness he would receive in the Paladin stronghold.

As he set the jug back down on the table, the lock clicked again and the old man entered the room. He stood near the doorway and beckoned Salem forward.

"I don't think I can move from this bed, good sir. My body feels broken." His throat didn't feel nearly as raw, and it was no longer painful to speak, merely uncomfortable.

The old man simply stared at Salem in silence and continued to beckon him forward. With a sigh, Salem swung his legs over the side of the bed and slowly pushed himself to his feet. The man led him through a dim and narrow hallway, footsteps echoing against the dusty floorboards. They followed a series of twists and turns and, after some time, arrived at a door. The old man knocked twice and opened it.

Salem followed him into the room. The floor here was made of stone, and the walls surged upward, twenty feet high, ending in vaulted ceilings with ornate latticework carved into wooden beams. Torches were lit in sconces, creating shadows that twisted and flickered across the walls and floors. In the middle of the room on a raised dais sat the Paladin Council. At least twenty grim-faced guards surrounded them, each holding a dragon bone pistol. One word from the Council, and Salem was sure there would be twenty bullets riddling his corpse.

He took a deep breath and squared his shoulders. The collar, the harrowing journey, the injuries he had sustained—everything paled in comparison to this moment. He had to find a way to convince the Council to help him find Simza, and he had to keep himself alive long enough to do it. He refused to believe it had all been for nothing. After facing Viktor a number of times, he would be a fool to think he stood a chance alone. He had to keep believing he could find Simza and rescue her, and he needed the Council to help him. Never mind that he would simply be trading one threat for another. When Simza was safe, he would worry about how to escape the Council. But, for now…

"I have a plan," he said.

***

Two hooded figures crouched in front of a fire. The flames reached up, shooting tendrils of smoke and bits of ash into the air. The coals burned hot and white, tinged with purple. Viktor muttered something quietly, almost unintelligible over the crackling and snapping of burning wood. Lifting a hand, he made a gesture toward the fire. The purple-tinged coals flared, and the fire roared higher, shades of violet and crimson streaking through the blaze. A face emerged from the flames, grotesquely flickering in and out, losing shape and then forming again as the flames danced through the air. Two horns curved from the top of the face, tapering off into trails of smoke.

"Is it done?" The voice was distorted and deep, filled with the rage and turmoil of a thousand burning suns. Viktor hadn't heard his master's voice, but now that his master had grown accustomed to this plane, Viktor recognized the language.

He lifted the hood of his cloak. "It is done, Conqueror. The girl is imprisoned as we speak, ready for you to do with as you will."

"What of the Wytch, the so-called Favored Son?"

"He's taken care of. He won't be escaping the clutches of the Paladin Council any time soon."

"The time draws near, then. Soon, I shall fill the heir of Magic with a darkness so deep, so endless, that the world will tremble. And I will watch as she destroys every last shred of her heritage. Magic stands no chance when the world is swallowed in night."

A smile spread across Viktor's face. When his master imbued Simza with the power of darkness and used her to destroy Magic, in turn destroying both the Wytches and the Paladins, Salem would be his. He could almost feel the blood dripping off his hands, pooling on the ground as he tore Salem's heart from his chest. He could almost taste the power, so ancient and so strong, that he would consume. He would have more strength than any man alive, and together, with Simza...

The deep voice cut through the darkness, drawing Viktor's attention back to the flames. "And you, girl."

Huddled next to the fire, Branwen winced. Lifting the hood, she replied, "Yes, my Lord?"

"You will help Viktor see to it that my plans are successful."

A fleeting look of chagrin brushed her features. "Of course, my Lord. I shall not fail you."

"See that you do not. Everything must go according to plan. My daughter of darkness is a vital part of that plan. Keep a close eye on her. She is stronger than you think. She cannot be allowed to escape."

***

Branwen's lips pressed together in a thin line, and her hands dug into the folds of her cloak, twisting the fabric. She glanced sideways at Viktor, studying him. How had it come to this? She should be the one in charge, not Viktor. She should be the one carrying out the master's plans. She should be the one elevated to glory when the world crumbled to dust.

She could still remember the day it happened. She'd come across a Paladin and she'd done what any Wytch would have done. She'd spoken the words that ended his life. It wasn't until after she'd killed him that she realized this man was so much more than she could ever have imagined. As she stared into his eyes, watching the haunting shadow of pain flickering behind the glaze of death, she'd realized who he was. He was the man for whom Magic had walked the Earth. He was the man for whom Magic had borne a child. It mattered not that he had taken the child and hidden her from Magic—the bond was still there—and Branwen realized she had made a fatal error when she used her power, Magic's power, to end his life. In that moment, a darkness had crept across Branwen. She had felt Magic abandoning her, leeching out through her pores, leaving her bereft of power. As Magic fled, something else began to take root. Something darker. It seeped in, filling the void Magic had left. She'd felt it churning violently in her heart, roiling like a heaving ocean, diseased but delightful. She had welcomed this new power. It nearly made her feel whole again, and for a while, she had reveled in it.

When Viktor appeared, things had changed. The master had slowly torn Branwen's power away from her, giving more and more of it to Viktor until she was forced to follow the machinations of this power-hungry maggot of a man as her master watched on silently.

She ripped her eyes away from Viktor and stared back into the fire. Soon enough, the master would realize her value.

Eyes gleaming violet in the light of the flames, she smiled and nodded.

CHAPTER 24

A s the Conqueror left, the fire dimmed, returning the campsite to near darkness, the flicking tendrils of light licking the edges of the circle. Viktor moved to the outside of the grove of trees where Simza lay. Trails of sand marked a pentagon on the ground around her. With her soul trapped in the elemental plane, her physical presence was unconscious, tortured. The tendons in her legs were taught, limbs outstretched—her fists clenched and the veins in her neck and face were swollen, red, pulsating with blood as adrenaline fueled her psychosis.

To the left, a rope hung from one of the oak trees, the aged, knotted bark creating deep shadows which moved and flickered in the firelight. A shadow drifted across the ground as the near-naked body above swung from the rope. The slipknot clung tightly to the Paladin's neck, his weight holding it in place. A barely perceptible breath passed his lips, the pale, clammy skin indicating that he clung to life. Imperceptibly.

Viktor approached his captive.

"You, my friend…" He paused, watching the body swing back toward him. "Your time has come. I need you for a greater purpose."

He placed a wooden bowl under the Paladin, then steadied the body with his left hand. His right hand moved to his belt and withdrew a small knife. A short, slightly curved blade designed for one purpose—the taking of life. Holding the handle of the knife between his hand and first finger so the blade pointed up, he ran the palm of his hand over the man's belly. He closed his eyes, positioning his hand, then stopped. Opening his eyes, he used his left hand to pull down on the stomach, then placed the point of the blade on the left; he pressed hard, making a precise cut into and below the skin before drawing the incision all the way across to the right side. The belly bulged as internal organs became visible and blood oozed. Viktor pressed from above and below. The cut popped open, and large coils of intestine showed through the gaping wound. The disembowelment would hasten death, but it would be slow and painful, further torturing the Paladin's body and soul. The projection of intense emotion—pain—into the astral plane through the use of blood would magnify the effect of the ritual.

Viktor now focused his attention on the neck. He slowly slid the blunt, outside edge of the blade down the throat of his victim, gently pressing against the Adam's apple, feeling the indentation as the skin yielded to the pressure. He had his mark; with practiced precision, he inverted the knife, creating a perfectly sized puncture wound in the artery. A jet of blood spurted into the bowl—hard, fast, easing slowly, draining life away. Viktor waited until he was satisfied with his work, then collected the bowl and walked back to Simza.

He shivered in anticipation at the ritual he was about to perform—a dark magic which hadn't been enacted since even before the time Paladins and Wytches had been a single tribe. He had collected Paladin blood, vigorous, young, fresh. He now needed Wytch blood. He walked into the pentagram, held his palm above Simza, and chanted.

"Uti hoc est corpus meum."

The hex on her brow shimmered, emitting a gentle silver glow like moonlight. He took the killing knife out again, except this time, he made a shallow incision, carving the pentagram across the surface of the tattoo. Blood gently oozed out of the wound, running down her forehead in globules, dripping into a small vial. The blood in the cut congealed, slowly healing. Viktor walked out of the pentagram, now ready to begin. He dipped the tips of his fingers in the larger bowl and slowly moved around the pentagram, spraying blood across the sand trails. The sand absorbed the dark crimson fluid, staining the surface. He did this slowly, patiently, ensuring there were no gaps in the trail he made, sealing the spell. Moving to the tip of the pentagram, he sat cross-legged on the ground, resting the backs of his hands on his knees, palms up, thumb to index finger. He closed his eyes and entered a trance.

"Infernum in terra."

A soundless yet perceptible vibration filled the air. The sensation was electric and would have raised the hairs on the arms of any Wytch. Inside the pentagram, the resonance increased in pitch. Tiny dust particles filled the air, hovering, shimmering.

Viktor's eyes flashed open. He reached down and dipped his fingers into the larger bowl of blood. His flicked the blood, expelling it in mid-air above Simza. Like the dust particles, they froze, hovered, then moved again, rotating, swirling. They formed a slow, gradual vortex, mesmerizing the eye. Next, he reached down to the small vial of blood from Simza. He again dipped his fingers, flicking the fluid across the space in front of him. It hovered in mid-air, mixing with the Paladin blood. The droplets touched and merged, rotating in a vortex before accelerating, increasing in speed. The static charge now changed to a low-pitched hum, a droning which filled and emanated from the space above Simza. The eye of the spell centered over Simza's mouth.

"Infernum in terra, Infernum in terra, Infernum in terra."

As he chanted, the vortex increased in speed and intensity. It gradually dropped, creeping lower and lower before touching Simza's lips. Then her flesh appeared to separate, molecule by molecule, atom by atom—caught in the vortex and trapped in the eye of the storm, disappearing. Like a virus, the disintegration of her flesh spread, gradually at first, then, as the vortex grew, more rapidly. Her lips, nostrils, cheeks, and eyes—the whole head. The spiraling, magical entity curved upward as it tracked across her body, destroying everything it touched, tearing the physical form away from the earth to which it was attached. It moved down her torso, enveloping, covering, devouring her.

Then silence.

Viktor stared into the clearing. No birds, no wind. Utter stillness. Simza was gone.

***

Simza didn't know what had happened after she thought she was loosening her bonds, almost free. Viktor had done something; she knew she no longer inhabited her body. She could hear, she could touch, she could sense. She felt Magic, felt her aura, and how much stronger her presence was. She knew she was in the astral plane; she had seen Salem communicate closely with Magic, sensed the departure of his soul. His body remained unresponsive, unconscious, and she knew that her body must be similarly prone in the physical world. Yet here, she had no physical body, so she knew she couldn't "see," even though she had "sight." Her soul was the astral projection of her mind, and she remained connected to her body by a slender thread of consciousness.

Then the darkness enveloped her. She remained in the astral plane, but she lost all awareness of the features around her, lost sensation of nearby beings and entities. Her link with Magic was severed, and she knew the Conqueror was trying to inhabit her. She felt his sentience, his presence, but he did not come from Wytch or Paladin blood. He wasn't human. Elements of his consciousness translated into human traits—anger, rage, spite, venom, vengeance, loathing. But it was more than that. Deeply rooted, there was a primal delight, a pleasure, from the ability to deliver pain and anguish. That was the beginning—the well from which his soul fed. But physical torture wasn't enough. His power, his arcane energy, was derived from the rituals used to inflict the wounds on his captives. He fed off magical energy in the astral plane that came from a victim's consciousness, a result of their willing acceptance of grievous pain and, ultimately, a death in agony. The release of the mortal from his earthly body shattered the chains, anchoring the soul to the living and releasing him to the afterlife. The Conqueror usurped the right of the individual in the life beyond, stripping their spirit of elemental force and condemning them to a life of eternal damnation. The steady flow of incoming knowledge ignited a new sense of panic. He literally fed off life.

A desperation entered her soul; she wasn't just alone, she

was cut off and hidden. She expanded her astral presence and focused her mental energy on the blackness surrounding her. She prodded, feeling around, but it fully enclosed her, blanketing the space she occupied. The prodding became more intense and repeated, a mental hammering against the prison walls.

She knew Viktor had prepared the ritual; her physical body responded to her consciousness and adrenaline pumped through her veins. The skeletal frame became rigid as muscles tensed violently. Desperation now turned to anger; she was a caged animal. The Conqueror had her trapped, but she now felt no fear at the prospect of death. She wanted a focus for her anger, a focus to enable her to challenge her captor. Rage.

Rage filled her, occupying the space left when her link to Magic had been severed. Rage at the sudden appearance of Wolfeye, rage at the blindness—the incompetence—of the Paladin Council, rage at the impudence of Salem and her willing response, rage at being taken by Viktor. But the eye of her rage came from her entrapment by the Conqueror, and the fulfilling completion to rage was revenge.

The deep well of emotion, of anger, turned into a whirlpool, spinning and rotating, dragging in energy from outside her mind and her body. The thread of her soul still connected to her body, and this became engorged with electric, magical energy. It fizzed as it grew and expanded—Viktor had completed the ritual, and Simza's body was gone. She heard him gasp at the blinding light that erupted where she had been. It was as if night had become day, but it was a white light—pure, living, magical energy.

The whirlpool of energy grew, drawing in vast fluxes of power. Simza's rage was focused on centuries of heritage which enabled the Romni blood to flow in her veins. The elemental energy cascaded and multiplied. She waited for it to concentrate, biding her time, gently caressing and teasing the walls that caged and enraged her. Then, with the swiftness of a warrior, she drew upon the deep well of swirling power enveloping her. She aimed for the weakest point and unleashed concentrated mental energy. The intensity of the strike crackled as force met force. The Conqueror's imprisonment began to diminish. The initial explosion of power now built, the whirlpool of consciousness with her living body deepening—no longer a slender thread but a raging torrent of power pulling in all earthly energy, adding to her resources.

Viktor seemed to realize, too late, the purpose of the ritual he had enacted. The whirlpool rotated faster, deepening, but this was no ordinary aquatic phenomenon. It was magical—a parasitic, ancient link, tearing asunder the bonds that separated the astral and physical planes. The source of this energy was the magical entities themselves which lived and traversed through the physical realm. They were sucked dry of their innate essence, left as empty vessels. Like Simza, Viktor's body drew into the powerful torrent. His arm was dragged toward the eye. As it touched the magical link, his physical being disintegrated. Slowly, his body disappeared into the void, his being now part of the huge resources Simza had built. Simza's astral energy peaked. She felt the Conqueror yield and back away from her point of impact as her power exploded in a mental fireball.

Then he struck back.

He channeled her power back into her consciousness through the link she had created in the physical realm. The fire bolt shot back to Earth and detonated in the clearing, flattening all that surrounded it. Trees blew over, and a pressure wave of energy washed over the landscape. The vortex glimmered in the night, a shimmering cylinder of energy, permanently fixed in the land-scape.

With deep, evil laughter, the two-horned figure of the Con-queror appeared before a bewildered Simza.

"Thank you for releasing me from the astral plane Ama-latuu—you have been foolish."

The gaping whirlpool momentarily stood open, a swirling, writhing torrent of energy. The Conqueror extended his arm, touching the void. With a blinding flash and explosion, he disap-peared, the vortex closing behind him.

***

In the clearing, a light breeze rustled the leaves on the flat-tened trees. The form of the now dead Paladin was nestled amongst them, lifeless and disemboweled, his soul disembodied. Simza's body stood inside the pentagram, surveying the scene of destruc-tion. Her eyes glowed purple and she cackled.

"I have returned," the Conqueror whispered gleefully. "This body...my daughter... We are now one."

He sensed her presence first, then walked across the clear-ing to the prone form of Branwen.

"You, girl," he commanded.

Branwen stirred, looking up, confused. "Simza, how did you—"

"Paladin Slayer, there is work."

Branwen paused before cautious recognition dawned on her face. "My Lord? You have returned!"

"We go," he replied. "We must find Salem Taker."

***

The blast cast Simza asunder, leaving her disoriented and dazed, the vortex no longer visible.

Is my link with the physical realm severed? she thought.

Panic set in as the implications of being cut adrift in the astral plane spiraled in her mind.

Then she felt it—unfamiliar and unnatural. She was still connected to her physical body, the slender conscious thread present, but faint. Yet it was different. Her soul probed again, using the slightest of touches. It was familiar while being unrecognizable, all at the same time. She paused before the thought came to her. The soul in her body was not hers. The Conqueror had seized it, filled it with his presence, leaving her in the astral plane. He had complete control of her physically, but for now, she still had her soul.

CHAPTER 25

Atticus stood on a field of stone stretching out to the eons. The dead, still air gave him chills like no wind ever had in his life. No living soul had ever moved through or breathed out the air in this plane.

He touched his sleeve. Though he perceived it to be the coarse fabric of his usual garb, his gut told him he was no longer corporeal.

It had been a snake, hadn't it? The creature which had killed him. A conjured snake with rubies for eyes. Atticus had been relatively fond of snakes before this. In part, it was the way their shed skins were ghosts of themselves. But more, it was the way a snake would look at him with seething disinterest, knowing it could kill him, and he it, then go on its way. As arbitrator of the Druids, he had not had the freedom to give someone so much as a stink-eye in centuries.

Perhaps it was death's way to dredge up memories, but Atticus suddenly found himself in his boyhood days, when a glare was all the hatred a little boy could muster.

He would miss his Brothers. It seemed they had yet to bury him; this was not the afterlife Magic had foretold for her children. He could have sworn rivers would have been here. Rivers and...forests? Thoughts of the living world escaped him now, and he was left only with a sense that he'd had purpose and camaraderie in his life.

The horizon shook and refined itself. It had been gray stone against gray sky, the contrast barely perceptible, but now an inky gap stretched and howled.

"Atticu—"

The Druid trembled in fear of this unnatural unknown. He wished for a memory to cling to, to hide in, even his own name.

"At—A—"

He had been a Druid with purpose and camaraderie, one not to cower before fear but to let it flow through him and settle.

A glowing silhouette of a woman in a dress cut through the dark. He kneeled in wonder.

"Atticus," said the woman. "How sad but good we meet here."

"I know you," he said. He pondered his words. He had meant to say, "You know me," but it had come out all jumbled up. Still, he felt the words to be true. A backward truth. The Druid chuckled.

The woman rested her radiant hand on his shoulder. "I am sorry to do this to you, friend, but I must return to the physical plane."

"My Brothers," he said. The physical plane was where he had been, where they still were. "I'd like to go back there."

"You died, Atticus," said the woman. "A Diabolical's snake golem."

The Druid did not understand the words—Diabolical, Atticus, golem. They felt more gibberish than language. "But you are here, so you have died. Why do you get to go back?"

"I did not die the normal way," said the woman. "The Conqueror stripped my soul from my body, and once he has destroyed the Paladin Council and the Wytch Born, he'll come back here for my soul."

"Why do you get to go back?" he asked again. He had no grasp of what the physical plane would be like; he knew only that he did not like it here on this still, cold plane with darkness creeping about the horizons.

"I have to warn them, get my body back, end the Conqueror for good."

"Why do you get to go back?" He said the words now only in memory that he had just said them a moment before. He wondered why he had said those words and how many times before they had been said.

"I will not disgrace your memory too long, dear Brother."

An inky tendril lashed out from the shadows, outlining the woman's luminescence. It kissed his neck, and the landscape blinked away, leaving his soul in an unholy dark.

***

Long after the fire had died and shortly after the sun nudged the horizon, Ansgar, Tarlak, and Morvyn awoke to Michael screaming. Tarlak didn't move, still wary.

"Stay back, demon! You're lying!" Michael's threats were tear-choked and quavering.

"Calm down, kid," said a low voice from around the corner of the bar.

"What's wrong?" Ansgar rushed to Michael's side, following his gaze to the man standing in front of them. "Demon! How dare you defile our Brother? Out with you!"

Morvyn and Tarlak ran to meet him and saw their dearly departed Atticus leaning against the side of the bar, his hands raised in caution, his eyes glowing bright.

"Mother, lend me power that I may rend this demon out from the sacred flesh of our Brother."

Nothing happened.

"It's all right," said Atticus. "Please, just let me explain."

"It speaks," said Tarlak. "I've never met an unholy creature with no form of its own yet sentient enough for speech."

"And its eyes glow bright," said Morvyn. "There is no aura of darkness about it."

"Give me your gun, Michael. I'll deal with this fiend, magic or no magic," said Ansgar.

"Magic is in danger," said Atticus, or whatever beast possessed him. "Are you not concerned that she did not come to your aid?"

"How is she in danger?" Tarlak looked around, noting that Magic was indeed missing, along with Salem and Simza.

"A Paladin named Wolfeye came in the night. That's too far back and there isn't time. The Conqueror means to destroy both the Paladin Council and the Wytch Born, and he'll use Simza Adenah to do it. We must stop him."

"What can we do?" asked Tarlak.

"Don't believe that thing!" yelled Ansgar. "It disgraces our Brother."

"And in my time I shall take my leave of him," said the fiend or whatever it may be. "But do listen, for tide nor time is in your favor."

"Who are you, then?" asked Michael.

Atticus smiled. "Would you believe I am Simza? But, in a way, I am not…just what remains of a piece of my soul. Such trifles do not matter. Branwen is to play the role of Paladin Slayer, and Simza's body the role of Magic Slayer. You must follow Magic's path into the desert and defend her against Simza."

"And what of Salem?" asked Tarlak.

"Do you believe it?" Ansgar asked. "No creature capable of such desecration could possibly mean well."

"I take no pleasure in this act," said Atticus. "Please, leave me be to tell my tale, and I will burden you with my presence no longer."

"There is no harm in hearing it out," said Tarlak. "Do you know where Salem Taker is?"

"Much happened in the night while you slept," said Atticus. "Should all go well, Salem and Simza shall reveal the tale to you over a well-earned brew, but should all not go well, it shan't be because I delayed you with details. What matters is that Salem stands before the Paladin Council in the Bredon Woods, which is about to be destroyed by Branwen. Magic waits in the desert for the Magic Slayer."

"So, who do you say we save?" Morvyn crossed his arms over his chest. "Salem and the Paladins or Magic?"

"Should Magic die, the Wytches will have no way to defend themselves when the Conqueror comes for their souls."

"Aha!" said Ansgar. "I've discovered the root of its trick. It distracts us with two oh so very important choices, a dilemma indeed, but it's rouse is for use to forget about Atticus—who stands right before us, mind you, rotting—to forget and leave him unburied, that this creature may permanently inhabit our Brother."

"Grief has rattled your brains, dear Brother," said Tarlak. "Supposing you ever had any."

"Now I must return to the astral plane. The soul of Simza Adenah can take the burden of being both here and there, lost and found, no longer. We disgrace our Brother no longer."

The bright light died in Atticus' eyes, and his corpse crumpled, lifeless once again.

"Oh," said Ansgar. "I suppose you lot will take this as evidence it was deceiving you. Well I won't. I'm taking Atticus back to the mountain right now to give him his proper burial. Who will come with me?"

Michael picked up his satchel. "I must warn Salem. I will go north to Bredon Woods."

"You won't get there in time," said Ansgar. "And you don't know where the Paladin Council meets in Bredon Woods."

Tarlak eased a spark of magic into his fingertips and brushed it against Michael's forehead. "Just as before, the images in your mind will lead you to Salem. Look for his surroundings."

Morvyn raised his arms to the sky. "Winds grant me this boon. Carry our young friend to the Bredon Woods northbound."

A ramming wind tore through the town of Reunion Pass and plucked Michael from the ground.

***

Ansgar did his best to restrain his anger. His Brothers would not see reason if he continued to lash out, and he knew it.

"Look," said Ansgar. "There's no true evidence that anything that thing, or that essence of who she says she is, said is true.

I can sense her true motive is simply to obtain a body. Why don't you believe me?"

"Don't be so hardheaded, Ansgar," said Tarlak. "If you truly feel you must bury Atticus, then do so. But I place my duty to Magic and my Brothers above all else. I go east to the desert to defend the Mother." He transformed into his beast form and charged eastward.

"And you?" Ansgar asked Morvyn.

"I will meditate." He sat cross-legged and stiff in the middle of the road. It was not as open as the mountain valley he had made his habit of meditating in, but it would suffice.

"You expect me to bury Atticus alone while you sit here?"

"Simza's soul is lost."

"So implies whatever creature sullied our Brother."

"I will find Simza's soul and offer her what counsel I can. Whatever being granted her the power to visit us, whether friend or foe, is an unknown Simza should not face alone." Morvyn closed his eyes, and his aura shifted to a wavering form as though underwater.

Ansgar knew Morvyn was now beyond reach, so he hefted Atticus over his shoulders and began the long trek back to the mountain. Perhaps at the town's edge, he would transform and make the job easier, but for the moment, it seemed too callous to clutch his Brother in claws, trying not to mangle him too greatly.

CHAPTER 26

Salem stood in front of the Paladin Council, his feet planted firmly on the dirt floor. Sweat dripped down his neck, but he didn't dare reach to wipe it away with so many dragon bone pistols in the room. The last time he was here, Simza had pushed him out so quickly, he had hardly seen the place. This time, he saw the eight men sitting on the raised timber platform with a gaping space, making the circle incomplete and imperfect. The room was candle-lit and smelled of incense and tree resin. The Council sat patiently, waiting to hear his plan.

"I know Simza has been deemed a traitor," Salem said. The candles flickered as soft murmurs filled the room. "I also understand your view of Wytch magic. But I think we have to move forward and defeat the forces destroying both our kinds." More murmurs. "Those forces have Simza," he continued.

At that moment, there was a loud crash, and the structure

around them trembled. Shards of rock fell from the walls. Wolfeye wrapped an arm around Salem's neck as the falconer launched out the door. The screech of the falcon, a thud, and then a boy's cry made Salem's stomach turn. It was Michael.

"What the hell is going on?" Wolfeye growled into Salem's ear.

The Council was perfectly still, all hands on pistols.

The falconer pushed Michael through the door, who stumbled to his knees. Salem refrained from going to the boy.

"You come here using Wytch magic. Again, you defile our sacred ground," one man said. The man in the center addressed him as Ahtunowhiho, and Salem figured since he was in the center, he was the Grand Inquisitor.

Then Ahtunowhiho turned to Salem. "Is this part of your plan?"

"No, I had no plans of bringing anyone else here. But the boy is my responsibility. Any punishment should be directed at me."

"And it shall be," Ahtunowhiho said. He nodded, and the falconer dragged Michael back toward the iron door.

"Wait," the Grand Inquisitor said. The quiet voice held years of wisdom and the weight of power. He stood and walked to the cauldron. He held his fist over the boiling ceremonial herbs and released a fine line of sand into it. The brew steamed and hissed, and he breathed it in. "Bring these two to my chamber," he said and made his way to a back room.

Wolfeye gave a low growl and released Salem only to grab his shirt and pull him outside. He signaled to the falconer to follow with the boy.

"Where are we going?" Salem asked.

Wolfeye didn't answer. They walked through thick trees on mossy ground to a clearing. "Sit," Wolfeye said, pointing to the bench. "You will be cleansed before going into the Grand Inquisitor's chamber." Then Wolfeye took his leave, but the falconer remained in the shade of the trees.

"That was quite an entrance," Salem said, grinning at Michael. "I'm guessing Morvyn conjured the wind for you, but I've never seen someone slammed into their destination."

"Yes, well, I climbed a tree, thinking I could listen through the chimney," Michael said.

"And then what?"

"I don't know. I'm here to warn you."

An old Paladin servant walked toward them with a basin and folded white linens. He placed the linens on the bench, kneeled down in front of Salem, and reached for his boot. Salem pulled his foot away and immediately heard the flapping of the falcon's wings. The servant waited with his head down until Salem put his foot back on the ground. With gnarled hands from swollen joints, his feet were washed in cold, green water that smelled of salt and algae.

"Have you heard from Simza?" Salem asked.

"Yes, you could say that," Michael said.

The servant moved to Michael's feet and continued the cleansing.

"Is she all right?"

"I'd have to say no to that. She appeared in Atticus' body. She says she's trapped in the astral plane," Michael said.

A heavy weight pressed on Salem's chest.

"She came to warn us that the Conqueror is using her body to kill you and Magic. Branwen will come too."

Salem gripped the edge of the bench. "Are you sure it was her?"

"Tarlak thought so. He went to the desert to defend Magic."

"We've got to warn the Paladin Council, or they'll think I set this up," Salem said.

The servant pointed to the linens and signaled that they remove their clothes and wear the white robes on the bench. Salem and Michael reluctantly undressed and pulled on the robes. These would be less than ideal if they needed to make a quick exit. Michael shook violently from the cold, or maybe from fear. Salem put his hand on the boy's shoulder.

"It's going to be fine. You did the right thing coming here," Salem said, even though he felt like a gun had been at his head since he'd been here, and now at Michael's too.

The boy's eyes were wet, and he looked like he might collapse any minute. They sat on the bench, and Salem put his arm around Michael to try to infuse some warmth into his icy body. He wondered how he could protect the boy, get them both out of there, and find Simza too.

Wolfeye appeared in the clearing. "Let's go."

Salem and Michael were led into a back door of the Paladin Council's hut, and they stopped at a scrim. They could hear the Grand Inquisitor chanting quietly. They entered the small room with smoke-stained stone walls. He sat on a red woven rug, facing a wall with a circle of candles in front of him.

"Katar." He introduced himself without looking at them. "Come sit."

Salem and Michael sat on the two rugs next to Katar. Although Salem was not familiar with their rituals, the room had a warm glow and a buzz of spiritual activity. Katar murmured in low, continuous verses as the sun sank completely behind the horizon.

"I've been holding séances since you and Simza were here last. Asking the Ancient Ones if the prophecy was coming now. There have been many times when war threatened, but never with the strong signs we have now," Katar said.

"Signs?" Salem asked.

"Yes. Stories of a boy and girl, born and bred to defend us. Separated to keep them safe. The Ancient Ones say they will find each other when it is necessary."

"Yes, I've come to believe that story," Salem said. "And now you believe it is time?"

"I am set in my ways, and sometimes we hear what we want to hear, and we can hope that change will not come."

"You believe Simza?"

"She was a Paladin and honored us in her duty. But once she learned who she really was, she could not go back. I know that to be true."

"Inquisitor, I must warn you that someone, or something, that looks like Simza is on its way here. I'm afraid it might be my fault."

"Yes. I've seen the half-boy in the water and the flames coming to warn us. I thought perhaps it was you when you first came here. But, alas, it is him."

Katar looked at Michael, and the boy could only gape at him in confusion.

"What do you mean half-boy?" Salem asked.

"He straddles two worlds, this one. Wytch and human."

Salem looked at Michael and understood it was the Wytch blood that drove his need to protect him. And something about the lanky kid's loud voice. But Michael looked more confused. Half-Wytches were usually killed because they had enough magic to get them into trouble but not enough to defend themselves.

"Why was I the one you saw?" Michael asked, his voice unsteady.

Katar gave a gap-toothed smile. "I have a secret to share. I may be the Grand Inquisitor, but I don't always have an explanation. I think that change is in the air and perhaps you are a sign that we must open our minds to things different from ourselves."

Michael's eyes were wide.

"And we need to protect ourselves from whatever comes," Salem said.

"Was that your plan?" Katar asked.

"No. My plan was to set a meeting with the Paladin Council and the Thirteen. I thought if we could meet on neutral ground, I could prove it was the Diabolicals who killed everyone in Reunion Pass, that all would agree it is time for unification."

"And where is Simza?"

"She's trapped in the astral plane. But I can sense her. I feel our bond, and I will find her. But right now, her body hosting The Conqueror is on its way."

Katar turned and nodded at Wolfeye, who stood at attention near the entrance. "Wolfeye will get the others in our safe house and we will put up wards. The army is prepared."

"Michael, you go to the safe house," Salem said.

"No, I want to stay with you. I can help," Michael said.

Katar pulled himself to his feet with his walking stick. He waved it over the candles to the rhythm of a final incantation, then took slow steps toward the door. Once he was gone, the room turned cold.

"You need to go to the safe house. This could be really bad," Salem said.

"I want to fight. I don't want to hide. I've spent my life hiding because I didn't belong anywhere. I had no father, my mother and brother died. I hid so I wouldn't be shipped off to some work camp for orphans. I don't want to hide."

"Michael, this is all new to you. But you are half-Wytch,

and this fight is no place for any amount of human. I can teach you, in the future, how to use your powers and to put up the proper defenses so you cannot be possessed again. But right now, you need to be safe."

"I've already felt my Wytch blood. I felt it battle the possession."

Salem knew the boy was undeterred, and it scared the hell out of him. He had not been able to draw on the power of the Mother, and without that, he would struggle to defend himself, let alone Michael.

"And Simza. She needs our help. She doesn't know where she belongs either," Michael said.

Salem smirked and threw a fake punch to Michael's shoulder. "How did you get so smart?"

Michael shrugged and beamed the first genuine smile Salem had seen on the boy's face.

***

In the astral plane, Simza wandered through the gray light on the gray surface, searching for something to attach to, anything to give her the weight of a body on Earth. But she only felt the tugging of her soul toward the evil of the Conqueror. And the deep sense of dread for Salem and what was to come. She tried to concentrate on keeping her soul, finding Salem, and connecting with the Mother.

***

Salem signaled from his perch in a two-hundred-foot white pine to Wolfeye across the way. The dark aura he felt approaching made him shiver. It was dawn, and the sun was dim, allowing the sordid, gray nighttime clouds to hang in the sky. Salem glanced up at Michael twenty feet above him, looking to the east to see who or what might come from the desert. Katar and the Paladin Council had blessed all the warriors who would defend against the on-slaught—the onslaught that looked like two women walking on the path to the stone hut. He could see Simza's figure now, so familiar to him, and felt his heart speed up. But he didn't feel her the way he had when she was near. Salem shut his eyes tight and tried once more to feel the real Simza, and this time, he did. A spark shot up his spine and light glowed behind his eyes. She was trying to find him, too.

"Soul. Danger," the faint voice said.

He reached to Magic to ask for her help. "Mother, as your child, I ask you to bring me the power to fight this evil in the form of two women. And to find the woman I need to end this war."

But there was nothing. He was on his own, and so was Simza.

The two women stopped under Salem's tree. His hands felt numb against the rifle Wolfeye had given him even though he was sure this would not be played out with guns.

Simza's body kneeled down, her arms held out over the ground. Gusts of wind made their way through the trees, causing them to sway. The pine needles and dirt swirled beneath her hands. The Conqueror was creating his weapon right before their eyes. But this was no sand golem like Viktor had conjured. The vortex seemed to open up the earth and create a black mass in the middle.

Salem saw Wolfeye make his way down from his tree. Was he summoning the troops for an offensive? The vortex burned on the outside and, as Simza stood and raised her arms to the sky, the swirling, burning mass did too.

Salem signaled to Michael to take the zip-line back toward the treehouse where the Paladin Council waited. He made his way down the tree in time to see the army coming through the forest. If only Ansgar was here to figure out a strategy. They rushed past him and lined up around the two women and the vortex. A wave of panic hit Salem as he realized that if they shot Simza's body, it might be beyond saving, and she'd never regain it if she found a way back to the physical plane.

Branwen opened her mouth to speak. "Salem Taker, sur-render to us now and we will spare the Paladin Council and its army."

Salem made his way out of the trees when an arm slid around his neck.

"Well, this is familiar," Wolfeye said.

"Let me go. They are going to burn this place to high heaven, and I don't have Morvyn here to put out the hellfire."

"We'll fight them."

"If I don't go, there won't be anyone left to fight. Can't you see that?"

Wolfeye dropped his arm when a massive tongue of fire reached out from the vortex and burned the trees and the men on the opposite side of the path. Wails from charred bodies rose up, and the trees singed into black twigs. Salem leaped from the trees and ran to the women, believing he had to stop them on his own or die trying.

"Stop!"

The flames reined in once again, contained by the vortex. He stood before Simza and Branwen and imagined armor of his own making holding him steady as their red eyes bored into him. The smell of burnt flesh and timber polluted the air, and the force of the vortex grew stronger. Salem felt its pull like a siren's song but much darker. The red eyes flamed and danced, and he could not turn away.

Minutes passed as Salem fought the darkness luring him into the vortex. He could see Michael in the trees with a gun and Wolfeye coming up behind the two women with what looked like a large burlap sack. Then, a small ball of fire pierced through Branwen's head, leaving a gaping hole in her forehead. As she fell, the wound closed immediately. Simza screamed an ungodly sound, then leaped at Salem.

CHAPTER 27

Salem did not flinch. He stood his ground and caught her in his arms, calling her name. He closed his eyes so the red eyes of the Conqueror staring out of her body could not control him or stop him from doing what he was determined to do. He kissed her, long and hard. He acknowledged his love for Simza and allowed it to consume him. It flowed from his soul in the physical plane to reach out and touch her in the astral plane. Her soul responded in kind. The Conqueror's power was based on hatred and cruelty; unfettered true love was not only completely foreign to him, it was dangerous as well. As light will vanquish the darkness, love will dispel hatred. Love was not the only thing working against the evil being, but also the power of Wytch blood calling to Wytch blood.

The Conqueror struggled within Simza's body to capture

her soul as it gravitated toward Salem, but it was pure and clean, and he feared its strength. He could not grasp it before it joined Salem's soul between the two physical bodies. The Conqueror's spirit shrank away from Salem's tight embrace, but Salem held firm. In a last ditch effort to be released, the demon used Simza's teeth to sink deep into Salem's lower lip until blood flowed. Salem put his hand behind her head and forced it down against the thick muscle of his shoulder.

The Conqueror had become desperate. While he fought, his control over the immediate surroundings began to slip. He had to concentrate on remaining in Simza's body, so the vortex that tried to suck Salem in began to lose its strength. Rather than allow that to happen, the Conqueror concentrated his will for a single moment on producing a ring of flame around Branwen, Simza's body, and Salem. His intent was to set the male Wytch on fire, which would force him to let go of Simza's body. When that happened, the Conqueror would grab Simza's soul, still hovering nearby.

Salem pulled Simza's body closer to protect it as he tried to back out through the ring of fire and escape the vortex before it could suck him in permanently. The heat reached Salem before the flames did, but he refused to let go of the woman he loved. If she was going to die, he would die with her, and they would both be free. He knew the Conqueror would not remain in a body being consumed by its own supernatural fire.

Just before the flames could catch hold of their clothing, a deluge of water descended upon the three forms within the vortex. The ring of hellfire disappeared. Salem looked around to see Morvyn arriving through the swath of burnt trees across the path. A steady rain fell upon the trees and doused the embers. He pulled Simza's body as far away from the vortex as he could get with the Conqueror still inside her, struggling to get free.

***

Branwen was still on the ground even though the hole in her head was healed. She was at a loss as to what to do. She was supposed to be the Paladin Slayer, and yet she hadn't been given the chance to do that, and she resented it. The Paladin Council was still in the safe house, though their army had been reduced somewhat by the Conqueror's hellfire. She wasn't getting any commands from her master, and she had no weapons with which to fight the Paladins. When the water hit her back, she was driven closer to the heart of the vortex. Her head and shoulders began to slide into it, and she was powerless to stop herself. The Conqueror no longer gave her power. He needed all he had to protect himself.

***

Simza and Salem were free of the vortex. Wolfeye ran forward with his large burlap sack and threw it over Simza's head. It had been treated with many spells in the Paladin safe house to protect the woman but to draw the foreign spirit of the Conqueror from her.

The Conqueror decided he might just cut his losses and take Simza's body without her soul, but then he saw Magic and Tarlak coming through the woods, and it changed his mind.

He knew he couldn't defeat so much power in one place without help, so he decided he'd have to retreat and regroup. He left Simza's body and entered Branwen. She pulled herself up and kneeled in the center of the vortex, her arms waving in a circle above her head. The vortex opened and swallowed Branwen whole.

***

As soon as the Conqueror left Simza's body, her soul re-entered it, and she slumped to the ground. Salem kneeled beside her and put his arms around her. She buried her face in his chest. She didn't cry, but she had to really fight the urge. She had been a fearless Paladin. Now, she was just a woman with some Wytch blood in her. She had never felt so weak or so strong.

"Are you all right, Simza?" he asked.

She nodded, too tired to speak. Morvyn was the first to join them, then Magic, and all eight members of the Paladin Council. Michael came down from his perch in the pine tree. Luckily, he had been on the other side of the path, out of the Conqueror's sight and bursts of flame.

Katar approached the small band of Wytches, all sitting or kneeling on the ground near Simza and Salem. He addressed Magic directly. "We have all had a difficult day. I wish to offer one of our cabins not far from here where all of you may spend the night. Food and water will be made available to you. I think we are probably safe, at least for tonight. We will post guards for our own safety, and I assume you will do the same," he said.

"Thank you, Katar. I will gladly accept your hospitality," Magic said. "Tomorrow, I think it would be wise to discuss what comes next. The Conqueror is obviously a great danger to both our clans. It might be wise to join forces against him. I believe that now is the time of the prophecy, fulfilled in Salem and Simza. She is the Uniter, both Paladin and Wytch."

"I agree that we must put aside the past, cease hostilities toward each other, and work toward a future of peace. If we don't do that, the Conqueror will destroy us separately. Today is a perfect example of what may be. Come, I will show you where you can sleep tonight," Katar said.

The Wytches rose to their feet and followed the Grand Inquisitor into the woods, where a sturdy-looking log house stood. Inside, a healthy fire burned brightly in the fire pit beside a wooden table and benches. Along the walls hung wide, low wooden shelves for sleeping. Magic thanked Katar and told him they would speak in the morning. Fruit and vegetables had been laid out on the table, and a boar roasted on the spit—pewter plates and wooden spoons provided.

"How did you find us, Morvyn?" Salem asked.

"The winds found you. I simply followed them. When I saw the smoke and the burning trees from a distance, I feared I was too late," Morvyn said.

"You were just in time," Simza smiled.

"We thought you were in the desert, Magic," Salem said.

"I was, but I had a vision, informing me that I must come here to see the Council and protect you against the Conqueror. It seems I was too late. You defeated him without me." Magic sighed.

"Oh, no. I don't think so," Simza said. "When he was inside my body, I was aware of his thoughts. He had no intention of giving up until he saw you. He was going to use my Wytch powers against the Paladins if he had been able to capture my soul, but Salem prevented that."

After the meal, Magic put a protective spell around the log house while they slept. Tomorrow, they would send for the thirteen elder Wytches, negotiate peace with the Paladins, and discuss strategies for dealing with the Conqueror.

CHAPTER 28

The Thirteen arrived by mid-morning, and they gathered in the log house with the Paladin Council, Simza, Salem, and the other Wytches. An elder Wytch, not as old as Carabin but close to it, approached Simza.

"Is this the Uniter?" she said, the corners of her mouth quirking.

"I'm Simza Adenah," Simza said, nervously averting her eyes. She wasn't sure how she felt about the title Magic had bestowed upon her.

"And Taker," the Wytch said to Salem, who stood beside Simza. She looked both him and Simza up and down with narrowed eyes.

"Eloran of the Givan tribe," Salem told Simza by way of introduction.

"Has he taken your heart, too?" Eloran asked Simza, her brown eyes twinkling.

Simza chuckled. "It seems he has, and I his."

"And so they say you are the girl and the boy of the prophecy, set to unite Wytches and Paladins once more, eh?"

"That is what Magic said," Simza answered.

"That's the thing about prophecies," said Eloran. "There's at least one every generation, and more than half of 'em come to naught. But if someone gets it into their head that someone or some event fits, then boom, they bring the prophecy to fruition."

"There's a prophecy every generation?" asked Simza.

"In my generation, there was a prophecy said a great flood would come and wipe out the betrayal of the Paladins. That, of course, didn't happen."

"The way the Paladins tell it, it was the Wytches who betrayed them." said Simza.

"That is the way of history. There are many sides. Much like love, the stories we tell can mend and destroy," Eloran said.

Salem looked at Eloran with concern. "You're saying love can destroy?"

Eloran let a slow slip of a smile cross her lips. "Oh, yes. How do you think there came to be Paladins and Wytches in the first place?"

Salem frowned. "Hostility among two tribes led to murder. The murdering tribe lost their Wytch Born powers."

"That is the simple version of it." Eloran nodded.

"Simple?" asked Simza.

"I know more of what happened. What really happened? That is hard to know for certain."

"What happened?" Simza asked. If she was to unite Paladins and Wytches, it would help to know why they'd split.

"That is a story for sitting. My old feet are tired from travelin'." Eloran's eyes wandered around the room to rest on the benches at the table. "Besides, we best get things underway." With that, she made her slow way across the room to the table, where the Paladin Council and the twelve other elder Wytches were already seated or preparing to do so.

For the next three hours, the Wytches and Paladins discussed the terms of their treaty. It was exhausting, and Simza struggled to listen as they took turns discussing a past whose existence she now questioned. In the end, they decided to call a truce on their current hostilities in order to focus on the Conqueror, a conclusion Simza thought they had intended to make in the first place. They knew he would return sooner than later and with more Diabolicals.

"Do you think he will try to take Simza again?" Salem asked.

"He will likely try if he can get her alone again," said Wolfeye.

Katar squeezed the bridge of his nose and said, "I think a break is in order. Perhaps some food? Then we can discuss strategies for defeating the Conqueror for good."

The Paladins and Wytches muttered their agreement. Soon, fruits and vegetables covered the table, along with pewter mugs of water.

Simza grabbed an apple and watched Eloran move to the fire. The elder Wytch pulled a green cushion from the bag strapped across her shoulder and sat on it. Simza looked at Salem, jerking her head in Eloran's direction, and walked toward the fire to sit beside the elder Wytch. Salem followed shortly. Magic stood leaning against a wall across the room, her eyes on the three of them with a look of hopeful curiosity. Simza offered a nod of acknowledgement but turned to face Eloran when the woman spoke.

"You want to know about the tribes you came from," said Eloran, rubbing her hands above the fire. "My grandmother was a child when it happened. She told the tale to my mother, who told it to me. At that time, one tribe was large and powerful. So powerful, in fact, that there were many rumors of corruption within it, which caused more hostility between the two tribes. In the midst of this background was a young Wytch named Ella who fell in love with a mortal named Kaillie. When her family found out, they forbade her from seeing him. Back then, as today, for a Wytch to marry a mortal was looked down upon.

"Between the three of us, and Magic over there, I think the reason has always been a fear that some of our power would diminish if we consummated with mortals. That and a fear of sharin' our power with anyone else," Eloran said in a hushed voice. "To deter Ella, her family sought to arrange a marriage for her with Mallyn Collecgar, whose family was part of the more powerful tribe. Ella defied her family, secretly meeting with Kaillie for months. Mallyn discovered what his bride-to-be was doin', and one night, Ella went to meet with Kaillie only to learn from her parents that Kaillie had been killed earlier that evenin'. There were no witnesses, but Kaillie's body was found burned horrifically in Ella's own bed. Neither her bedsheets nor her room had been touched by fire. Only Kaillie. Ella was devastated and enraged. She could smell the magic in the room, and she knew Mallyn was particularly talented in controlling fire.

"When Ella left their home, she confronted Mallyn and two other Wytches. They reasoned that if Ella told Kaillie's parents that her kind were responsible for Kaillie's death, they would rally the town to turn against the Wytches. So, they had come to kill off

Kaillie's family. Fueled by grief, Ella fought them, killing Mallyn's two companion Wytches. Mallyn himself escaped, returning
to his tribe. Ella feared that so long as Mallyn lived, Kaillie's family was not safe. She realized she had forfeited her life by killing
two fellow Wytches. So she appointed herself their guard and
warded their home with magic. The next night, Mallyn returned.
This time, he brought his family, Ella's family, and members of
both their tribes. They fought hard to convince her that Wytch
Born belonged only with Wytch Born, but when their pleas failed,
they grabbed Ella and held her with magic.

"Afterward, a great argument rose up between the families.
Mallyn and his family demanded Ella's blood for the two members
of their tribe whom she'd killed. Ella's family, on the other hand,
contended that Mallyn had no right to kill Kaillie or her parents
and that it was for their tribe to decide. Mallyn proclaimed that his
position as husband-to-be gave him the right to make said
choice. The quarrel raged for hours. Ella's tribe refused to give her
up for justice at the hands of Mallyn's. Sometime during the ar-
guin', Mallyn and a few others of his tribe slipped away and killed
Kaillie's parents and burned their house to the ground.

"Ella's tribe fled in a rage, prepared to rally against Mallyn's people. However, Mallyn's tribe called upon the ancients to
see justice served. Ella's tribe was stripped of their Wytch Born
powers. Instead of headin' into war, they headed out of town. Ella
rose as a leader among them. Recruiting other dissatisfied members of the tribe as well as mortals, she created the Paladins. They
saw the corruption among the Wytches and vowed to root it
out…by any means necessary. A decade after she left her home as
a disgraced Wytch, Ella returned as a Paladin. She laid waste to
Mallyn, who by then had become a leader among his tribe. The

survivors were warned, 'We are the Paladins, the Wytch hunters. We will hunt you down one by one as you take flight.'

"And so…here we are. Perhaps love can mend what love of power and control consumed."

Simza and Salem sat there, shocked by the story they'd heard. Salem thought of Dan Pearly and his mortal wife, who was murdered.

"We should get back to planning," Magic said suddenly, pushing herself off the wall and heading back toward the table.

Simza stood and reached a hand down to help Eloran stand.

"Thank you, Simza," said Eloran, patting Simza's shoulder once she stood. "Don't worry. We'll beat him. The prophecy implies it."

"Didn't you say prophecies were basically self-fulfilling?"

Eloran chuckled. "That's why you needn't worry."

***

Shortly thereafter, the Paladins and Wytches returned to arguing out a strategy for dealing with the Conqueror. They were no closer to a real plan as the sun set and a tremor cascaded across the ground, sending everyone to the floor. The tremor was followed by a shout from Morvyn, who was on guard duty after the break.

A wave of heat spread through the log house. Salem looked out the window and saw an unending fire. Knowing they were protected by Magic's spell, he yanked open the door.

"Morvyn?" he called. "Atan?" He hoped the Paladin guarding alongside Morvyn might hear him if his Brother could not.

For a moment, all Salem could hear was the roar of the fire licking angrily at the sides of the log cabin. Then he heard a moan. Scouring the ground, he spotted a foot in the flames. He reached out, ignoring the agony of burning, and pulled the foot and the body attached to it into the log house.

The Wytches immediately doused the flames eating at Morvyn's clothing and flesh. Carefully, they carried him to one of the wide sleeping shelves, where Magic and the Wytch Fleurin began their healing spells.

The other Wytches set to putting out the flames. Once they succeeded, they saw Atan's body two feet from the log house door. He was dead, his skin blackened and near-unrecognizable. As the Paladins prepared to take Atan's body off for burial, two figures emerged from the trees.

They looked like women with long, flowing, flame-red dresses and crow-black hair. Their eyes glowed copper as they stared at the house. When they spoke, the Wytches and Paladins heard the Conqueror's voice. "Will you hide away, little mice? Or will you come out to play? Will you hand me Simza and the world? Or do I get the joy of forcing them from your hands?"

The women smiled. They didn't wait for an answer as snakes of black fire zipped out of their upturned hands toward the cabin. Ansgar led a charge of Wytches toward the snakes.

Just beyond the trees, in the clearing where they had battled the day before, a large vortex appeared. Branwen stepped from it, poised like a queen and followed by a dozen or more Diabolicals just like the women at the cabin. Now that the Conqueror had returned, the war had begun.

CHAPTER 29

A volley of gunshots exploded from the defenders of the cabin. Bullets whipped through the incoming army of black vipers, and snakes disintegrated into black mist only to reform and continue slithering forward.

Salem reloaded his pistol. Simza laid her hand over his, stopping him from raising the gun once more. He looked in her eyes, and she called on Magic. "Mother, in protection of Wytches and Paladin alike, imbue these bullets with mystical power to strike down thy enemies. Allow thy humble servant, the Favored Son, to conquer."

Releasing his hand, Simza stepped back. Salem fired at the nearest snake. A translucent blue trail followed the bullet as it traveled from pistol to snake. The head of the serpent exploded in a mist of black and red, dissipating into the air. He fired again and again.

Turning to the other Wytches, he shouted, "Call upon Magic to power the bullets. Pair up with a Paladin and work together!"

Blue trails arced across the battleground, the final snake dispatched by a shot from Michael.

"Look!" Eloran shouted, pointing toward the clearing. Clouds swirled above the clearing. Violet lightning bolts flashed across the open portal.

A crushing roar shook the cabin as a column of flame erupted skyward, engulfing the closest pine tree. Another set of Diabolicals, red dresses swirling around their feet, stepped into view. One pointed at a second pine tree, and flames shot from the ground with a resounding boom.

"Ansgar, Tarlak! We need to do something!" shouted Salem.

"You and Michael focus on those two," said Tarlak, pointing at the new set of enemies. "Ansgar, take the snake ladies. The rest of you, put out those flames!"

Ansgar unsheathed a pair of twin scimitar daggers and moved off the porch. Tarlak followed, his staff glowing with power.

Salem gestured to Michael. "Load up." The two moved in the opposite direction, Salem gathering magic into his hands.

From behind them, a burst of water shot from the combined hands of three of the Thirteen. It struck the first column of flame, which disappeared in a hiss of steam.

Ansgar moved in front of Tarlak, scanning the area with extreme focus. The ground immediately around the two Diabolicals writhed and pulsed in black smoke. A serpent struck from the darkness. Ansgar pivoted left, his left scimitar slicing off the snake's head. Flipping his right dagger into a backward grip, he swung forward, the dagger sweeping upward, chopping off another head. Using the momentum, he dropped to his knees midspin, stabbing through the mouth of a third snake. His movements blurred together as he cleared the area.

Tarlak moved behind Ansgar and raised the staff above his head. With a downward thrust, he brought the staff to the ground, causing a shockwave of energy. Waves of magic shot through the earth in four directions, leaving small ditches in its wake. Each beam of magic struck an obsidian stone, standing in each of the four cardinal directions, and white runes glowed upon the black rock. A white bolt of magic shot from one stone to another, creating a magical barrier—the cabin, Wytches, and Paladins inside, cutting off access from the portal and army of Diabolicals. Four of the monsters were trapped in with the defenders.

***

Branwen stopped. She felt the magic radiating off the newly formed boundaries. Motioning for one of her followers, she ordered, "Bring it down!"

A Diabolical thrust her hand out, black magic shooting toward the barrier. As the line of black connected, a bolt of white shot back, striking the Diabolical in the stomach. She screamed in pain.

The snake-forming Diabolicals turned toward each other and grasped hands, chanting in a strange tongue. Wind whipped at their dresses. The columns of fire swayed in the breeze, and as the chant grew louder, the wind increased. The flames danced, twisting and turning in the ever-stronger wind.

A shrill scream came from the cabin. The closest column twisted itself into a fire tornado, the tail lifting from the ground and inching closer to the wooden walls.

***

Wytches and Paladins scattered from the porch. A crack thundered through the air as the fire tornado ripped the porch from the cabin and flung it through the air. It landed with a crash, fire licking its broken beams, spreading to nearby trees.

Ansgar danced closer to the Diabolicals. He leaped upward, rotating into a flip, daggers glinting in the firelight. Landing next to the monsters, he rolled under their outstretched arms, both scimitars flashing out to slice through flesh. Hellish screams filled the air. Ansgar spun on his right heel, daggers arcing upward, both Diabolicals exploded into black smoke, their screams echoing across the clearing.

***

Salem and Michael moved away from the cabin, passing behind the column of flame, the unbearable heat pushing them farther from the cabin. A gunshot rang out, and Salem felt the wind of the bullet as it whizzed past his ear. The shot hit a snake mid-strike, interrupting the straight line to Salem's neck. He looked back. Wolfeye sat in the eaves of the cabin, a smoking rifle in his hand. Salem nodded and moved on.

"The wind is getting stronger," yelled Michael. Salem saw the boy's white knuckles clutching his pistol in a death grip.

They were now across from two Diabolicals who had mirrored the other two, chanting in the foreign tongue.

"Stay here. Line up your shot on the closer of the two," said

Salem. "I'll move farther around for a better shot. Wait for my signal and watch out for snakes." He moved off into the forest.

The wind howled now. Glancing back, Salem saw the columns of flames beginning to move.

A scream came from the cabin—Simza's scream. Reaching inward, Salem felt her presence. No, she was safe, for now. Thinking of her, he picked up the pace.

A loud crack and a whoosh of wind brought him back to reality. Instinctively, he ducked into a crouch. The burning ruins of the porch impacted the forest in front of him, followed by a set of unearthly screams. He could now see the second Diabolical. Lining up his shot, he glanced at Michael. The boy was staring at him. Wood smoke wafted through the trees, the air hazy and heavy. He nodded at Michael. When he squeezed the trigger, his gun bucked in his hand. A black serpent rose from the ground, intercepting the bullet. He fired again, and another snake exploded into mist. Michael's shots did the same.

Holstering his pistol, Salem spread his arms wide, palms pointing to heaven. "Mother, bless this Favored Son. Open the fierce power of the cleansing force and aid me in our struggles against the evil ones."

Green flames burst forth, covering his hands. Salem sprinted forward. A snake reared its head, then exploded into mist. A second struck and disintegrated before it could find its target. Michael ran in time with Salem, firing at the snakes. The deeper report of a rifle boomed from the cabin, Wolfeye covering his progress, snakes exploding on each side.

As he approached the Diabolicals, Salem raised his left arm and thrust it forward. A ball of green flame shot out, engulfing the nearest Diabolical. The second turned, a bestial growl rumbling from her throat. She leaped into the air, just escaping Salem's attack.

Pain raced down Salem's back as metallic claws carved down through his flesh, the monster landing behind him. He dove forward, the second claw whistling through the space where his head had just been.

***

"No!" Simza shrieked as she watched the Diabolical's claws rip into Salem's back. She stepped out from behind the tree and thrust her right hand at the flaming tornado. Closing her fist, she jerked her arm, and the tornado obeyed her movement. Repeating the process with the other hand, she found she now had control of both raging vortexes. She clapped her hands together and the twisters collided in front of the cabin, merging into one. She watched Salem dive to avoid the Diabolical's deadly talons. As he took cover behind a tree, she reared her arm back and threw the tornado at his enemy. The cyclone mowed through the trees, the Diabolical disappearing into the flame and the tornado erupting against Tarlak's barriers.

Tarlak dropped to his knees, the impact of the twister against the barrier draining his magical energy. Ansgar dropped next to Tarlak, and Simza turned away, feeling the Brothers' shared magic.

She rushed forward, reaching Salem at the same time as Michael. "Are you all right?" she asked.

He looked at her, cocked his head to the side, and replied with a grin, "Never better." But he grimaced as he tried to stand.

"Hold still," she said, waving her hands over his wounds. Bright light emitted from her fingertips, caressing his back, sealing the cuts.

"You're learning quick." Salem didn't hide his surprise, but she just smiled weakly.

***

Branwen watched powerlessly as four Diabolicals were defeated. The strength of the Uniter to control not just one but two fire tornadoes surprised her. The level of magic exhibited by the young woman was intoxicating. She would possess that power!

Facing the portal, she spread her hands wide above her head in supplication. "Powers of the Depths, Powers of the Shades, bring forth the denizens of darkness, the shades of war, the creatures of the abyss."

***

A distant roar sounded through the swirling darkness of the portal. The exhausted Wytches and Paladins all turned at the sound. Ansgar tightened his grip on Tarlak, all of their attention on the darkness.

An aged claw emerged, settling on the ground. It pulled back, scratching deep rifts in the earth. A muzzle appeared, the maw opening and letting out another roar. Two rows of razor teeth lined the mouth. Strips of dead skin hung from its head and long neck. Four powerful legs supported the huge body, three gray claws on each foot, and a double row of spikes adorned its neck and back, ending at the edge of the tail. Yellow eyes surveyed the battlefield, nose sniffing at the magic in the air. The creature reared its head back and roared at the sky.

"Servant, ye olde Denizen of the abyss, you know who the

Conqueror needs. Kill the rest," Branwen yelled.

The creature charged, the earth shaking with each footfall.

"Move back behind the cabin!" ordered Ansgar when he saw the beast.

The Wytches and Paladins retreated, placing as much distance as possible between themselves and the creature from the portal. The beast reached the boundary, and lifting itself on its hind legs with a thunderous roar, it plunged its claws into the magical barrier.

The barrier exploded outward in a flash of magnificent light. The creature flew backward, landing with a crash and a growl.

Tarlak and Ansgar soared through the air, crashing onto their backs. Four separate cracks splintered the air as the obsidian rune stones ruptured.

Branwen and the army of Diabolicals surged forward, unobstructed, to finish off the defenders.

CHAPTER 30

Simza shielded her eyes as the bright light of the broken barrier reflected the crimson roar of the flames. Even with her vision momentarily obstructed, she could feel the earth wailing under the weight of the Denizen's pounce. It terrified her to see how the creature so easily tore through a defense crafted by one of the Wytches strongest in the presence of Magic herself. In all reality, she should have expected the Conqueror to have boundless tricks up his sleeve, but the heat of battle often left no room for imagination.

Everything she did was her body's first instinct. There existed no time for thought, the need for action consuming her movements. When she had seen the Diabolical's claw pierce Salem, rage had set two tornados upon the beast. When she had seen his life dripping from his back, anxiety kicked in and closed his wounds. Her acceptance of Magic controlled her reflexes completely.

A thought like that would have disgusted her weeks ago when she was Paladin at heart. Though unfamiliar to the true workings of Magic, the concept of moving on someone else's accord all pointed to manipulation. Simza would have seen it as a Wytch being nothing more than a pawn without willpower. But now, in the face of battle surrounded by shouts and screams, she found comfort in knowing her power bridged the gap created by her lack of formal training. She had been raised a killer, but a calculated one. Everything she had done was carefully planned out, each step meticulously carried through. In certain instances, she'd spent weeks setting up a scene before going in for the kill.

But not anymore.

As the horrifying beast jumped in the air, her hands flung out in front of her, words of magic wildly dancing around her brain. A gust of wind shot forward, but the Denizen's momentum resulted in his movements being barely stinted, throwing Simza backward instead.

She didn't even had time to brace herself for the crash. The speed of her fall knocked the wind out of her. Gasping for air, she was vaguely aware of people crying her name. To her left and right, she could make out the shapes of her comrades, old and new, fighting against the Conqueror's forces. Gritting her teeth, she heaved her body to a standing position. The Denizen had moved on to others, ruthlessly pouncing and snapping its blade-like teeth. Its goal wasn't her; it wanted casualties.

Incantations of Magic mixed in her mind while she attempted to weaken the creature as it attacked others. Her actions were swift, mindless, short bursts of strong energy. She had been tired prior to the barrier being obliterated, and resting within her adrenaline rush was exhaustion. Spells may have become more natural to her, but she had yet to build up the stamina required to maintain such strong magic.

She ran on pure emotion.

"Simza!"

Halting her onslaught of attacks, she twirled around to find Salem running toward her. Meeting him halfway, she felt time slow when he grabbed her forearms.

"What are you doing?" he shouted over the crashes echoing around them.

"I'm trying to fend off the Denizen! It's not after me—"

"You need to slow down!" Salem interrupted, shaking her slightly. "You're wasting your energy by just using any spell that comes to mind."

"My reflexes were what sparked the tornadoes!"

"And that was a good time to depend on your reflexes, but you said it yourself, the Denizen isn't trying to kill you. Don't react, love. Act."

At his words, Simza's thoughts stilled. The amount of energy she had been heedlessly expending crashed down on her like a ton of bricks. Giving Salem a sharp nod, she watched him nod back before running back into the war. Her eyes followed his retreating figure until dust swallowed him up.

Taking a deep breath, she forced herself to analyze the situation. Her physical body was exhausted. The pure nature of the situation surrounding her took its toll on her body, especially now that she was clearing her mind. The invincibility adrenaline had given her was wearing off, but even though her limbs felt as though they could sleep for a thousand days, she felt magic coursing through her veins. Her pool of energy in that sense was still relatively full.

Others called her the Uniter, and it was time she showed what that truly meant.

Her choice of weapon may have been Wytch Born, but she still had the mind of a Paladin.

In the flurry of bodies sprinting and crashing around her, she could make out Tarlak and Wolfeye to her left fighting off a group of Diabolicals. While she did not know Tarlak's fighting style all that well, she knew Wolfeye's. He was strong and clever, but in the seemingly endless wave of Diabolicals, she could see his frustration. He had a temper—one that had caused her to attempt to end the possibility of continuing his family name—and that temper was rising. His shots were becoming faster, more erratic. He and Tarlak fought on the same side but not together. It was only a matter of time before they became twisted in their movements and shot each other.

Dashing forward, she shot a blast at a tree near the Paladin and Wytch, knocking it over. At the sound of the crash, both their gazes briefly flickered toward her.

Still running, she yelled, "Pay attention!"

Neither acknowledged her words, but she knew she'd made her point.

"Aw, look at you playing Uniter."

Whipping her head around, she saw Branwen approach her. She tensed as the woman leisurely walked her way. Even from her distance, she could see the twisted delight madly dancing in Branwen's cold eyes. In her clear mentality, Simza had the chance to be thoroughly disgusted. The Conqueror had created the war of the century in order to attain her soul. This wasn't a history lesson with comprehensible means supporting the villain's actions, for no amount of context could make the Conqueror seem a noble being.

The Paladins and Wytches—those were people who fought for valid causes.

"Simza Adenah, I've missed you," cooed Branwen, stopping about ten feet away from where Simza stood. The woman's lips pulled into a wicked grin as she cocked her head to the side. The battles raging around them whipped Branwen's hair threateningly in the air.

Simza steadied her stance. "I can't say the feeling is mutual."

"What a typical line," Branwen sneered. From the dirt floating around Branwen materialized the figure of a man. From her distance, he appeared to stand a head taller than Branwen with shoulder-length, stark-black hair, hazel eyes, and mismatched clothing, but as the dust cleared, Simza's stomach twisted. His hair was a patchy, oily mixture of black and brown, as if he had run out of one color and was forced to steal from another. His left eye was hazel, his right gray, but both equally as void. His shirt and pants appeared to be from two different eras.

Simza fought the urge to retch as the man's thin lips pulled into a demonic smirk.

"Did you miss me?" he asked, his voice like gravel. "I regret that I can't greet you in a more attractive form, but when I smashed the bridge to the astral plane, I left in quite a compromising position."

This was his physical form—the Conqueror's. Stretching out her fingers, she steadied her breath. It was truly as crooked as he.

"You look sick, dear," he called. "It took all my energy to scrap together fragments of souls trapped in the astral plane. Why so confused? You thought the astral plane was unreachable forever? Insolent child, maybe to you Wytchlings, but not to the Conqueror. This," he hissed, referencing his body, "is the result of the broken connection and the physical manifestation of those souls. Now, won't you be a good little girl and come over here?"

Not moving a muscle, Simza glanced to the side. She could make out Michael's thin frame moving in and out of the action, shooting and yelling in different directions. It was crazy that they had only met weeks ago, for he had become such an integral part of the team. Raised as a killer, there were not many maternal instincts within her, but part of her ached seeing the young boy on a battlefield, despite that being how Paladins were raised.

Directing her attention back to the Conqueror, Simza steadied herself as the Denizen's landing in the near distance shook the earth. From the hellfire and the hellhound-like beast to the Diabolicals of dark matter and the evil incarnate leader, everything about this war was unnatural. If her short time being forced to adapt to her Wytch blood had taught her anything, it was that everything came at a cost. The repercussions for such unearthly forces were unforeseeable, and that made them all the more dangerous.

"What are you thinking about? Let me see!" The Conqueror lunged at Simza.

Dashing to her left, she called upon the winds and used them against a nearby tree to propel herself backward. The Conqueror's pursuit continued as Simza sprinted through the trees. Looking behind her, her breath caught as she felt her foot catch against something. Hitting the ground, she forced herself not to think of the throbbing in her ankle. Quickly, she turned onto her back just in time for Branwen to jump on top of her, straddling her waist.

"I'll have your soul and I'll destroy every shred of hope you fragile creatures ever had of peace!" snarled the Conqueror.

Looming behind Branwen, he brought his hands toward Simza's face as she struggled. Everything happened in slow motion—magic danced on her fingertips. Before she could raise her arms to try something—anything—a blast knocked Branwen off Simza's body and into the Conqueror, and the two collided several feet away.

Gasping at the pain as she immediately stood up, Simza looked to find Michael standing in the distance with his gun pointed their way. The hit had been effective in freeing her, but not enough to banish the Conqueror. Branwen heaved in pain, clutching her side, as the Conqueror pushed her away to pull himself up on all fours.

The Conqueror flung his arm out in Michael's direction. As he turned to his right, the Denizen lunged down at him from above, mouth wide open.

A scream tore through Simza's throat as the beast's razor teeth snapped. Simza stood still and the world around her fell victim to chaos.

The ease with which he was tossed around sickened her. She was the Uniter—a symbol of hope to Paladin and Wytch Born alike, and she had watched as a sixteen-year-old boy was devoured. Eaten. Michael.

It wasn't fair. He was only a kid. Only pure chance had dragged him into this mess. He hadn't asked to be possessed, but he was, and he'd joined their team. He gave up a life of growing into a man, getting married, and having children to be part of their crazy world, and now, he would not even be alive to see the result of what he'd helped achieve.

Clenching her fists, she stared at the ground.

It wasn't fair.

He did not even know the reality of what they were fighting for, but he was willing to fight in order to see a brighter day.

Her ankle throbbed, her head ached, her eyes stung, but they were nothing compared to the way her heart twisted. She was sad, she was horrified, but most importantly, she was livid.

"How dare you?" she whispered, feeling Magic whisper soothing thoughts in her ear. Energy flooded her system, patching her up. All the physical ailments would heal in seconds, but her mental and emotional ones would take time. The Conqueror wanted her soul? She'd show him just how strong it was. She'd make both the Conqueror and Branwen feel the prickling sensation of a thousand needles she felt inside. She'd drag the process out. Each cry they released would be a prayer for Michael. Simza Adenah would end this.

"He was only a boy!" she shouted.

Eyes snapping up, magic on her tongue, she charged.

CHAPTER 31

Great anger had taken over the Uniter. She wanted to crush the Conqueror, his accomplices, and all the mindless parasites following his lead. He was right there in front of her, a centuries-old demon after her soul, and she would send him back to the pile of dirt from which he'd come. As for Branwen, it would be easy to take her out; still writhing on the ground, quite a few minutes would have to pass before she healed completely. Simza had changed her course of attack when she realized the Conqueror would be ready for her, but thankfully, Branwen wasn't. Now, Simza marched toward them.

Still, no matter how determined she was to put an end to the war, she had not fully mastered her abilities yet. Her raw energy was still untamed, her spirit off balance. Half a dozen Diabolicals gathered in front of the Conqueror, shielding him.

***

Branwen did not need to be on her feet to act. Instead, she spoke words in a language unknown to mortals, Wytches, or Paladins, commanding her army to regroup and prepare to defend her. Above all, she commanded them to defend the Conqueror. With blood dripping down its mouth and pieces of flesh stuck in its sharp teeth, the Denizen turned its head to them. If neither Branwen nor the Conqueror gave instruction, it would carry on its murderous destruction.

***

Simza, quickly realizing that she could not fight them all alone, stopped charging and instead tread slowly backward.

Nearby, Tarlak and Wolfeye, more aware of their surroundings after Simza's interjection, fought back to back. One after another, creatures of darkness fell by Tarlak's staff, both by skillful direct hits and impact caused by Tarlak's spells. Wolfeye's smoking gun delivered magically imbued bullets to several heads, limbs, and guts belonging to a never-ending swarm of enemies.

"How about finishing off that corrupt sorceress?" Tarlak called over the deafening noise his staff made at every burst of lightning flowing through it.

"Will do." Wolfeye changed targets by calmly moving his outstretched, gun-wielding arm from pointing at the amber eye of a snake Diabolical to pointing at Branwen's lower forehead, right between her eyes. Eager and confident in his skills, the towering Paladin pulled the trigger.

***

As if in slow motion, Branwen saw the luminous blue trail of the bullet out of the corner of her eye. Without having to move, think, or speak, a transparent round shield with a fiery red circumference appeared in front of her, and the bullet stuck in it mid-air. Attracted by the commotion, a fresh, small group of Diabolicals gathered quickly around Branwen.

Once the shield dissolved and the bullet fell to the ground, Wolfeye only had a clear shot of the Diabolicals around Branwen. "Damn you, fiends!" he yelled as he shot down two of them.

***

The more the Paladins cooperated with the Wytches, the stronger Simza became. The radius and the impact of her spells, however clumsy they occasionally were, had increased. Casting them did not make her feel as drained as she initially felt. In fact, every time a hideous monster exploded, evaporated, or simply hit the ground, it energized her. But, she was not the only one feeling this way. Even if the malevolent beings rose in numbers, the bond of the alliance would not easily break. Shadows might have been recalled from the depths of the abyss, but their force was no weaker than that of Wytch Born and Paladins united.

***

With green flames pouring out of his hands and eyes, the wound on his back healed and the pain having subsided, Salem threw large, gleaming fireballs at his enemies. Hitting his targets more frequently than not, his spirits began to lift. Slowly but steadily, he knew Simza was learning how to handle her role, her heritage. There they were, two factions which had once hated each other, fighting side by side for a common goal. How different his life and the whole world had been back when he played cards at the Frontier House of Vice. How little he knew then.

But then the wind changed. A whisper crawled into his mind, interrupting his thoughts and causing him to miss hits consecutively. *Fall back. You will lose this battle. Fall back. You have to fall back, Salem.* He could not understand from whom the message had come. Was it from Magic? Where was she? She had been offering her powers to her children, he knew, else he'd still be suffering wounds, but it still couldn't have been her. Neither the tone nor the voice resembled Magic's in any way. *Pay attention, Taker. If you carry on, all the Paladins on these plains will be slaughtered. You may think you are winning right now, but you are not. Retreat to the clearing at once.*

Puzzled and disturbed, Salem stopped shooting fireballs and held his head. The whispers had multiplied, causing him intense pain. Idle as he was in the middle of the battlefield, he had become an easy target. It did not take long before a throwing axe hit him in his upper right back. He cried in pain, then kneeled, unable to hold his own weight any longer.

"Lark…" was all Salem had the strength to utter, the green flames no longer illuminating his eyes and hands.

***

"Salem!" Simza's scream rolled through the battlefield when she saw him on the ground. She ran toward him, hoping he did not have any wounds she could not heal. As her powers were still new, she was still not completely sure of her limits, but she would not give up without a fight. She could certainly not let Salem suffer the same fate as Michael. Not while she was there.

Three snake Diabolicals stood, one next to another, chanting spells. Before Simza could reach Salem, a new vortex appeared before the creatures, neither narrower nor less intimidating than the first one. As soon as it fully formed, more shadow entities jumped out from within. Crocodile-headed Diabolicals with wolf paws for hands and hooves for feet, along with purple floating robes worn by individuals invisible to the naked eye, became the latest addition the Conqueror's small army blocking Simza's path to Salem.

Overwhelmed by her need to reach Salem and the number of creatures between them, Simza attempted to cast a fire blast by channeling her energy to the skies. Clouds of red and black fire formed over the battlefield, crackling over their heads. No longer requiring Magic's aid, neither to heal nor destruct, was an experience both liberating and daunting.

Recognizing her power in the clouds, she intensified her focus, creating in her mind's eye images of burning Diabolicals scattering under a pouring rain of fire. When she felt that the clouds had charged enough with her fury, she raised her arms to the sky and brought them back down. Following her action, a heavy downpour of burning beads the size of musket bullets pierced the ground, hitting everyone exposed. To her surprise and horror, the Diabolicals seemed unaffected by them, while Paladins and Wytches alike sustained skin injuries.

"Why? What did I do wrong?" She looked around for an answer, trying to protect her face from the painful particles burning her clothes and hands. She also tried to contact Magic, both by calling out to her and through her mind, but that failed too. Fortunately for herself and her allies, her confusion and loss of concentration caused the clouds of fire to disperse.

Simza could no longer see Salem, who had been surrounded. At that moment, she reminded herself that the only way for her to help him was not by rushing to him, or acting on impulse like Wolfeye used to do, but by standing perfectly still. In her mind, she repeated Salem's words, which would become her mantra. Slow down. Don't react. Act. She had to force herself to focus for everyone's sake. Especially for Salem's sake.

Despite her great urge to dash at the Diabolicals, Simza closed her eyes and emptied her mind of all thoughts, hopes, and fears. That momentary emptiness gave her the peace she needed to gather her energy and transform it into something greater, something completely new and more powerful than her own self. She imagined life coming down from the sky. Tough, vigorous, aerial life to strengthen the Uniter, prepared to stand by her until the very end. Life that would fight darkness with its light. Once again, she raised her arms to the sky. As she spoke, the diamond-shaped Hex tattoo on her forehead flickered.

"I, the Uniter, command you. Make your appearance in our time of need. Shed the radiant light that flows through you on my enemies and make them see, or crush them if they are too far gone into the night to wake up. I shall await you."

Simza opened her eyes. Her orange petticoat blew in the wind picking up. She knew this time that the call had succeeded and realized she had conjured and brought to life her own powerful being, using solely her own power and will. She could already hear the flapping wings in the distance.

A majestic white griffin appeared through the clouds and glided through the air, landing on its lion paws, lifting a cloud of thick dust around it. Half-eagle, half-feline, its bow-shaped claws and sharp beak were ready to tear through anyone who stood in its way. Blue flames jumped from its eyes. Its pointed ears heard every necessary sound, and its long tail could grab and toss anyone several feet away.

***

Intrigued, with smoke coming out of its nostrils and re- mains lingering where it still chewed on its latest victim, the Den- izen let out a growl and approached the griffin until they stood face to face.

CHAPTER 32

The griffin's screech peeled between the trees. For a moment, Salem watched the Diabolicals slow in their attacks then turn to view the mighty beast which had joined the Paladin and Wytch alliance. The Denizen too seemed frozen before opening its slavering jowls wide and snapping them shut again, only a second after the winged griffin withdrew out of range.

The battle of these two great beasts seemed to have taken over the focus of the melee, and Salem, weakened and confused, used the moment to his advantage; he had a feeling it might be the only chance he'd receive. "Wolfeye!" he groaned, calling to the first ally he saw. He watched the Paladin exchange a glance with Tarlak, who blasted back three Diabolicals headed his way, offering defensive cover for Wolfeye to remove himself from their closest battle.

"Taker," Wolfeye panted, taking a knee beside the Favored

Son and placing a gentle, concerned hand above the wounds on Salem's back.

Salem gasped in fatigue and haste, turning to meet the Paladin's gaze. "We need to fall back," he grunted. Wolfeye only gave him an anxious stare in response. "I've received a message…"

"From Magic?"

Salem found it odd to hear the Mother's name so informally upon a Paladin's lips, without spite or malice, but he pushed the sensation aside. "I don't know," he replied with a sigh of defeat. "But I've been told the Paladins will not survive the day if we linger here. We cannot continue this battle."

"What of Simza?" Wolfeye asked, pain flashing behind his eyes.

The few seconds it took Salem to look across the battleground and find the tall, commanding form of Simza Adenah, imbued with more power than he ever remembered seeing, felt like eternities. "I hardly think she falls into any of our categories anymore," he whispered. When he turned back to Wolfeye, he found a steely determination and a surprising amount of trust in the Paladin's gaze. "The message said we had to get to the clearing, but I don't—"

"I know," Wolfeye interrupted. "I know a place that might serve. And it's close. I'll alert the others." He stood, and Salem reached out to grip the Paladin's forearm, stopping him briefly.

"We have to be quick. I don't know what's coming, but whatever it is, it cares little for those left behind."

Wolfeye grunted in agreement and turned to sprint back to Tarlak. Salem tried to call out when he saw the Denizen hurtling through the air toward the Paladin. The huge, snarling creature slid across the ground, throwing up great showers of earth and rock as it righted itself in its flight. Wolfeye barely managed to skirt around the beast before the griffin flapped its mighty wings and pounced upon its foe once more. The pair of enormous creatures tousled among the trees, and Salem found only enough strength in himself to stare in awe. He hardly thought the victor of that battle would decide the day's fate, but it seemed impossible to focus on any other violence around him than that being wrought by two fearsome creatures who seemed to produce more damage than the rest of them put together.

He heard a shout, then turned to see Tarlak shifting into his beast form. The huge primate the Druid had become now lumbered off through the trees, followed by Wolfeye on his horse. Almost as if in slow motion, Salem glanced about and saw his Wytches and their Paladin allies calling to one another, repeating the order to fall back and follow Wolfeye. He tried to stand, to force his body to move toward the others, but the pain in his back screamed against the movement and he almost collapsed into the dirt.

Turning, Salem's gaze fell on Simza once more. She resembled a goddess to him, completely accepting of the powers with which she'd been born, standing against the Conqueror with hardly any attention paid to the growing chaos around her. She truly had embraced herself as the Uniter, as the one with the power here to sway the fate of so many worlds, and yet she did not see him. Salem wondered, with fleeting bitterness, whether he'd ever see her again—whether, if he did, she'd even be the same Lark with whom he'd fallen in love. The chances of Simza changing completely into what prophecy had ordained, leaving no traces of her former self behind, seemed far too great now.

Salem wanted her to look at him, to see him one last time. He felt his strength failing and somehow, surprisingly quickly, had resigned himself to the fact that he would not survive the day. The wounds in his back burned, fiery and heated, across his flesh, and he found himself almost completely unable to garner the strength to move at all, let alone call out. At least he'd saved the others, he reasoned. At least he'd given them a chance.

Staring at Simza as she hurled flaming death, the elements of her powers now wielded through Magic and her mixed blood, at Diabolicals closing in all around her. Salem barely noticed when something pinched his shoulders. A strong force wrapped around his upper arms, and the ground flailed and spun beneath him. He was whisked away from the battleground, and when he looked down, the earth below him shrunk with every second. Two Diabolicals closed in on the space where, moments before, he'd just been ready to die. Looking up slowly in an addled haze, Salem found himself staring up at the dark, feathery underside of what seemed a giant bird—Ansgar!

The screeching of the griffin and the thunderous roar of the Denizen as they clashed in perpetual battle followed close on their heels. Through slow, labored blinking, Salem was only vaguely aware of the ground rushing by below him, of the trees coming perilously close to touching him as he hurtled through the air in Ansgar's grasp, of the dozens of Wytches and Paladins below him, following the Paladin on the black stallion.

Their retreat seemed to take forever, but then Salem felt the ground gently coming up to meet him, and he toppled onto his side when Ansgar released him. The Wytch's features smoothed from the angular beak and feathery wings into the Druid's brown robes, and Ansgar kneeled beside Salem, quickly taking the time to inspect his wounds.

Salem looked around, fighting what felt like some sort of drug in his system—fighting to stay awake. The sounds of battle had quieted by far, and he gazed around to see familiar faces standing only feet away. Wytches and Paladins alike held each other up to catch their breath. Most of them now looked to him for guidance—what had Wolfeye told them? Their robes and jackets were covered in blood and dirt, the fatigue of their battle smeared across their faces and buried deep in the pain behind their eyes. Salem lurched when another bout of excruciating pain shot through his back, and he wondered suddenly if the message he'd heard hadn't, in fact, been some sort of hallucination from the agony of his wounds.

Then he realized they actually had made it to a clearing, though if it was the clearing of his anonymous warning, he couldn't be sure. He hoped Wolfeye had sufficient reason to have chosen this particular place, but he lacked the strength or the willpower to question the Paladin at this point. The clearing seemed to be at the top of a small rise in the forest, elevated from where they'd just fought the Diabolicals—where Simza now faced the Conqueror on her own. Strangely, there was no fear in Salem's heart for the battle Simza Adenah now faced; his fear only lay in the possibility of what she might become afterward.

There seemed a long moment of what felt like complete silence, and Salem wondered why their party hadn't been pursued. Then, as if in answer to his question, a giant explosion wracked the forest below them. Huge bursts of green and purple light blossomed out among the trees, mushrooming outward with the force of a hundred Wytches' powers, called forth from the Mother herself. The very air around Salem seemed to split with the crackling electricity, and he could only watch in mute horror as the light faded to reveal a circle of barren wasteland in the forest below. Tendrils of blood-red smoke oozed from the cracked earth, slithering upward into the dark gray of the sky.

Nothing existed anymore within that circle—no Diabolicals, no Branwen, no Denizen fighting the griffin. The Conqueror and Simza Adenah, too, had vanished.

Salem felt a scream about to erupt within his chest, but it was cut short by an unfamiliar tinkling of foreign metal. He reached out to find purchase on Ansgar's arm, who still kneeled beside him, and tried to find the source of the sound. When he turned, he found himself momentarily blinded by a flash of white light.

"That is why I told you to run," a deep voice called. Salem's allies in the clearing turned as well, all to face the shimmering, glowing figure of the intruder in their midst. Then the light faded and winked out, and Salem realized it had only been reflected off the glowing-white armor which covered every inch of the stranger. "Taker," the stranger continued, "it's been eons since last I met a Favored Son. The timing of the Universe is more unpredictable than even I imagined. On behalf of the Ancient Ones, I must thank you for being open to our call. Now, we can only wait."

***

It took almost every ounce of power she had to keep her eyes open in that moment. And when she did, everything she thought she knew about the world became irrelevant.

The storm swirled around Simza, a terror of her own making, and she couldn't quite believe the things before her. The very air shimmered around her through the veil of reality—it seemed she peered through smoke and fire, through a curtain of wavering time. To her right, a trio of Diabolicals were locked in perpetual battle with a foe even Simza could no longer see. Their mouths were open in a shock of rage, hands extended like hooked claws, yet they neither moved nor made a single sound. A noxious wind like sulphur blew around her, and within its howling torrent, it blew away pieces of the frozen Diabolicals, inch by inch, their flesh washing away in the breeze like ash from a fire that had blazed all night.

The ground below her feet seemed neither stone nor earth—nothing recognizable from the physical plane. She saw no sky, no land, no color. As she stared around the bleakness before her, a tiny well sprang and overflowed in her heart when she saw only Diabolicals wasting away in the ethereal wind—no sign of Wytch or Paladin could be found. Had they escaped?

Even the Denizen, she saw, had no power in this place. It seemed to stare straight at her, a snarl on its gaping maw, the eyes burning a fiery red but snuffing out as the breeze too stole whatever physical representation the creature had left. And then it was gone—she assumed never to return.

But still, Simza Adenah, the Uniter, did not feel safe in this place. She remembered then what had brought her here—the battle with the Conquerer, a flash of power stronger than she'd ever felt, and a need to take the melee somewhere over which she'd have far more control. And she realized that power had come from her. She had done this.

Movement on the hazy gray horizon caught her eye, and the Conquerer's form seemed to materialize both from a space very far away and right in front of her at the same time. The utter silence of the void in which she now stood was broken by the roar coming from his footsteps, the breath escaping him like tongues of flame and screams of the dying. Here, in this place, Simza realized she saw him for the first time as he truly was. She'd called him to be even more present on this plane, even though the others of her own kind would never have survived the journey. Not as she did now.

A low chuckle rumbled across the toxic fumes of the air

around her, and she had a flash of memory from a time that seemed very, very long ago. She'd seen that form before, as ever-moving and ungraspable as the starlight in the valley—this was the creature from her dream, the one that had wanted her, called to her, lusted for her. She felt that pull again now, as strongly as she had then, but it gave her no pain. No misery. The Uniter felt a certain dutiful acceptance overcome her, though she had absolutely no idea what she was to do next. Her powers had come at the right moment, it seemed, but the explanation for them, the direction, had not.

"You've made this far too easy for me," the Conqueror hissed, taking slow, deliberate steps closer. A slit opened in the center of the demon's face, the wielder of all that was evil across so many universes, and Simza steeled herself.

She was finally ready to face the thing for which she'd been made.

CHAPTER 33

"Who are you?" Wolfeye shouted at the stranger in glowing armor.

Salem turned to glower at the Paladin, feeling the strength in Tarlak and Ansgar's stares as they, too, glared piercingly at the man. He'd obviously spoken out of turn, had obviously no idea who the Ancient Ones were. Did the Paladins teach their kind nothing of the Old Ways anymore?

Tarlak then moved briefly toward Wolfeye in anger, but the stranger held up a gauntleted hand to stop him. "No, 'tis a fair question. I will have it heard that anyone who wishes to speak here has an open invitation. The time for secrecy is over…if we are lucky." He blinked slowly, sadly, and turned to address Wolfeye. "You may call me Davryn. There are few of us Ancient Ones left in the planes of existence, and I am nigh the youngest."

"How old are you?"

Salem turned toward the sound of the childish question and recognized Fleurin staring wide-eyed at the self-proclaimed Ancient One.

"Older than this universe," Davryn replied. "Younger than others. None of that will matter, though, if Simza Adenah does not pass her current trial."

Salem felt his heart wrench at the mention of his Lark. The sting in his back hardly registered when Ansgar began an incantation in a low hum, holding his hands just inches above the gaping wounds. "Do you know where she is?" he asked.

Davryn frowned. "Somewhere none of us can follow. Except, perhaps, for the Mother, if we've performed our duties. And even then, that's one decision Magic will never manage to repeat."

"Do you have any answers that aren't riddles?" Wolfeye snarled.

"Wolfeye—" Salem started.

"No, Taker," Davryn interrupted. "I stand by my word. Every voice is welcome here." The Ancient One turned, his armor shining in a blinding flash against the setting sun, and raised his arms to address both Wytch and Paladin alike in the clearing. "My sons and daughters, gather. I will tell you what the battle you've so bravely fought here today means, for each of you and for all realms of existence. Perhaps the story and your long-awaited fellowship will lend the Uniter strength while we palaver."

***

It took all the strength the Mother had just to keep herself in one piece. The swirling vortex of darkness moved all around her, buffeting her against the storm of itself, threatening to tear her apart.

292

She could have been in here for minutes or days—time no longer existed on this plane, nor did anything else.

The Ancient Ones had finally intervened in their world again, had fixed the rip in the astral plane, and they'd sent her here instead with their last combined force. Magic had asked them to, so the fear she felt now had nothing to do with the unexpected. She knew exactly what she'd gotten herself into and exactly what would be required of her should she make it out of this place of nothingness…or should she find the one thing that existed within the vacant expanse.

As the battle had raged on the hill, while her Wytch children and their new Paladin allies had fought the Conqueror and his Diabolicals, Magic's focus had been torn in two. For what felt like hours, she'd concentrated half her mind on defending her children, on healing those who needed Magic's touch of life just in time and in striking down the evil which had attacked them. The other half of her had been far away, calling through space and time, hoping for the Ancient Ones to give her one last sign of their existence— one last hope that they still heard her call. She'd realized, then, that this was how her own Wytch Born children must have felt every time they called for her aid and succor. Desperate. Pleading. Unknowing.

Then, Davryn had appeared to her. It had been centuries upon centuries, in so many different worlds, but she'd recognized him immediately. He was the last of his kind, the Ancient Ones, as much as she was the first of her own. Her Wytches might not ever know just how far back their lineage went. They traced it to the Mother, but she traced herself back to those Ancient Ones, back to the shining stars amidst the darkness of chaos and despair, going back further than the visage in shining white armor appearing before her.

Davryn had known her plight in that moment, had read her mind and her intentions on one dimension while she battled beside her children in the forest on another. "You know what this means?" he'd asked her, though it sounded far more like a statement, an echo of her own shadowy prophecy.

"I do."

"Very well," he'd said. "The astral plane has been repaired just enough for us to send you through it to reach the end. It will be the last place you ever venture." His eyes, shimmering in the wavering form of their own unreality, regarded her calmly with acceptance.

"Let it be so." Those had been Magic's last words on the physical plane of that world, and she'd sealed her fate.

Then Davryn's shining visage had disappeared, the air had been sucked away from her as though in a vacuum, and Magic had appeared in this place. Gone were the trees of the forest around her. Gone were her Wytches, her children, and those who fought beside them. Gone were their enemies. Gone.

Now, she trudged through the nothingness, praying for one more moment of sanity before all her faculties left her—though there was no one here to respond to those prayers. Even the Ancient Ones couldn't hear her now. After centuries of devotion, of learning, of honing her craft and teaching it to others, surely she'd have the strength to do this one last thing.

Magic became distinctly aware of the fact that she no longer felt solid ground beneath her feet, but she could not discern how long that sensation had been missed. She raised a hand to her forehead in a gesture of concentration only to find that she no longer seemed to have a hand or a forehead. The sinking despair of disappointment hit her hard because she did not have the direction she'd so hoped to receive here. She had nothing.

Then she saw it, seemingly off in the distance yet right before her. A flash of dark purple light pulsed with luminescence, power, and purpose. She felt within and around that light two distinct polarities. One was the all-encompassing, ravaging, cold-as-death evil of the Conqueror—an essence she'd expected to feel here but had only just noticed its previous absence as it appeared suddenly within this space-less void. The second spirit gave her hope she'd thought had completely abandoned her. It was Simza Adenah, the Uniter—her daughter.

Renewed by her one remaining purpose, Magic propelled herself through the darkness toward that purple light. This one last thing, she could do.

***

Simza felt herself both compelled by and simultaneously rejecting the awful force of power before her. This was the Conqueror, the energy which had called to her in her dreams, terrorized her faith in the knowledge she'd possessed, ravaged her body with the fever of longing, and pulled her through the most terrifying of her own transformations. Now, this beast of a being existed before her in a plane unlike any she'd ever known, smiling at her with a gaping void in its face that made her quiver.

"You might have lasted a little longer if you'd stayed where you belong," the creature rumbled, taking step by slow, agonizing step toward her. "You did not listen to your clan, did not listen to your blood, and now you are mine."

"Where are we?" The words tumbled out of her mouth, though she fought to keep her voice from shaking. Simza was not afraid of her surroundings, was not afraid of the looming creature before her. She was terrified of the fact that she wanted him to come nearer. That unnatural thing which had haunted her for so long was a part of her, she knew, and with that knowledge she understood that the closer the Conqueror came to her, the less she'd be able to resist him. She had to stall.

The demon paused, tilted its massive, writhing head, and gargled a laugh. "This is my realm," he boomed. "This is the Nothingness, the Void, the bowels of my domain. I am everything here, where there is nothing, and you cannot resist me, Amalatuu." He spat the word as a mocking curse.

"And you wish to destroy me here," Simza added.

Another rumble of chaotic laughter escaped the Conqueror, and the very air vibrated with the force of that tremor. Simza thought her head would split.

"You are so naïve," the Conqueror purred. "So foolish. I have never wanted to destroy you, Amalatuu. I only want to make you mine. You possess a power of which I've dreamed, imprisoned away in the underbelly of this world, and I've coveted your soul since the day you were born. Your life force was created to exist with mine in the most unholy union only I can provide. And you've fought me every step of the way." More laughter echoed from within the darkness around them. "Now you have reached the end."

He seemed closer now, stronger, and Simza felt the weakness building within her. This was no time to doubt herself, but she had no idea what to do, and there was no one here to help her.

In a last attempt at fighting, she hurled a blaze of purple fire at the Conqueror, feeling her power surge within her like hatred and longing combined. The peace of her goodness and the tempest of whatever evil had laid dormant in her battled one another, and she used her weapons on the demon.

More laughter resonated around them, and Simza realized

only too quickly that her attacks did absolutely nothing. The Conqueror flashed the same purple color as Simza's fire, raising his arms as if to embrace what should have destroyed him. "Delicious," he growled.

Panic seized Simza Adenah's heart. If she could not defeat the Conqueror, if she could not withstand him and keep her own soul intact, all hope truly was lost. And she was truly the wrong person—she was never meant to be the Uniter.

Then, she felt a sudden third presence there with them, and it took her a moment to realize that it was not part of the Conqueror's plan. Slowly, Simza turned to the right and saw a shimmering form in the apparent distance. This time, the figure did look far away, as if coming from a different plane or dimension.

She recognized, in a flash of relief and horror, Magic coming toward them. Simza tried to shout to her, to tell her to get out of there, to leave them. She wanted to tell the Mother—her mother—that this was her own destiny and no one could interfere. But the sound died in her throat and she could barely utter a choking cough.

Magic met Simza's gaze, her eyes flickering with hope and determination, and the sight of it made Simza's heart sink. Magic had resigned herself to something, perhaps even condemned herself, and the Uniter had a very strong feeling that this page of history had already been written for quite some time.

The roiling, rocking laughter emanated from the Conqueror yet again around them, and Simza reached out toward Magic's outstretched hand. But it was too late. With a roar, the Conqueror flicked his arm toward the Mother of Wytches and shot a writhing black stream from his hooked claws. The attack struck Magic in the chest, shattering her visage in a flash of blinding white light, sending shards of what she once had been shimmering all around them like the ashes of the defeated Diabolicals. Finally, Simza screamed.

Magic was gone. Destroyed. Obliterated in this void of nothingness and despair, never to exist in any other realm again. Simza knew this with every fiber of her being as though it had been written on her very heart, and the pain she felt at this knowledge surprised her. She felt herself drop to her knees and onto the non-existent ground below her, doubling over in defeat. This was never supposed to happen. She was never supposed to bring about the end of Magic as the world knew her. She had failed them all.

She felt the Conqueror's hot, fiery breath on her shoulders as though he stood over her now. Simza imagined the demon licking his slavering jowls with that horrid slit of a smile, hungering intensely for the chance to consume her spirit. To make her a part of his own destruction. And she could not move, ashamed of her own powerlessness to stop it. Ashamed of the small part of her that welcomed his sinful embrace.

A light prickle of sensation washed over her, and Simza slowly opened her eyes. The pieces of Magic, like so many stars in an endless sky, swirled around her as she kneeled. Shimmering, they held the pearlescent reality of hope, of something unforeseen. She watched each shining particle come toward her with their last vestiges of sentience—touch her skin and become a part of her.

Magic had given her daughter one last gift, though it existed in the Mother's death.

The Uniter felt the power of Magic, of her mother and the Mother of all Wytches, burning through her veins like fire, growing stronger with each passing particle entering her semi-body on this plane. She felt knowledge, strength, hope, power, and above all, understanding. A flash of heat wracked her body, and when she looked up, she found the Conqueror where he'd always been, as if no time had passed.

Simza understood exactly what she was meant to do. It made sense now, why she'd always felt a sickly pull to the Conqueror and the evil of his seduction. It made sense now, why neither Magic nor Wytch nor Paladin could explain to her the full extent of her powers. It made sense why the Blood of the Ancients named her Amalatuu, but it was not merely to unite the warring factions of Wytches and Paladins. That much had been crucial, yes, but it was not Simza Adenah's truest purpose.

Knowing this, a fevered grin spread across her lips. She'd unite them, all right, and nothing would stop her now. Not after what those who believed in her had already sacrificed.

The fiery demon of smoke and shadow before her did not seem to notice her revelation, nor the shift in her powers. Slowly, as if savoring the moment in its exquisite end, the Conqueror finally stepped toward Simza, close enough that she could feel the lure of his existence pulling at the darkest parts of her. And she let him approach.

"Now I shall have you, Amalatuu," he growled, all semblance of patience now removed.

With dreadful intent, Simza lifted her bowed head from the dimensionless expanse of the void and stared into the terrible, glowing eyes of her centuries-old foe. "No," she whispered, grinning beneath her cold, deadly gaze. "You are mine."

Summoning every ounce of power, every filament of life energy from every plane of existence, Simza Adenah clenched both fists, opened her arms, and called her magic. A shuddering crack echoed through the Nothingness, sending ripples of power shooting out from their source in the Uniter. Her skin burned hot, like fire in her veins, and the tattoos running up her arms seemed to crack like the crusted earth above a molten core. The runic lines on her skin burst with a deep purple light, and she breathed heavily with the strength of her own curse.

The Conqueror stopped in his approach, the embodiment of confusion flashing across his demonic face. The confusion then turned to terror, and he let out a wild groan that shook his domain almost as harshly as Simza's final call to him. But it did not shake the Uniter from her purpose.

The howling void was filled with Simza's screams and the soul-splitting shrieks of her ancient enemy. She opened her arms wider, welcoming the pain, the destruction, and called the Conqueror to her. The demon scrabbled for purchase, unable to grasp a solid escape from his ultimate doom in this world. His form wavered, flickered briefly out of existence, and then his body was forced toward Simza's and into her.

The purple light of her tattoos burned even brighter, and a great flash of light exploded around her. Then, there truly was nothing.

***

Davryn had almost finished his story, it seemed to Salem, but stopped suddenly in mid-sentence. The Ancient One put a gauntleted hand to his chest, almost as if to ease some deep pain there, and turned a devastated gaze on those gathered around him.

"Magic is gone," he said solemnly.

A muffled hush of disbelief rose through the allied warriors, and Salem put his own hand to his own heart. No one said a word. They'd all heard Davryn's story, understood that Magic had to make the ultimate sacrifice to give Simza what she needed to defeat their true enemy. But it had seemed just a harmless story while the Ancient One spoke, something that had already happened to someone else, or something that would happen far after any of their lifetimes. It was a shock to realize that Davryn had explained the prophecies and Magic's intentions to them in real time, as they were happening, and Salem was sure that each Wytch there felt the Mother's absence just as strongly and as surely as they felt their own existence in the clearing.

Then, an explosion of screams and thunder echoed through the forest, and each of them stood from where they'd gathered, immediately on guard. Salem winced as he stood—Ansgar had healed what he could of the wounds, and Davryn had spoken incantations, but Taker still needed time for true healing. When he turned, though, all notion of pain escaped him.

The forest was bathed in a deep purple light, blooming around them in what had seemed twilight before but now could only be called total darkness in comparison. It was Simza's light, he knew, but he did not know if it came from her victory or destruction.

Whispers of trepidation and awe ran through the small band, each gripping their weapons in preparation for whatever might arise from the forest below them. A branch cracked, he saw Wolfeye raise his bow and take aim, and then a figure stepped out from behind the trees.

Simza. His Simza. Walking tall and straight and apparently unharmed. A shout of joy escaped Salem's lips and he moved to run toward her. But then he felt Davryn's hand upon his shoulder, urging him to remain where he was. "Wait," the Ancient One whispered.

That was when Salem noticed the difference—a wavering glisten to his Lark, her hair and coat billowing as though a small breeze blew only around her. He caught sight of the faint purple light along her tattoos and noticed the violet glow coming from deep within her eyes. He swallowed the lump in his throat, feeling his worst fears had come true. Simza had returned, but not as herself.

She stopped a few feet from those gathered around him, taking seconds to look over each familiar face. A few Wytches bowed their heads, some gasped, and one or two Paladins followed suit. Salem turned to look at Wolfeye. The man's face ran with hot tears. Then, Simza locked gazes with Davryn, who fell to his knees in a salute. "Amalatuu," the Ancient One whispered.

"We have consumed him," she said. Her voice rang out loud and strong, but oddly dissonant, as though two voices spoke through her instead of only one. It was a terrifying sound, and Salem felt the cold sweat trickle down his back. "His evil no longer exists in this world. He will try again in others, but for now, for the next age of this Earth, the Conqueror is gone."

Then, the purple light faded completely from the runes on her body and from within her wide-eyed gaze, and Simza stumbled, supporting herself on a nearby tree. Salem didn't even think—the sight of her in any form of distress spurred him into action. He was at her side immediately, helping her up as she panted in shuddered breaths, recovering from whatever overwhelming power had finally subsided within her.

Simza looked up into his eyes and blinked rapidly, a wry smile on her lips. Awestruck, Salem could only tuck a stray piece of hair behind her ear and whisper, "You did it."

"Well," she sighed, taking a deep breath, "you did something to help, I'm sure."

He could only laugh in disbelief at her jest and brought her mouth to his in a last attempt to show her what his words would surely fail to convey.

***

Three days later, Davryn of the Ancient Ones, Simza Adenah, and Salem Taker stood at the edge of the Bredon Woods for their final goodbye. The Paladin Council had met with the Thirteen at this very place, a border between their lands, to hold palaver with the Ancient One and Amalatuu. A truce had been struck between the factions, perhaps temporary but hopefully for the remainder of each tribe's future. The truths had been revealed, histories smoothed over, and a surprisingly bitter-less understanding had been reached—there were far greater evils to overcome in the word, this world and others, than what had previously driven them to destroy each other. So, for now, they remained allies.

Davryn had told them that he'd done what he could for this era of mankind, both Wytch, Paladin, and human, and that he thought he lacked the strength to return again. Better, he said, that Simza Adenah now held the world's magic in her fingertips. She had, essentially, become Magic herself—taken up her mother's mantel—and the Ancient One expressed his faith in her ability to protect the Wytch Born just as well as, if not better than, her predecessor had.

"Find some peace," he told them softly, "and treasure it. Peace is such a precious thing."

They barely had a chance to thank the figure in glowing white armor before he disappeared in a flash, leaving them alone at the edge of the woods.

Salem had been dreading this moment since he first saw Simza appear from behind the trees after her battle with the Conqueror. He did not think she was his Lark anymore, but something more—something greater. Something even he could not dare to comprehend or match with what little powers he held himself. No doubt Simza Adenah the Uniter would have enough on her hands without the added advances of a pitiful Wytch's spurned feelings. So, in true Taker form, he did not say a thing to her about it.

She had opened a portal along the edge of the woods, which led, he could see, back to what once had been Magic's Clearing. Salem remembered only too vividly being called there himself, the first time in so long and what seemed even longer ago, to meet with Magic. She had told him then of her mistakes, of the Conqueror's threat, and he had learned of Simza. Now, the woman he'd fallen in love with—that unattainable creature, now more than ever—would return to her Mother's realm to take Magic's place. And Salem Taker would remain in this realm until the end of his days, watching over the other Wytches, as was his place. It made only too much sense.

"I suppose a farewell is in order, Lark," he mumbled, trying to meet her gaze but only managing to stare at the tree branch behind her head. He stuck out his hand, waiting for her to take it.

"Yes. Farewell, then," she replied. If he didn't know better, Salem would have thought she was making fun of him. But she took his hand and shook it firmly. When he finally did bring himself to look at her, he caught only an amused smile on her face beneath the twinkle in her eyes.

The Uniter took one step through the portal she'd created, and Salem watched her silently, already preparing himself for a lifetime of trying to forget her.

But then she stopped, turned, and looked back at him in a mimicry of admonishment. "You know, Taker," she started, pouting playfully, "you are still a Favored Son." Then she bit her lip, still smiling, and reached a hand out toward him in invitation. She said words beyond words in just that one gesture—everything Salem Taker needed to hear.

Grinning, he took her strong hand and stepped through the portal.

THE END

The Choosing
By James Dinsdale

The usual sounds of twilight were silenced by a piercing scream. Tents arranged around a central fire pit were barely visible in the fading light, their sides flickering from the dancing flames. In one of the farthermost tents, a scream full of anguish and shame echoed out again. Scattered around the tent, members of the tribe tried to ignore the sounds from both the tent and near the fire pit, where several of the tribe's elders gathered beside an animated man dressed in the garb of a shaman. The shaman talked and gestured toward the screaming, clearly unhappy.

Inside the tent, a young man lay on an animal skin pallet, clearly in a lot of pain, the gouge marks from his recent misfortunate hunt raw and inflamed. A young woman probed the wound, picking out detritus and dirt, cleaning it as best she could. She wasn't the tribe's shaman nor was she part of the shaman's retinue, but people had sought her out because of her natural ability to heal. She too tried to ignore the increasingly manic words of the tribe's new shaman as he ranted at the elders, his voice rising with each sentence. She concentrated instead on this young hunter, trying to save his leg.

The young woman had never imagined she would become a healer, normally the remit of a shaman, but her innate ability to understand what was needed and her success in curing some of the more serious ailments had thrust her into the role. It seemed as if the answers to what was needed just appeared in her thoughts, and the herbs she sought for treatment, previously unknown to her, appeared to glow when she searched for them. She had never questioned how or why this happened and she never lauded her ability. She was a member of the tribe, and her duty toward its survival was of more import. Her own personal desires were secondary; she lived as long as the tribe survived.

She was so deep in concentration that she never noticed the sudden silence. She didn't even notice the tent flap being torn aside as men entered and reached for her. Her focus shattered as strong arms grabbed her and ripped her from her patient, dragging her to her feet, the young hunter screaming as his leg was suddenly dropped. Her head snapped from left to right as she sought out those who had interrupted her, her eyes seeing the men who had grabbed her and the vicious grin of the tribe's shaman as he stood close, directing them.

"Take her outside," he commanded, and the men holding her pulled her outside into the warm night. Even now, when her mind was a riot of confusion, not knowing or understanding what had happened, she could sense the warmth of the earth and feel the life forces around her. Animals, insects, plants, trees—everything that lived, everything that grew nearby seemed to be reaching out to her.

As she was dragged to a tree near a rocky outcrop on the outskirts of the camp, the shaman yelled to the men, "That is far enough. Stop here." He approached the small group of men with the woman held between them. "Make sure she can't get away," he ordered.

Where would I go? the young woman thought, then to the men around her asked, "What's happening? Why are you doing this? Let me go, Cha'el. You have no right!" The shock and disorientation finally leaving her, she glared defiantly at Cha'el, the tribe's new shaman. She shook off the arms holding her and stood before him. The shocked men who had been restraining her tried to understand how such a waif of a woman had been able to shrug them off so easily.

Cha'el stepped backward away from the angry woman, shock and fear etched on his face. He was the tribe's shaman and therefore, technically, sacrosanct, but he had only recently come into the position after his master's death and was still trying to leave the mantle of pupil behind. His bluster was all show, but his inner, less confident self remained that of a petty, selfish bully. As he tried to back away from the young woman, he tripped over a small rock and landed unceremoniously on his back.

Winded, scared, and trying to scrabble upright, Cha'el screeched at the men, *"Get her! Get her away from me!"*

The young woman just stood over the shaman, seeing the fear and, for the first time, seeing how much danger she was in. Cha'el was not a confident man and saw the young woman as a threat to his position. As she let herself be dragged back by the men, the shaman found his footing and stood upright. Cha'el's fear fueled his temper, and now fury consumed him. Even the men who held the young woman could see that the shaman was beyond sanity and stepped back, dragging the young woman with them.

"Tie her arms and legs. Make sure she can't move," Cha'el commanded. He had regained some dignity if not composure, and his voice was a sharp whisper.

The young woman let herself be bound. She understood that the men only did what they had to do, not what they wanted to do. Her hands were tied, and she realized how reluctant the men really were. Instead of tying her hands behind her head, as they would an enemy, they had tied them to rest in her lap. They tied her ankles and not un-gently guided her to the ground so she lay on her back.

Cha'el's wild eyes flicked over the woman now lying prone before him. As the other men stepped back, he stepped forward and kicked the woman hard. Her grunt of pain did not appease him, and he kicked her again. When the woman moved, trying to protect herself from the blow, he screeched, "I said make sure she can't move!" Cha'el had not realized that the men had backed farther away, trying to distance themselves from what was happening. He didn't try to hide the contempt on his face as he muttered, "Must I do everything myself?"

Looking around, he smiled when he spied what he sought. The young woman's eyes followed him as he approached and picked up a thick piece of wood, one of the many felled for firewood recently; it made for a sizable club as long as a man's arm. Walking back over to the prone woman, he hefted the club in both hands and swung it at her knees. Anticipating the move, the woman lifted her legs and rolled out of the way of the very clumsy attack. This only added more fuel to the fire that was Cha'el's fury, and he howled in frustration, swinging the log club violently toward the woman and not caring where it struck her.

One of Cha'el's wild swings glanced off the young woman's head and dazed her. Incapacitated, she didn't see his next swing directed toward her legs. The thud of it hitting her thigh was followed by a moan from the still dazed woman as her body jerked from the attack. Cha'el's next swing was better aimed, and the club hit the young woman's knees with enough force to shatter them. The sickening sound of bones splintering reached even the men who had backed off a fair distance from the apoplectic shaman. One of them rushed in to try to stop the shaman from killing the woman outright but failed to prevent another blow glancing off the young woman's head. As the man grabbed the club from Cha'el, he saw that the woman had been rendered unconscious—probably a blessing.

Cha'el's fury was about to be unleashed upon the man who had dared stop him when a voice said, "Enough." It wasn't loud, but the authority it carried was unmistakable. Cha'el's eyes sought out the peon who dared undermine his authority but met the gaze of one of the tribal elders instead.

"Enough," the elder repeated, this time with more force. "The girl is not to be harmed further."

Cha'el could not counter the command without severe repercussions to himself. Nodding at the elder, he walked back to the tents, seething to himself and planning his next move.

"Sam'an." The elder looked at one of the men who had brought the woman to this place. "Stay and look out for her. The rest of you, return." Without saying anything else, the elder turned and walked back behind the shaman. All but one of the other men followed him. Sam'an, one of the tribe's gatherers, squatted next to the unconscious woman and waited.

"Be calm," the warm voice told her. "All will be as it should be."

"Where am I?" asked the woman, confused. All was dark, and she could not feel the ground on which she thought she lay.

"You are here, as you should be."

"Here?" queried the woman.

"As you should be," replied the voice.

"Who are you?" asked the woman.

"I am the soil. I am the rock. Me and my kin are everything."

The answer was such a simple statement of fact that, even though it didn't answer the woman's questions, it somehow felt right. She wasn't afraid and she couldn't feel any pain.

"Your form is broken," the voice told her.

"My form?"

"The form by which you move upon me," the voice said.

"My body?"

"The form by which you move," the voice repeated.

"And my body is broken? How?" asked the woman.

"Your form is broken, but this is how it should be," the voice stated as a matter of fact.

"As it should be?"

"Be calm when you return. We are with you," the voice said.

"When I return? Who is 'we'? Where are…" The woman did not get to complete her sentence when she felt everything tilt, and her head spun.

"Be calm," the faint voice instructed. "Calm."

The woman groaned some time later. Sam'an, squatting silently next to her, turned and looked as the woman fought her way back to consciousness. She was still bound and lying on the sandy ground but moving slightly. Glancing at her legs, Sam'an saw that one of them had been broken and was swollen. The injury looked very serious, and Sam'an recalled the viciousness of Cha'el's attack. He didn't know why the shaman held so much hatred toward this woman. If anything, Sam'an had nothing but respect for her. She had, after all, helped his younger brother heal when he had been sick some time ago. Sam'an turned to look toward the tents and wondered what was happening.

Her eyes opened. It was dark and she was lying on sandy ground. Her mind tried to recall how she had ended up here, and she tried to move her arms in order to stand but felt something stopping her. She glanced toward her hands and saw that they were bound. Why? She struggled to remember what had happened, and the memories came rushing back.

The shaman was practically ranting, the elder thought. He and the others had been siting, listening to the shaman for some time now, and he was getting bored of it. The elder did not entirely trust this new shaman but had kept his peace when Cha'el's former master had named him before he died. The elders had little choice in the matter, as it was tradition for the shaman to name his successor. That didn't mean he had to like it. Cha'el had always been a petty boy, prone to moods and outbursts when he thought he had been slighted. Fortunately, the boy had been chosen as the old shaman's pupil; he would not have found a place in the tribe otherwise. The petty boy had grown to be a conceited and arrogant man. Unfortunately, he was now the tribe's shaman. The elder's shoulders sagged slightly as he considered what this would mean for the tribe's future.

The young woman looked down toward her legs and gasped when she saw the damage. The sound drew a look from the man standing near. He didn't say anything, but she saw the empathy in his eyes. He quickly looked away, as if fearful she may ask something from him. *This is how it should be?* she thought as she recalled the voice from her dream. She wasn't so sure she liked the current situation as it was, but she had very little say in the matter. She looked back toward her injured leg. *Surely it should hurt,* she thought. She felt no pain but was sure that she wouldn't be able to move the leg if she tried. She paused a moment, took a breath, and, holding it within her, tried to move her legs. The un-injured one moved slightly, restricted by the bindings on her ankles, but the injured leg was unresponsive. There still wasn't any pain, and for that, she was thankful.

The night was dark and the moon had yet to rise. She had been looking upward toward the lights in the sky, seeing patterns and shapes. The sound of the men approaching made her look toward the tents to see who was coming. Her temper flared when she saw Cha'el flanked by several men. Not one for anger, she calmed herself, allowing the warmth of the ground to flow into her.

"Good…" She started when she heard the voice, unbidden, in her mind.

The woman didn't have time to ponder as the men were upon her, staring down at her.

"Get her up," Cha'el commanded. "And bring her back to the fire." He turned away as the men reached for the woman and helped her upright.

She was still surprised to feel no pain from her injured leg. Two men lifted her between them, their arms linked behind her back and under her buttocks in a makeshift seat. Her 'guard' followed behind them silently.

Cha'el looked back and scowled when he saw how the men carried her rather than dragged her, as he would have preferred. He didn't say anything; he had been working hard toward this moment, and although he would have liked to succumb to his pettiness, he restrained himself. His prize was near.

They took her to the gathering of the tribe near the fire. Torches had been lit to illuminate the tented camp. She saw the faces of many people she had helped—faces of her friends and her neighbors. All of them showed surprise and shock at her treatment. They were confused and eager to understand what was happening, the young woman included.

Cha'el walked toward where the tribe's elders sat, facing the large fire, with a large, semi-circular space opened up before them. The shaman stopped in the large space and turned to face the men bringing the woman toward him. They gently lowered her to the ground, where she sat upright, her legs in front of her and her bound arms supporting her.

"Unbind her," one of the elders commanded. "She is not going to run anywhere with a bad leg."

Cha'el turned to complain but kept his peace. He saw the elder's eyes on him, judging, and Cha'el finished his turn with a slight bow toward the elder in mock acquiescence. Men cut the woman's bindings, and she propped an arm on either side of herself for better support. She didn't try to move her legs and remained seated in front of the elders.

The elder who had commanded her unbound stood and looked out toward the faces watching the young woman. Cha'el felt a surge of pleasure rush up his body as he anticipated what was about to happen. This was one of the few elders who didn't look at him as if he were something unpleasant; the man had been the most receptive to Cha'el's case against her.

"This woman has been accused of unnatural magic," the elder said with no preamble.

"What?" the woman exclaimed.

"Hush. Be calm. This is how it should be."

The young woman bit off what she was about to say. Was the voice real?

"Yes. We are here."

Who was here? What was happening to her? She started to worry that she was losing her mind when she needed it the most.

"Hush. We are real and we are with you. Do not fight what should be. Accept."

The woman reflected upon the voice. All her life, she had trusted her instincts and feelings, and they had always been right. She knew that she should trust her intuitions and not fight. She wasn't sure about what she should accept, but she was pretty sure that she would find out soon enough.

She realized that Cha'el had been talking while the voice had distracted her. Of all the times to be distracted! Then she looked up and saw everyone staring at her.

"Do you have anything to say about this?" the standing elder asked her.

"Peace."

She looked toward the elder, knowing that even if she wanted to say something, she had no idea what was happening or what to say in defense. She hung her head, staring at her injured leg.

Cha'el smiled in triumph. He had never dreamed that it would be this easy to get rid of the woman who had made the tribe—his tribe—look down at him. It was because of her that he had not received the respect he was due. It was because the tribe would rather seek her out than him. She was the cancer eating at the tribe, blinding them to what he really was.

Voices shouted out from the tribespeople gathered around them. Some supported the woman, some of them condemned her for what she had allegedly done. The elder let the shouting continue for some time before he raised his arms. Waiting for the people to quiet down, he looked toward Cha'el and saw the shaman smiling to himself. Other elders saw the smile on the shaman's face, some spitting into the dirt at their feet. When there was quiet, the standing elder spoke.

"What does our shaman require?"

Cha'el, grin replaced with an expression of seriousness, looked toward the elder and said, "Cleansing by fire!"

Shouting started again, some of the tribe surging into the semi-circle before the elders, clearly angry with the proceedings. The elder thrust his arms into the air again, waiting for the order to be followed. Eventually, the shouting and arguing stopped, and the only sound was that of the fire spitting and crackling.

"She will be cleansed by fire! Bind her now!"

The woman was grabbed and held while her arms were bound, now behind her back. She offered no resistance, trusting her instincts and feelings. She knew she should be terrified; they were going to burn her alive! It was a very rare form of ritual, and she had no memory of it ever happening during her short life.

"You stay calm. Good." This time, the voice was different, like a breeze whispering to her.

Other men stacked firewood onto the pyre, creating a large blaze in the normally subdued fire pit. The woman looked at the elders, and they at her. Her face remained impassive, no emotions showing at all. Some of the elders, however, looked distinctly uncomfortable with the proceedings but remained quiet. The shaman seemed as if he wanted to dance from foot to foot.

After a remarkably short time, the standing elder looked from the now roaring fire to the young woman. He didn't say a word, simply nodded, and the men holding her led her, limping badly, to the edge of the fire. A woman of the tribe rushed from the crowd and tried to stop them. She screamed at them, hitting their arms and chests. The young woman looked at her—a young mother who'd had a difficult labor. She said nothing but, catching the young mother's eyes, smiled and shook her head. The young mother's attack faltered as she sobbed and was led back to the side by her nervous husband.

"The choice is good," a sharp, crackling voice said in her head.

As the men prepared to lift the young woman—the ritual involved throwing the accused into the roaring flames—she simply told them, "There is no need." The men look at her, confusion apparent on their various faces. Without another word, she simply limped into the flames, her eyes clenched shut, the smoke from the fire causing them to water and tears to stream down her face.

Everyone went silent, stunned by her actions. Nobody had ever heard of, let alone witnessed, such an act. Who would willingly step into an inferno to their certain death? They each held their breath as the young woman threw herself into the center of the blaze.

The flames roared and flew higher into the night sky. As the crowd looked up, a growl like thunder shook most of them from their feet, including the elder and the shaman, who dropped to the ground like felled trees. Then the ground shook.

"I am FIRE and I claim this person!"

The crowd looked toward the fire as the crackling voice sounded out. They stood in awe as the flames around the woman receded, forming a circle of fire and leaving her on a bed of smoldering embers.

"I am AIR and I claim this person!"

As the second voice sounded, a breeze appeared from nowhere and blew the smoke from the embers out of the circle of flames. All could see the young woman lying in the circle, burned and covered in soot.

"I am WATER and I claim this person!"

As the third voice called out, a light cloud appeared over the young woman, dousing the embers and enveloping her with cool, cleaning mist.

"I am EARTH and I claim this person!"

The earth shook with the sounding of the fourth voice, and the crowd gasped as green shoots sprang up from the circle of embers and the wounds on the young woman, caused by the shaman and the fire, healed before their eyes.

A sharp brightness pierced the night, causing the crowd to shield their eyes, and a fifth voice rang out. "I am LIGHT and I claim this person!"

The few who braved the piercing light through the hands covering their eyes saw the young woman enveloped in a halo of white. She stood in the circle of fire, her bare feet upon fresh grass, shimmering as she gazed out toward the crowd. A sad smile appeared on her face before the light grew in intensity.

Even the bravest amongst the tribe had to keep their eyes tightly shut against the intensity of the glow. Then everything went dark again. When the tribespeople looked at the fire pit once more, the young woman was gone.

"What has happened?" the young woman asked.

"You have been chosen by my kin and myself," the fourth voice, that of Earth, said to her.

"Chosen for what?"

"You have been chosen to guide those such as yourself. Those who will come after you from all manner of tribes and peoples."

"I am to guide people? What am I to teach or show?" the young woman questioned.

"You will learn and you will nurture. No more shall the ignorant destroy our creations. We have seen too many who understand our nature killed by those who do not." This time, the fifth voice, that of Light, spoke to her.

"They will be as your children to guide and teach in our ways," the voice of Air whispered.

"You shall be their Mother," crackled Fire.

"THE Mother!" they called to her.

The Map
Chapter 1

Rain fell, heavy and cold, on the small rural town. Though it was still early autumn, a chilling breeze swept through Main Street, carrying a thick mist across the pavement. Only a few cars drove through the storm, rushing to get home to warmth and cover. The unkempt street went straight through what was known as 'downtown', though the tallest buildings were only two stories high. Nestled beneath an abandoned apartment and tucked between an empty general store and an insurance office, sat the Bridle Cafe. The thick drops of rain beat against the wide glass windows.

Kaitlyn Hart gazed longingly out at the dreary sky, sighing as a passing car splashed a wave of misty rain over the window she stood beside, blurring her view. The water running down the glass gave the street beyond a surreal look to it; everything was dark and gray, despite being almost noon. She picked up the plates and silverware that had been left behind on the cafe table.

Carrying the tray of dirty dishes with one hand, she lightly touched the arm of an elderly man sitting at the bar. "Need anything else, Troy?"

"Maybe another cup of coffee would be nice," he replied. His drawn-out voice was as shaky as his hands and he moved slowly, but Kaitlyn waited patiently for him to hand her his mug.

"No problem at all," she said kindly.

A few minutes later, she returned his mug to him, filled with steaming hot coffee. She looked down the bar at the row of empty red barstools. The only other patron in the cafe was also an elderly man, who had just walked in and taken a seat in a booth by the entrance. Troy was a regular, but Kaitlyn didn't recognize this other man.

"Morning," she said with a friendly smile. "Can I get you anything?"

The burly old man unfolded a newspaper, never looking up at her. "Cuppa Joe. Black."

He didn't say anything further, and his stiff demeanor suggested he wasn't interested in conversation. Pursing her lips in confusion, she straightened her shoulders, nodded and turned back to the kitchen. Must be having a bad morning, she mused.

Just after three in the afternoon, another waitress, Maya, came in for the evening rush—which didn't seem like it would be all that rushed, given the rain—and sat talking to Kaitlyn for a few minutes.

"Why don't you head home early? You have a new husband to get back to, after all."

"True." Kaitlyn grinned. "I still can't believe I'm married!" She looked down at her diamond ring, sparkling in the florescent light. "It's all moved so fast. But Brandon is just...amazing. The last three months have been incredible. I can't even remember living without him."

"You're so lucky. I wish a handsome businessman would swoop in and put a ring on my finger next."

"One just might!" Kaitlyn giggled. "You never know, if it can happen to me, I'm sure it can happen to you."

"Sure thing. I'll just keep holding out for that." Maya rolled her eyes. "Go home. Make him dinner or something. Breed some handsome babies with that eye-candy of yours."

Kaitlyn's cheeks flushed a deep red, and she shrugged her shoulders. "What if the dinner rush hits and you're alone?" Both women looked out at the now-empty diner, then looked back to each other and laughed.

"Go on, honey, go home. I bet it'll be a nice surprise for him."

After a few more minutes of polite refusal, Kaitlyn finally agreed to take off early. She hung her apron on a hook in the back room and called a farewell to the chef, who sat behind the stovetops watching a soap opera on a small TV. He stole a quick glance over his shoulder, waving back, before being sucked into his show once more.

Shaking her head with a chuckle, Kaitlyn pulled her long golden hair back into a loose ponytail at the nape of her neck, then tugged on her oversized gray sweater. Hugging her arms tightly around her waist, she went out the door into the cold, windy streets, soaked instantly by the downpour that hadn't stopped since sunrise. She ducked her head down and stayed as close to the row of buildings as possible as she followed them around to the back, where her car sat alone in the empty parking lot.

The drive home was uneventful. It continued to rain, and the ditches overflowed into the streets. Kaitlyn drove slowly, her windshield wipers drumming a steady beat as the raindrops played their melody. Despite the downcast grays and muddy browns, she loved the rain and enjoyed watching the wind ripple through the streams as they fell over the pastures. It was like the water danced to its own song. The imagery was enough to put her in a good mood, and by the time she pulled up into her gravel driveway, she had a content smile and a gleam in her eyes.

It had only been a week since she and Brandon had tied the knot; the ring was still unfamiliar on her finger and the ink of her new last name still wet on the marriage license. Their relationship had indeed moved quickly. When he first walked into the diner three months ago, his suave suit and dashing smile had stolen her attention. When she walked up to take his order, his honeyed voice and smooth tongue had captured her heart. After just four dates, she had known she was in love. He had proposed, and she hadn't hesitated to say yes.

She walked into the small country house, removing her wet flats and sweater at the door. He had recently bought the home when he came here from the city, and she moved in as soon as they'd said 'I do'.

"Brandon, sweetie?" she called out from the short hallway. "I'm home early."

There was no answer. Having seen his car in the driveway, she knew he was home; he must have been taking a nap, or possibly a shower. Deciding to surprise him with dinner, Kaitlyn went into the kitchen and rummaged through the fridge. She pulled out a block of cheddar cheese and a few packages of deli meats. She set the temperature on the oven and sliced a few thick chunks of cheese. Just as she turned back to the fridge to grab a can of flaky biscuits, a muffled crack rang through the house.

For a moment, she just stood there with her fingers curled around the handle of the refrigerator. She blinked and took in the silence, wondering whether or not she had actually heard anything at all. She removed the can of biscuits from the fridge and set them on the counter, then wiped her hands on a dish towel and strode into the living room.

"Brandon?" There was no one there. Just the furniture and shelves full of collectable, decorative glass soda bottles. She headed into the hallway, checking the bathroom. She opened the door, but the light was off and the room was empty.

Her and Brandon's bedroom door was also closed. She thought she saw a shadow move across the crack at the bottom of the door and called out again. "Brandon, is that you?"

Turning the handle, she slowly pushed the door open. Her bed was still made, nice and neat, just the way she had left it. The curtains were open wide, offering a view of the small, barren flower garden in the backyard, flooded by the rain, with the woods in the distance. The trees were just beginning to change colors, and through the storm she could see glimpses of reds and yellows on the tree line.

As she pushed her door open further, her eyes fell on the floor at the foot of her bed, and she froze in her tracks. Lying on the hardwood floor was a middle-aged man in a black suit. He was face-down, his hair was short and dark, and his shoes had slipped off his feet. His head lay in a pool of deep, dark red, and his light skin was unnaturally pale. Her stomach heaved, and without hesitation she rushed back into the bathroom and vomited into the sink.

Once she felt the nausea pass—and knew there was nothing left in her stomach to void—she rinsed out her mouth and washed her face with a towel. With shaking hands and her stomach still in the back of her throat, she forced herself to stagger back to her bedroom.

Her eyes ran over the corpse once again, but this time she was able to swallow back her nausea. She realized with relief that it wasn't Brandon. His hair was longer than that, and his suits were always well-pressed, never as wrinkled as the one on the lifeless man before her. She took a step closer and bent down, reaching out a hand. She wanted to flip him over, to see his face, but she hesitated. She had never touched a dead body before and didn't want to start now.

Behind her, the door to the master bathroom swung open, and she heard the sound of the light switch being flicked off. She leapt to her feet and spun around, coming face to face with her husband.

She couldn't manage to speak. His expression was blank, but as he looked into her eyes and saw her fear and confusion, a thin smile crossed his lips.

"Oh, Kaitlyn," he said, sounding disappointed. He shook his head slowly, walking into the room. She backed up slowly as he approached her, never taking her eyes off the long black pistol that hung from his hip, fastened just beneath his unbuttoned suit jacket.

She tried to ask what had happened, who the man was, why he had a gun like that...but all she managed to do was stammer, "Wh-what..." She felt her heel bump into something stiff and glanced over her shoulder to see that she had backed into the dead man's leg. She vaguely heard footsteps behind her but couldn't tear her gaze away from her husband.

"I'm so sorry, Katy." Her husband shifted his eyes to the bedroom door and gave a slight nod. "I really wish you hadn't seen this."

Before she could say a word, the burly older man from the cafe walked in the room. He took a hold of Kaitlyn, squeezing her arm tightly in his grasp and yanking her away from the man on the floor to bring her closer to himself.

"No!" Kaitlyn said, finally finding her voice. She tried to break free, but he was too strong. When she swung her other arm around to slap the man, he caught her wrist and spun her around, pinning her with her back against his chest and her arms crossing in front of her. "No, stop! Let me go! What is going on here?" She looked frantically between Brandon before her and the older man behind her, waiting—hoping—for an answer.

"I really wish you would have called first, Pumpkin. I could have had this whole mess straightened out. But now...well, I'm sure you understand that you can't be free to tell people about this little mishap." He pulled the pistol out of its holster at his side.

"Wait! What are you—"

"Now, now, don't fret. I can't very well kill my wife. Besides, I need your help. I was hoping to wait until after we had been married a month or so, but you've forced my hand."

"What do you want? Please, just let me go and I'll do whatever you ask." Tears streamed down her face as countless scenarios played out in her head, none of which answered the questions of what had happened here and what was about to happen to her. Her eyes wandered back to the corpse. "Please, just let me go."

He ran the back of his hand lightly down the side of her face, wiping away her tears. "I need your father's journal. He drew out a map...we'll talk about it later. I have a mess to clean and a few phone calls to make." He paused and offered a sympathetic smile. "I'm sorry, Pumpkin." Brandon raised the gun in the air and brought it down fast and hard against her temple, and with a burst of white before her eyes, Kaitlyn lost consciousness.

The Map is CWC's fifth novel and is set to be published late 2016. Look out for the official release date and excerpts from the ongoing story on the CWC website or Facebook page.

ABOUT CW PUBLISHING HOUSE

CWPH was founded in 2015, dedicated to publishing CWC novels. Due to numerous requests, we have opened our doors to submissions from completed collaborative novels and will work exclusively with collaborative novels written by two or more authors. CWPH has also arranged a number of Anthologies, with more to come. To learn more about our books and our authors, please visit: www.cwpublishinghouse.com

www.ingramcontent.com/pod-product-compliance
Lightning Source LLC
Chambersburg PA
CBHW060518180626
46817CB00002B/397